BREATH

AND

STARSHINE

MEDICUS CORPUS BOOK TWO

KAMI KING LARSEN

For my wonderful parents.

Natural forces within us are the true
healers of disease.

-Hippocrates

BREATH AND STARSHINE

1

HALE

The letter was tucked between Aurelia's couch cushions.

Sleeping on the lumpy sofa wasn't something I did often, but when I found her door unlocked, I decided to go in and wait for her.

I'd meant to stay awake long enough to see her when she returned from her shift, but I was just as exhausted as she was. These shifts were draining us all. Even Roe's charm and energy were falling prey to the rigors of the clinic.

Our schedules wouldn't overlap enough for me to spend some actual quality time with Auri for another few days. I was aching from being on my feet for hours but also aching with something far deeper. Something I had trouble naming.

Despite the sofa's scratchy material and uncomfortable padding, as well as the watery light filling the room, I'd drifted off before she got home and slept straight through until after she'd crashed in her own bed. Waking to the shifted light, in a pool of my own sweat, I cringed when I thought what I must have looked like to her when she returned. She hadn't even woken me. I found her sleeping face

1

down with her arms tucked under her cheeks. In only a tank and briefs.

Before I knew what I was doing, I stepped toward her beautiful terracotta skin and dark curls. I was bending to place a kiss on her cheek when I caught myself. I was many things. A total creeper was not one of them. Blowing out a shaking breath, I drug myself into a pivot and left her room before I did something I shouldn't. When I kissed her again, I would make sure it was perfect. And she was awake to enjoy it.

It was time to get back to my own apartment for a shower before heading into the clinic for the night, but I needed a minute to collect myself. I slumped back onto the same couch where I'd left a drool spot and sighed. The cushions shifted and a corner of worn brown paper poked up. She must have been sitting here reading at some point. I lifted the missive and moved to place it on the small table at my feet. As I set it down, the edge unfolded and I glimpsed the signature—Lita. My hands shook, and the paper vibrated. Had the little boy died? The debate in my mind lasted approximately two point five seconds before I unfolded the paper and read.

Aurelia,

Your notes are so truly appreciated. I can't tell you how emotional it makes me to know you are still thinking of us. Yes, Jonaten is still struggling. He seemed to have perked up a bit after you left us those weeks ago, but his health is flagging once again.

As to your offer, I can't imagine what more you could do for him in Devil's Meadows than what was available here, but I will think on it. The journey for us would be rather difficult given his current condition, but if by some miracle I am able to find a group heading south, I will see if we can join them.

In the meantime, I cherish each day with my sweet boy and think of your kindness often. With hope that we may see each other again,
    Lita

I wasn't sure how to react. Aurelia was walking a fine balancing act, and she needed to be careful. If Medicus Corpus got wind of why she wanted Lita and her son to make the harrowing journey from their small settlement in the north, it wouldn't end well for her.

We'd all come too far for her to lose it all now.

2

AURELIA

It wasn't yet mid morning, but sweat had pooled under my hair and below the band of my bra. Even the shade of the building provided little relief. A breeze blew from the south, but rather than cooling me, it simply baked the perspiration into a thin salty crust over my skin.

"Still not acclimated, huh?" Geneva smiled as I drug a wrist across my forehead.

"You can't honestly tell me *anyone* ever gets acclimated to this," I replied, trying and failing to keep the exasperation out of my voice.

She chuckled, but her lovely youthful face became somber as she prepared to tell me whatever she'd tracked me down for.

"So, look, Auri. I want you to be extra careful when you're out and about." Tucking a golden blonde strand behind one ear, she seemed to weigh her next words. "I don't mean to be alarmist, but there have been some attacks along the central corridor in the last couple of weeks. All on young women. And all of them fatal."

The blood drained from my face. "There have been attacks? Here?"

Gen pursed her lips and nodded. Devil's Meadows was a large hub settlement, but it wasn't so large that this kind of news wouldn't have been talked about. People here were close and surely someone would have known someone who had heard *something*.

"How many?" Not that it mattered really. *One* was too many.

"A few."

I raised my eyebrows and gave her the *I'd like more details please* look.

"Three," she amended.

"You're telling me *three* young women have been killed in the last two weeks and no one is talking about it? I find that both difficult to believe and ridiculously inappropriate. People need to know."

"If it makes you feel better, I agree. The other escorts and I are pushing the hub leaders to start informing the settlers. It won't stay quiet for long."

As ever, Geneva's face betrayed little emotion. She was too good an escort for that. Still, she meant what she said.

"It doesn't make me feel better, but I appreciate you letting me know."

"I understand, but look. . ." She glanced over her shoulder with a sigh. "There's something else. It isn't simply that they've been killed. It's the manner of the deaths that's a bit more unsettling."

With it being relatively the temperature of the sun this morning, not many folks were out and about. Not a soul stood near enough to overhear, but Gen seemed hesitant to continue. What could be so bad she was concerned about being overheard?

Finally she leaned in closer, her voice just above a whisper. "They were all suffocated."

A tingle ran down my spine. If it had been anyone else, I'd think the whisper was just for effect.

Not Geneva though. She was worried and didn't want anyone to know it.

My head flinched back of its own volition. I wasn't sure what I expected to hear, but having the life snuffed out like a candle sounded terrible. Not a quick death but a horrifying one.

Now that she was talking, Gen ignored my discomfort and continued, "And the scenes were pretty odd. All of the victims had some measure of defensive wounds but no signs of strangulation. Just some bruising on the face. It appears they were killed where the bodies were found, but who does that? How do you subdue someone in public long enough to suffocate them and risk not being seen?"

Definitely not what I was expecting to hear this morning. Clearing my throat and shaking my head, I looked at the woman who had become so much more than a guard or my chaperone. Geneva was part of my life here, a dear friend. Part of my family. The small furrow between her brows told me she would worry about me until whoever had committed these horrible attacks was found and dealt with.

She owed her life to me. Well, technically, she owed it to Holdan Listerman and me. While she wasn't as concerned with Holdan's safety, she would do everything in her power to keep me out of harm's way.

"I'll be as wary as possible," I said.

Her face grew stern. "You need to be more than wary. Until we know more about what is happening, when you aren't at the clinic or the housing complex, don't travel anywhere alone. Particularly at night. As best we can tell, all of these attacks have occurred after the sun goes down."

That wasn't in and of itself surprising. Most of the inhabitants here were primarily productive in the early morning or late evening during the summer months. In the height of the afternoon, the sun was a blazing orb, blistering skin and melting productivity. I was told it would be different when winter—or what passed for winter in the desert—arrived and the days became shorter, the temperatures more bearable.

"Okay, Gen. I'll try."

"Don't *try*, Auri. Do it. Drag Roe or Hale with you when you're out. Hell, even Holdan or one of the junior escorts from the clinic would be acceptable. If you can't get one of them, send word to Asher or me. We can escort you to and from work."

Runners were available all over the large hub, willing to carry a message in a relatively speedy timeframe, but most of them were kids and a good portion were girls. She wouldn't expect me to risk one of them to fetch protection for myself.

"I will try," I hedged, "but you know I can't promise. Now, I need to get into the clinic before someone becomes angry at me for relieving them late."

She sighed, shook her head, and gave me a brief hug before I raced inside to see who I could heal that day.

As a testament to the power of Medicus Corpus among the settlements, the clinic was housed in one of the better-preserved buildings in Devil's Meadows. It was situated along the central corridor of the settlement, stood four stories tall, and was divided into levels—each one dedicated to the types of patients being treated there. The first floor was for emergencies and quick in and out visits—broken bones, lacerations, simple medications, and other quick fixes. Each of us took turns staffing the first floor.

Hale spent a good bit of his time on the second floor where all things surgical—from tooth extractions to complicated amputations and delivering babies—took place. In a separate space along the north-facing windows, a series of cots separated by hanging drapes accommodated patients who needed to stay in the clinic for several days after their procedures.

The third floor housed the pharmacy, lab area, and exam spaces for adult patients who required more time with a practitioner. When I wasn't manning the first floor, I spent the bulk of my time with the fourth floor patients or with the occasional foray into the pharm lab.

It was the fourth floor and its sweet little patients for me this morning. As I exited the stairwell onto the landing, a world of colored paint and bright imagery overtook me.

Years ago, Roe had lent me one of his many books, thinking the ancient story would distract me from some stress or other. The abbreviated tale had been taken from some long-lost text and told of a girl carried away by a storm who found herself in a magical land of tiny people and wondrous adventures. I hadn't experienced anything like that story before and had rarely found the time to enjoy similar frivolities since. But every time I entered the fourth floor of the clinic, that story sprang to mind.

It wasn't simply the pint-sized patients; it was the explosion of sensory stimuli. Whereas the lower three floors were worn and drab, the children's ward was a riot of bright hues and fun illustrations—many of them concocted by the kids themselves. Along the walls, every speck of available space was covered in animals and rainbows, stick figures and hearts. Some told intricate stories and others were merely chalk and paint spattered in puddles, smudges, and handprints.

Admiring a small flower and bumblebee, I didn't hear the footsteps behind me and jumped when a hand came down on my shoulder.

"Whoa. Easy tiger," a low familiar voice said above my head. "Although that was definitely more of a squeak than a roar."

My heart racing, I turned and craned my head back looking up at a handsome yet haggard face. "I might have squeaked, but it's your fault, Hale. You shouldn't sneak up on people."

His green eyes were tired and his golden hair tousled. Seeing him worn out made me remember how he'd looked when I came home the previous night to find him passed out on my couch. He'd looked so at peace, I hadn't bothered to wake him.

"I wasn't sneaking, but sure."

His hand dropped and I could have kicked myself. We had arrived in Devil's Meadows two months ago, and while Hale and I were certainly on better terms than we'd ever been, I was starting to believe I had imagined him kissing me in the ramshackle structure in the center of the desert. *When he thought I'd been dying.* Either my brain had been starved for air or I'd misread the situation entirely.

Thinking about it only depressed me, so I elected to ignore my feelings and pretend he was no more than he'd always been. My best friend's brother. At least he wasn't openly hostile toward me now.

"So, what's up?" I asked. "I feel like I haven't seen you in ages."

"Yeah, these damned shifts are going to kill us all, I think. Checking in on the littles?" He dipped his head in the direction of the children's ward.

"I am indeed. Figured I start up here before I head downstairs to tackle whatever comes through the door."

9

Hale rarely came to the fourth floor if he could help it, but he'd been on shift last night which meant he probably needed to sign out a kid to me. It was a rotation we all shared. Between the seven practitioners, one of us was always here to keep an eye on things and address any emergent needs. It meant we—Roe, Hale, and I—didn't see each other as much as I would have liked. Between day shifts, nights, and sleeping, we were lucky to have a day every other week to spend together. It wasn't all bad though. At least I could trust them to do what needed to be done if they were here and I wasn't.

Sure enough, he drew me to the side of the hall and lowered his voice. "One of your young patients wasn't doing so hot last night, so Sandy asked me to come take a look. I was scared the kid was going to crump on me."

"Crump?"

"It's just a thing I heard Theo Wong say last week. It seems to fit. They get so sick so fast. I never see it coming until. . ." He spread his fingers and mimed something exploding in his face.

"I completely understand the feeling."

"Yeah, but at least you have a backup plan. I sometimes feel like I'm all alone on an island here in the middle of the night." He rubbed his palms up and down his face.

I nodded. Maybe I did have a backup plan, but it wasn't one I could openly use and I still felt like I didn't know what I was doing half the time.

"Let me guess. Diego?" I asked.

Now it was his turn to nod.

"All right." I blew out a tired breath. I was going to need to step up my "treatment" of him.

As if reading my thoughts, Hale grabbed my hand and gently squeezed. He flicked his gorgeous eyes—made an even more vibrant green by the redness caused by a night of no sleep—from side to side and whispered, "As far as that backup plan goes. . . Just be careful, Aurelia. Do *not* let them catch you."

I smirked. "Nope. Not part of the plan."

Still holding my hand, he studied me for a moment. "I've only got one more night left then I'm off for a couple of days. Maybe we could, I don't know, grab dinner together?"

My smirk blossomed into a full-blown grin. I'd been waiting weeks for this invitation after all. "I would really like that."

"Well, then, it's a date."

"Sandy. . ." I drew the woman's name out in a singsong voice as I smiled and set down my bag at the central area where the practitioner assistants worked. "Heard Diego was giving you some grief last night."

Diego, a four-year-old with adorable dimples and atrocious lungs, was in the clinic more than he was out of it. He had a tough road ahead if we—the older practitioners and I—couldn't figure out a suitable way to keep his tiny airways from repeatedly filling with mucus.

"Could have been better," Sandy said and yawned. "Could also have been worse."

Sandy—not Sandra, as she was quick to remind folks—was a lovely, kind, and patient woman. Not only did she have her own daughters and three grandbabies relying on her, but also a large extended family and all of the sick children of the settlement. The frequent visitors to the children's floor all knew her warm smile and asked after her if she wasn't present on the wards. Like the practitioners themselves, the assistants shared shifts on a rotating basis and floated from floor to floor. Sandy always seemed happiest when she was covering nights upstairs.

"Will you be here all day, Miss Aurelia?" she asked, not using my formal title.

"Yes indeed. All morning and all afternoon. If I'm lucky, I'll be gone in time to meet Roe for dinner. But the gods of medicine are fickle, so"—I raised my arms to the side—"who knows."

Sandy chuckled but it was brief and strained. Worry creased her eyes.

"Why? What's up?" I asked.

"It's not much. Probably nothing in fact. But my niece hasn't been feeling well. If it's all right with you, I'm going to have my brother bring her by today and have you check her out. Not that I don't trust Duncan, but. . ."

Patting her on the shoulder, I smiled. "Say no more."

Jassika Duncan was one of a pair of practitioners who'd been serving the settlement here for more years than I'd probably been alive. There were also two others who were a handful of years older than me and the Belstrohms. Jassika tended to favor the pediatric patients as I did. She was dedicated and knowledgeable and maybe just the tiniest bit cranky and cynical. She'd taught me tons in the past two months, but I hoped I could also teach her a thing or two. It really didn't surprise me Sandy had asked me to see her niece. The teens tended to feel more comfortable with someone slightly closer to their own age.

"Can you ask them to be here by early afternoon? I really would love to meet up with Roe tonight. Our shifts are out of sync, and we keep missing each other." I picked up Diego's chart and flipped through it, not worrying Sandy would be offended I wasn't focused solely on the conversation. Multitasking had become such a necessity of late, and the assistants knew me well enough by now to realize I was still paying attention. This was a benefit of building the relationship I had with them all. It helped to talk *to* and not *at* them. To ask about their lives and not just the patients. It meant we were all part of the same team, which also meant I'd get woken up fewer times in the middle of the night for simple things they could handle themselves.

The cherubic nurse didn't smile, but she did look relieved when she nodded. "I will one hundred percent guarantee she'll get here in time. Thanks, Aurelia."

The remainder of the morning and afternoon sped by in the usual manner.

Under the guise of simple concern, I sat with Diego for several long minutes holding his hand until my arms and shoulders began tingling uncomfortably. By the time I stood to leave, I felt like I needed a nap, but his breathing was much less labored. The tingling and fatigue were the trade-offs of using my newfound gift—wonder-working.

When I placed my stethoscope on his chest, the wheezing and tightness were nearly gone— replaced by a smooth exchange of air in and out through his airways.

Despite this small success and otherwise routine nature of the day, my usual enjoyment in the clinic seemed to be missing. A tension filled the spaces around me, and while it was easy to blame it on the extreme temperature outside, the stuffy, sweaty space felt almost claustrophobic. I was antsy and looking forward to seeing Roe. Having a coolish beer and light conversation with my best friend was all the balm I needed. At least I didn't get hit with a whiff of ozone. My gift also triggered the olfactory sensation and warned me of impending danger. Even without the smell, the sense of foreboding weighed me down nonetheless.

Through the small windows, light trickled in and the shadows stretched and bent around the beds, cots, and workspaces. Evening was creeping closer, and Sandy's niece still hadn't arrived. So much for guaranteeing they'd be on time. Mentally I gave her fifteen more minutes, and if she didn't show, she would need to wait until the next day or be seen by whoever was covering tonight. That would be Hale, who would be less than thrilled.

I began packing up when Janet—the lead assistant and day shift coordinator—peeked her head into the small office we used for charting.

"Don't kill the messenger, but they just walked in." She faked a cringe as she said it.

"Of course they did." I sighed and plastered a smile on my face before hauling my butt out of my chair, slinging my stethoscope around my neck, and heading toward one of our exam spaces.

"Hi, Clarice, I'm Practitioner Morris. You can call me Aurelia if you prefer." My eyes fell on an ill-appearing girl somewhere between fifteen and eighteen years old. She mumbled a hello as I sat on my stool. Although her eyes were heavily shadowed and a bit hollow, her skin was flawless and I could tell she was a gorgeous girl.

An older man sat next to her and fidgeted with a simple yarn bracelet. His round face and short frame was a ringer for Sandy. "My sister sent us to you," he explained. "She says you're the best practitioner she's seen in years."

"That's kind of you—and her—to say, but I'm not sure that's true. All of our practitioners are quite skilled." The man held out his hand, and I clasped it in both of mine. His skin was papery and rough; his grip firm.

"I'm Conrad, by the way. Clarice is my daughter, but you already know that." He spoke with a nervous hesitancy.

"It's a pleasure to meet you both. Now why don't you tell me what's been troubling Clarice."

The teen answered, speaking with not only the confidence of youth but also something close to anger. "I don't really know what the big deal is. I've been managing just fine, but everyone keeps saying something's wrong with me. *Nothing's* wrong with me." She wasn't breathless exactly, but close. Her expression fierce. Gone were the downcast eyes and half-mumbled words. "What he's talking about started a couple of months ago. I started to feel tired all the time. Hard to catch my breath. Lots of easy bruising and some racing heart. Now I just feel like crap." Her eyes shifted to the side. "Sorry, Dad. Anyway, it's just normal stress. Dad doesn't agree. So here we are."

My pulse quickened and a flush ran through me. Feeling tired. Easy bruising. *Jonaten.* This girl's symptoms sounded eerily similar to his. What were the odds? Low, I reminded myself. The odds were low. Common things were common and uncommon things—things like leukemia—were not. This could very simply be nothing more than a case of mono or some other troubling but ultimately relatively benign illness.

"The other practitioner thought maybe it's anemia?" Conrad's eyes welled, and a single tear dripped from his lower lash line. "We haven't done any testing though. Only high iron foods. When we can get them."

I cocked my head slightly. "I got the impression from Sandy you hadn't seen any of the other practitioners."

"Well, not formally. I had her ask since it was . . . difficult to convince Clarice to come down here."

"Dad," the girl groaned. "It's no big deal. Don't get yourself so worked up." Her voice held real caring

15

as she squeezed her father's wrist. The mood swings were a thing to behold. "Really. I'm just a little stressed. A little run down. It's not like life is super chill, you know?" She crossed her arms over her chest and stared at her shoes.

Anger and confusion were common in lots of folks with chronic illness, but teens tended to be the worst. And she was right. Since we'd arrived in the hub, I hadn't seen many people with easy lives. In Devil's Meadows things ran the gamut from tough to horrid to downright hell for some. The fluctuations in Clarice from caring to frustrated to hostile weren't anything new to me either.

Doubtless she would be unhappy about getting a needle in her arm, but taking some blood was the first step to getting to the bottom of this.

"This isn't my girl." Conrad raised his hand in the general direction of his daughter. "She looks like she's on death's doorstep one minute and is happy and laughing the next. I just want some answers. I *need* some answers. *If* there are answers to be had. I've prayed to the heavens to cure her, but maybe the stars need a little help."

"I understand your frustration. Let me examine her and start some testing, see where that gets us." A fine balancing act existed between professional aptitude and soothing comfort. Straddling the two was difficult—I wanted the father to know I was proficient in my job and Clarice to trust me enough to get the answers I needed without putting her through undue pain or misery.

After a thorough exam and a multitude of questions—spanning everything from her past history to the foods in her typical diet—I still felt we were dealing with more unknowns than answers. I ticked off several possibilities on a mental checklist. No prolonged bleeding with her menses. No blood in her stool—a question received by Clarice with a look of utter revulsion. No bone or joint pain. No family history of similar symptoms. No. No. No. The negatives kept coming and despite my best efforts, they didn't lead me in any particular direction.

At the risk of being late to meet Roe, I pushed on. After gaining the girl's permission, I poked her finger and placed a drop of blood on a slide. I studied the cells under the microscope and returned to Clarice and Conrad. "It's a little odd. I expected to see a dip in the blood count on the slide I made, but rather than being low, her red blood count is actually quite high. Thicker you could say. I don't believe her diet is the culprit."

My mind flashed to a frail little boy and his devastated mother. I chided myself. This wasn't Jonaten. I couldn't let my attachment to one patient cloud my judgment with all others.

"I know it isn't convenient, but it would be in Clarice's best interest to have you return to the clinic tomorrow." The teen began to object, but I pushed on. "And plan to stay here a couple of days until we can sort out exactly what her affliction is."

Clarice was not only vocal but brutal in her objection—stopping just shy of getting physical. I understood her fear, but even that didn't seem reason to act as she did, lashing out with words better suited for a back alley brawl. She stormed out and down the hall in a flurry of teenage righteousness and murderous scowls. Her father, who needed no convincing, assured me they would be back bright and early the following morning. Then he ran after Clarice.

Checking the clock, I was shocked to see it was nearly seven. So much for getting out of here early. Electing not to change out of my olive cargo pants and the matching loose smock which made up my practitioner's uniform, I signed out to one of the older practitioners who was still around. Hale was on nights again, but I didn't have time to track him down.

The small open air tavern was a few blocks over. I hurried as fast as my short legs could take me, the anticipation of seeing Roe only barely outweighing the anticipation of a lukewarm beer or two.

Summer in Devil's Meadows was unlike anything I could have envisioned. Even as the sun melted behind the mountains to the west, the temperature remained stubbornly above the century mark. Admiring the smattering of stars that twinkled in the watercolor sky, I wondered at people who praised the lack of humidity. Claiming the dry heat was in some way better made no sense to me. Hot was hot.

Just as the thermometer amazed me daily, so too did the people who called DM home. Gen had been right all those long weeks ago. I was beginning to like it here because of the vibrant and rugged people. The night life alone would make anyone smile. Many waited to come out and mingle until the hard pack and pavement would be less inclined to melt the shoes from their feet.

Entering the open air space that served as a tavern, I could not wait to talk to Roe and unwind for an hour or two. Given the stress of our job and the limited free time, my social life—never previously robust—was all but nonexistent. When I wasn't working or tending my medicinal garden, I was practicing with Holdan, writing to my parents, or climbing up and down the stairs near our rooms. Gen had gently suggested the latter activity might be good for me. Having started our long trek from Renfield in less than optimal physical shape, I'd made some improvement to my stamina along the road and she didn't want to see me lose it.

Looking from table to table, I reveled in the idea of just relaxing with one of the people I loved most in the world. Roe could make me forget about medicine and patients and charting. His radiant smile and easy teasing helped me slip away from blood draws and screaming babies. Even better, he helped take my mind off my budding talent with miracles and wonder-working. He let me just be me.

The smile slid from my face as I scanned the area once more. Roe was nowhere to be seen. Was I that late? I didn't think so. Maybe he had been held up with his own patients and responsibilities. Assuming I was well behind him, I hadn't bothered to stop downstairs to check for him. Perhaps I should have and we could have walked over together.

Regardless of his whereabouts, I still needed to eat, so I grabbed a stool at the bar and picked up the chalkboard listing that day's options.

A middle-aged woman with deep smile lines, kind eyes, and coarse grey hair took my order of a bottle of beer along with a goat cheese and tomato sandwich.

Tarps stretched above the wooden bar top, and the desert breeze thrummed along the taut material, cooling the space a degree or two. Solar lights lined the poles behind the bar, their blue-white light casting distorted shadows across patrons' faces.

"Here you go, doll." The server set a dark green bottle of beer in front of me. "The sandwich'll be out in just a tick."

I smiled and nodded my thanks, eager to slurp the escaping foam from the neck of the scratched and worn bottle. I might have actually sighed audibly after the first long drink of the bitter liquid. Everything here lived multiple lives. How many people had used the same bottle before me? Had the same need of a little respite after a long and weary day in the desert heat?

Someone sat down next to me. Assuming it was Roe at last, I turned, but my sarcastic comment died on my lips. It wasn't the charismatic roguish face of my friend but the sallow complexion of a stranger looking back at me. Perhaps stranger wasn't the proper term. He was vaguely familiar. A man about my age whom I'd seen here and there about the settlement.

"Gary," he said by way of introduction. He grabbed my hand in his, and a wave of alcohol— something stronger than beer—hit me full force.

His sparse ratty little mustache accompanied by a smattering of hair on his chin brought to mind some sort of rodent. A desert rat.

He raised his eyebrows in an "I'm waiting" gesture. Against my better judgment, I replied "Aurelia" and tugged my hand free.

Where in *all the desert* was Roe?

"I've seen you around." His gaze flicked to my uniform. "You one of the Medicus people?"

"I sure am."

Choosing to take my chances with the sticky bar top in front of me, I turned away, silently praying for the server to arrive with my meal. If Roe was going to be a no-show, I wanted to eat and get out of there.

"My kid sister just got a job there at the clinic. She's not bright enough to be anything more than an assistant, but she's gotta do something."

I could feel the sourness spread across my face. The assistants worked just as hard as anybody. Most people—this guy included—wouldn't last more than a day doing what the Medicus assistants did.

As if reading my thoughts—or more likely the disgust on my face—he went on. "Must be a hard job, seeing sick people all day. Whining and crying about this or that. I myself am healthy as an ox." His complexion and the doughiness of his arms begged

20

to differ. "It's why you haven't seen me round the clinic."

Pursing my lips and nodding, I tapped my fingers on the wood.

I was going to kill my best friend.

"Maybe I should make something up." He leaned over and lowered his voice. "Then you could examine me."

My stomach rolled.

He chuckled when instead of answering I took another long drink of my beer.

"I never would have taken you for a beer drinker. You look too cute for that. Had you pegged for juice and spirits."

The last thing I wanted to do was answer him and encourage any further engagement, so I shrugged and bent forward, looking down the bar toward the server. With any luck she'd be bringing my food out shortly.

"I mean, you are cute, you know. Maybe if you lost the glasses you'd be almost hot."

Nope. Killing Roe was too just a punishment. I was going to torture him. Slowly.

Finally exasperated, I stood and headed toward the small lavatory situated in the corner farthest back from the road. As I moved between small scattered tables, I took in my surroundings. It was a small hope, but if I saw a familiar face, I would just grab my food and join someone else to finish my meal. Unfortunately, the crowd hadn't really picked up yet. A few couples were seated about, a group of older shop owners sat huddled around a larger table discussing business and trade opportunities, and two other singles occupied spaces at the bar. One of these was a man dressed in filthy work clothes who appeared to be drinking himself into oblivion. The other, hidden in the shadows at the end, seemed completely lost in his own thoughts.

21

Exiting the lav, I glanced at the second man again and realized he looked as lonely as I currently felt. Luckily for him, in this settlement lonely didn't need to last long. If one was so inclined, brothels and bars full of other lonely people could be found within an easy walk.

Fortunately my sandwich had arrived by the time I retuned to my beer. Unfortunately Gary remained firmly rooted to his spot next to them both. Hoping he'd take the hint, I grabbed the plate and my drink and relocated to a small unoccupied table near the edge of the road. Clearly he was either duller or drunker than I expected and didn't miss a beat before following in my wake.

The goat cheese and tomato were heaven on my tongue, but I was eating so fast I barely enjoyed the food. I wanted to get out of there and away from the droning talk of a bare knuckle boxing tournament Gary planned to compete in over the weekend. I could have taken the food to go, but I was still holding out hope Roe would arrive. Similarly, I could tell Gary I wasn't interested, but I didn't have the energy to engage.

Swallowing my last bite, I noticed the gaze fixed firmly on my chest. Creep. Thank all the stars I had elected to wear my loose smock uniform rather than changing into the light tank I had originally planned.

Standing, I drained the remaining liquid from the beer bottle. He was licking his lips. *Actually licking his lips* as he stared at me.

"For the love of all that is good," I muttered. Despite my fatigue, I couldn't just walk away. "Gary, is it? I don't appreciate being mentally undressed by some drunk I just met."

Instead of looking ashamed as I naively expected, he had the audacity to stand and lean into me. "We could go back to my place, and it could be a lot more than mentally."

I cringed at both the slurred words and the spittle glistening on his lips. The sickly sweet smell of his breath brought on as much loathing as the statement itself.

"You cannot be serious." I raised my arms, palms facing forward. "And yet for some reason I believe you are. I'm leaving now and desperately hope to never run into you again. But given the size of the settlement, it's pretty unlikely I'll get my wish. So when you do see me next, I suggest you turn around and walk the other way."

Slinging my bag over my shoulder, I stepped around the table. He grabbed me firmly above the elbow. I winced more from surprise than pain, as he swung my body around to face him. Yet again, I was reminded of my petite stature. This man wasn't tall, and he certainly wasn't fit, but he still had a few inches and at least fifty pounds on me.

"Hey, cutie. Don't be like that. I was only trying to break the ice a little."

From the corner of my eye, I noticed someone moving in our direction. The lonely guy from the end of the bar. Not knowing him or his intentions either, I elected to handle this myself.

"I am not going to say this twice. Let go of my arm and do not touch me again."

After a moment's hesitation, Gary's face creased and he slowly released his grip. I stepped away and out into the road, the conversation Gen and I'd had earlier crashing back on me. I glanced over my shoulder and noted Gary sitting with a petulant scowl aimed at his drink. Interestingly, my would-be rescuer was standing casually against the bar, sipping from his own dark green beer bottle. His gaze locked on mine, and he tipped his chin in the briefest of nods. I put my head down and hurried into the stream of pedestrians on the road.

3

ROE

Damn it all. I was late. Really late.

Goldie-Locks was going to be totally and righteously pissed.

In fairness, it wasn't altogether my fault. Not completely at least. After a ridiculously long day of treating diabetic foot ulcers, toenail fungus, peptic ulcers, and my all-time favorite—lice infestations—I'd realized I hadn't brought a clean change of clothes with me. I couldn't stomach the idea of eating in a uniform contaminated by at least one, if not all, of the flavors of contagion I'd seen and treated that day. The only suitable solution had been to run home as quickly as possible and change.

Racing back out, I'd bumped into Listerman. Normally I wouldn't have bothered to stop if he'd been bleeding out on the side of the road, much less for a chat, but he happened to be exiting from an unused sewer tunnel at the end of the block. Holdan Listerman, Mr. Dapper himself, satchel over his shoulder, in the remnants of a sewer system under Devil's Meadows. There had to be a story there. So I stopped.

"Practitioner Belstrohm." He dipped his chin to me.

25

"Listerman." I did the same. Maybe just a touch mockingly.

He sighed and kept walking, so I slowed the pedals of my bicycle and walked next to it, back the way I'd just come.

"Oh, come on! You *are* going to tell me what it was you were doing in an old sewer tunnel, aren't you?"

"Not at this juncture. No. I'm not."

I studied him for a moment and nodded. "Fair enough. But you know I'll find out eventually."

"And use it against me, I have no doubt. Suffice it to say, I am trying to do my best to leave the past seven years of my life behind. Leave them, as it were, in that all-forsaken desert where they belong."

Holdan had done some terrible things in his life. And while much of it was due to the psychotic she-demon who had enslaved him, I still hadn't forgiven him completely for his part in the nightmare we'd survived on the road months back. If he felt he could find redemption among the fossilized feces and waste from this ancient city, then more power to him. The idea of inviting him to dinner occurred to me. While I didn't think Auri would mind if he tagged along, I would. So I watched him walk back toward our housing building and climbed back onto my bike.

Trying to make up lost time, I pedaled all out. Barreling around a blind corner, I almost flattened the very person I was racing to meet. Auri slammed herself flat against the side of the closest building.

"I swear, Roe Belstrohm, I will murder you in your sleep one day."

Dropping my feet flat to the ground, I doubled over the handlebars cackling like a lunatic, trying and failing to contain my laughter and regain my breath. "I'm . . . so . . . so . . . sorry." A drop of sweat rolled down my nose and hit the dust on the center tube of my bike.

"You certainly don't seem sorry."

"I am. Really. . . It's just the look on your face."

"Mmm-hmm." She eyed me seriously then shook her head, chuckling as well. I was sure I had escaped unscathed until she slugged me in the arm.

"Ow. Tiny Badass." I finally reined in my laughter and swung my leg over the seat, moving to push the bicycle by the handlebars as we walked. "I really am sorry. I didn't want to miss our dinner. Did you at least get something to eat?"

"Yes. But now that you mention it, I'm more angry about you missing dinner with me than I am about you almost killing me."

She informed me of her unfortunate admirer as we strolled along. The guy sounded like a total ass, and while I knew Auri could handle herself, I told her I'd be on the lookout for him in the future. One slimy desert rat doughboy shouldn't be hard to miss among all the other desert rats.

The air remained warm, but with the sun down and the stars out, I didn't feel as much like a chicken in a convection stove as I had earlier in the day. It wasn't pleasant, but it wasn't hellish either.

"Well, you ate but I'm still ravenous. I've got some ciders at home and probably something relatively edible. Let's crack open a couple of bottles and swap nightmare stories. We haven't just hung out in ages."

She pushed up her glasses and smiled. "Sounds good to me."

I straddled the bicycle and tipped my head back and to the side. "All right then. Hop on. I'll pedal."

Bicycles weren't overly common in DM, but a week or so after arriving, I'd seen this one in a junk shop and negotiated a trade with the small leathery

27

proprietor. It had cost me a few hours of time—which I had in short supply—cleaning his windows and making him a batch of muscle-soothing salve. Off the clock and the record from Medicus of course. As it turned out, the bicycle was rickety and needed new tires, but it got me around faster than my own feet could.

Auri looked skeptical but obliged and seated herself behind me. She wrapped her arms around my waist, and I pushed off. It was a wobbly start, but we were flying up the road in no time. I was almost giddy as the hot dry air blew in my face. It really had been awhile since the two of us just spent time together. If one of us wasn't working nights, we were both too exhausted come the end of our shifts to socialize. Or more likely, I was too tired, and Auri was too busy practicing her newfound gifts with Holdan Listerman.

Way back when Hale, Specs, and I had matched together for this assignment, I had hoped the three of us would conquer life together. I had completely underestimated how little time we would actually have for ourselves or each other. The older practitioners assured me we would soon get into the swing of things and settle into a pattern that would allow us more free time. I hoped they were right.

Devil's Meadows was a good-sized hub settlement, but even here most of the settlers shared what they had. Men, women, and children all had the same rough around the edges look of folks who struggled to thrive, but it wasn't often you saw someone who looked more impoverished than everybody else. And rarer still was to see someone who looked as if they'd just crawled out from under one of the massive boulder formations scattered about. As we pulled off the main road onto the side street leading to our housing building, we encountered a man so covered in filth and dust, he looked like he'd done just that. Resembling a walking heap of earth and garbage, the man stood half in and half out of the roadway, head dropped and shoulders slumped.

As I slowed to move the bicycle around his disheveled form, Auri muttered into my ear, "I feel like we should stop—see if he needs help—but there's someone following us."

Slowing the bike fractionally, I checked over my shoulder. My eyes didn't catch on anyone or anything behind us, save for the occasional quail racing across the road. "You sure?"

"I'm pretty sure it's the guy from the bar."

"What'd you say his name was? Gary?" I asked.

"Yeah. Not him though. The other guy."

"You're starting to have quite the list of guys, aren't you?" I quipped.

She squeezed my ribs. "I'm serious. He's back there. I saw him."

Not daring to slow too much and risk toppling us into the road, I studied the form of the man ahead. To my dismay, he was shuffling farther out into the road. I picked up the rancid odor rising from his unwashed person and soiled clothing. Soiled with what, I could only imagine.

The solar light outside our housing complex was still a good fifty yards off, and the light it cast was weak and watery. Still, it transformed the man's gaunt face into that of a lunatic—eyes glowing an unnatural greenish yellow and hollow cheeks skeletal.

His appearance suggested a stiff breeze would topple him like one of the thousands of tumbleweeds around, but still unease grew claws in my stomach. Auri too must have sensed it. She was a stiff tight shell of muscle clinging to my back. For all I knew, that weird ozone smell was filling her nostrils and signaling to her things were about to go straight down the shitter.

29

The chain of the bike clicked slowly as we neared the dark figure. Her grip on my waist cinched even tighter, and she yelped, "Go, Roe. Now!"

Not knowing if it was the threat behind us or something else, I didn't question her, just pushed my weight into my legs and over the top of the handlebars, urging the bicycle onward.

We made it only a dozen or so feet before something slammed into our side and sent me tumbling away from the bike and Auri. I was up in a heartbeat, spinning to look for her. She lay flat on her back—the bike frame over one of her legs, its back wheel spinning in the air. The disheveled man sat perched on her chest. Long locks of matted hair hung to either side of Auri's face, partially obscuring my view of her, as he crushed his mouth over hers. She was thrashing wildly under his weight, and slight as he was, her efforts were futile.

Before I could think, I was driving my shoulder into his temple, my momentum carrying us both away from Auri's petite frame and onto the adjacent walkway. Years of athletics kept me on my feet, and I was able to run through my landing. The other man's body made a skidding sound as he bounced along the gravel, coming to rest in a rumpled heap. My first inclination was to crush his trachea beneath my hands until his eyes popped from their sockets, but the sound of Auri gasping and spitting had me stepping over him and to her side instead.

He couldn't have had her pinned for more than thirty seconds, but still she was gasping and purple as if she'd been submerged in water for five times that long. Tears streamed from her eyes. Miraculously her glasses had stayed firmly in place through the entire ordeal.

My own adrenaline had my hands trembling as I helped her into a sitting position. Doing a speedy

30

cursory check, I assessed for any major injuries. There didn't seem to be any, but still she shook with racking heaves, attempting to drag lungfuls of air into her chest.

"All right, Little-bit. Take deep slow breaths. You're all right now." Repeating the words, I kept one eye on the crumpled body to my right while still trying to scan the area for the second man Auri claimed to have seen. "Maybe we should get inside." She nodded and leaned against me as we walked the remainder of the way to our building. I'd come back for the bike later.

The night was unusually quiet—broken only by the humming drone of cicadas calling from the scraggly trees and the sound of Auri's ragged breaths. Neither the insectile noise nor the heavy panting did much to calm my jangled nerves.

One other bicycle—in worse shape than mine—and a small hand-pull cart occupied the space near the door to our building. No other inhabitants were out—unusual for this time of the evening but not unheard of.

We were nearing the door when Aurelia finally spoke. " I . . . can't . . . catch my . . . breath."

Tears still streamed from her eyes and pooled on the bottom frame of her glasses.

"Yes, you can. Slow. Inhale. Exhale."

I rubbed one hand down her back and reached for the door with the other. She drug in another gulping breath but then settled and slowly exhaled. A few more exchanges later and her voice still sounded hoarse, but her breathing was fractionally better. Slower and more steady. Still not good.

"What are the chances . . . I don't . . . have some communicable disease . . . now?"

"Come on, Tiny Badass. You're made of strong stuff. No germ would dare to pass those lips." I

31

chuckled to lighten the mood but felt it die on my lips as I looked over my shoulder. The huddled shape of Auri's attacker was gone. Terrific.

Despite the lack of a body and absence of others outside our building, I still had the feeling we were being watched.

"Inside now, Specs. Let's go."

We entered the small lobby of our building, the door clicking shut behind us. Auri's rooms were on the second floor. Mine and Hale's on the third. We were headed toward the stairs when the lobby door banged shut again. Spinning, I shoved Auri behind me and faced a man I'd never seen before.

He wasn't quite as tall as me, but he was broader through the chest and shoulders. Dark close-cropped hair covered his skull, and he wore an intense dark expression. Not menacing exactly, but way beyond serious.

"You," Aurelia hissed. "What do you want? Why are you . . . following me?" Her breath still sounded far too labored, each word whistling a little as it exited her body.

He held up his hands and stopped walking. "You need to be cautious. If I could follow you so easily, so could he." The man's voice was calm and easy. Something in his tone reminded me a bit of Asher. By "he," I could only assume he meant the lunatic outside.

"All the more reason for us to get behind a locked door, don't you think?" If I sounded like an ass, so be it. Desperate times and all that.

"Not necessarily." He took a step forward.

I tensed. "Far enough."

He looked like he wanted to argue but placed his raised foot back down and didn't come any closer.

"Neither of you know what you are dealing with. He's had a taste. Now he will not stop. You should have killed him when you had a chance." The man's eyes were penetrating—deepest dark brown and full of fire. *Now that he's had a taste?*

"I try not to make a habit of killing people. Quite the opposite actually."

"You should have made an exception." He looked over his shoulder to the glass door behind him. "I realize you both are more of the healing type, but trust me. In this situation dead would have been better. You don't know him like I do."

Whatever he meant by these cryptic warnings, I didn't like it. If he knew that psycho so well, why was he letting him run around attacking people?

"Our friends." Auri's breathless voice came from behind me. "They're escorts."

When he didn't respond, she added, "If anything happens to us. Things will get ugly . . . for whoever . . . is responsible."

Heavens love my clever little friend. We couldn't walk to either of our rooms and have this stranger—or worse, his deranged friend—follow directly to our door.

Apparently, he'd followed Auri from the tavern, and for all we knew the two of them were working together. This could all be some nefarious act to get us to trust him. I'd never seen this guy before. We hadn't been here long, but I'm fairly certain I would have noticed him if he was a regular member of the community. I mean—those eyes. I would have noticed those eyes.

"Let me help you. You're probably still short of breath." He was speaking now directly to Auri. As if I wasn't even there. "You need my help."

I squared my shoulders in front of her again. "We don't need anything from you. Now. Back. The hell. Up."

What we needed was to get out of this small space with a man who was taking up way too much of it. If we made a run for it, we might get as far as the building across the courtyard—the one Asher and Gen lived in. If I'd been by myself, it wouldn't be an issue. I was confident I could outrun this guy, but Auri was another matter entirely. Running wasn't exactly her thing.

"You were going to help me at the tavern." Ragged breath. "You followed me?"

He nodded and tried to look over and past my shoulder to my fierce little friend.

"It's hard to explain just now. I don't have the time. You don't trust me. Good. I can actually appreciate that, but I am being honest when I tell you I only want to help." Still neither of us moved. He shook his head and looked around as if the way to our trust was lying on the floor between us. "You mentioned your friends are escorts. You can think of me in a similar vein. It's not what we're called where I'm from, but it's close enough."

He was slowly inching forward again, and I pushed Aurelia back another step. I didn't want to listen to more of what he had to say, but we didn't have many options.

"The man that attacked you won't come back as long as he knows I'm here. I've been tracking him for a long time now and I believe he knows it."

Another step forward from him and another step backward from us.

Something about the way he spoke seemed legitimate, but there was no chance I was going to risk it. I'd been held captive once before, and one time was enough for anyone. Goldie-Locks didn't need that in her life either.

I could still feel Auri's breath hitting my shoulder blade, and to my dismay it was still a good bit quicker than it should have been. She was panting at a rate that threatened hyperventilation if she kept it up. I turned my head as far as I could to check on her but couldn't risk taking my eyes off the man in front of me.

"She needs to lie down. It's going to be a while before she feels well." As if I needed him to tell me she needed rest. He took another step forward. "Really. I do only want to help." He raised his hand toward me in what I'm sure he thought was a calming gesture.

"Roe . . . I . . . can't catch . . . my . . ."

I needed Auri to calm her breathing so I could think of something to do. We were backed up to the interior wall as far as we could go. There wasn't anywhere else. Not without getting around Mr. Dark and Dangerous.

Another step forward.

"Roe . . . I . . ." She slumped against me, and her body slipped down between me and the wall.

Turning to grab her, I heard a mumbled, "I really am sorry about this."

I didn't see the fist until it connected with my face and sent me into the black.

4

HALE

The baby squawked like a tiny bird of prey as I pulled her from her mother's womb in a flood of blood and amniotic fluid. As quickly as I could, I placed her on the young woman's abdomen and secured a set of clamps on her umbilical cord and cut cleanly between the two. The assistant with me crooned as she wiped the tiny screeching creature with warm towels and suctioned out her mouth while I waited patiently to deliver the placenta.

It was my first delivery in Devil's Meadows and a great way to finish up a long stretch of nights covering the clinic. I couldn't wait to get out of there, take a shower, and fall into a blissful sleep, knowing I had two whole days off coming up.

On second thought, maybe I'd wait around to tell Auri about the delivery first. She'd get a kick out of it, I was sure. Women's health certainly wasn't my forte, but I had enjoyed seeing this little life enter the world kicking and screaming.

After ensuring both mom and baby were doing well, I grabbed a cup of coffee and my surgical textbook and sank into what passed as a comfortable chair in the little space we used as a lounge. Because it was placed near an east-facing window, it was one of my least hated spots in the building. I could sit here and read while watching the sun come up over the rocky striated mountains in the distance. Most mornings, the incoming practitioners popped in here to chat with the night coverage, and today was no exception. Unfortunately the practitioner who banged open the door and pulled me from the sunrise wasn't the one I was hoping to see.

"Ah! Hale." Jassika Duncan dropped a stethoscope and a battered news periodical on the table and loaded a mug with way too much sugar and a splash of coffee. "How was your evening?"

"Not bad." I rolled my shoulders and stood. "I take that back. It was actually pretty good. Delivered a baby."

"Really?" She raised her eyebrows. "How's the kid?"

"Nice and pink. Mom's doing good too."

"Huh. Good for you." Jassika was an older woman who wore her medical acumen like a badge of honor. I didn't hate her, I just didn't *like* her very much. Of all the other established practitioners, she was the last one I wanted to work with. She knew what she was doing, which was great. She just seemed to resist anyone who did things slightly differently, which rubbed me wrong.

She ran her hand over her head, flattening her soft cap of short hair. The cut would have looked girlish had it not been the color of steel. I guess it matched the rod up her ass most of the time.

"Yeah," I responded. "It was good. You didn't see Aurelia on the way in, did you?"

It was still early, but Auri tended to be an early bird.

"No. As a matter of fact I haven't yet. I imagine she'll be in shortly though. I can update her on anything if you need to be getting home."

I contemplated telling her I'd wait, but then thought better of it. The last thing either of us needed was to have half the clinic staff wondering why I wanted to see Aurelia at such an ungodly hour.

"All right then. I've got nothing important to sign out." I was grabbing my bag to go when she stopped me.

"Actually, Hale. You might have a talk with your friend next time you see her."

That stopped me dead. I tilted my head and frowned in her direction.

"What might I be talking to her about?"

"Let her know that what she's doing isn't, shall we say . . . a good idea." She was staring at the mug in her hands as she swirled the steaming liquid as if all the secrets of the universe were hidden there.

"I'm not sure I follow."

"I think you do. And I think your brother likely does as well. People have noticed. Her patients here do very well. Normally, I commend a dedicated practitioner who has the skills to manage their patients well. But I think she may be a bit more than dedicated. Others around here might not be bold enough to say anything yet, but it will happen eventually."

I didn't know what to say, so I kept my mouth shut.

"The Grand Divagation happened for a reason, and Medicus's rules exist as they do for the same reason. The people of Devil's Meadows are lucky to have the three of you here. I'd like to see you stay awhile. Tell her to mind herself very carefully."

I nodded and left Jassika Duncan to tend to her patients.

5

AURELIA

Brass bells. The chiming of small bells. I was being hunted by a madwoman in a wagon covered in tiny brass bells.

But we'd escaped, hadn't we? Saved Roe and healed Gen and escaped the madness of Nanette months ago? Holdan was—not a friend exactly, but also not a monster. The bells had been left in the desert somewhere. I was sure.

But still the metallic tinkling rang on and I was running from them and swimming to the surface of consciousness and the brass chimes continued to ring.

Then I was choking—my air at first cut off by a foul breath seeping into my mouth. Then it morphed and moved to my neck. Invisible power looping around and strangling my airways as I fought and thrashed.

Rolling over, I snuck out a hand and banged it onto the tiny hammer atop my alarm clock and silenced the shrill wake-up call.

It wasn't the first time I'd woken in a panic at the sound of the damn clock, but as it was, I didn't have a substitute and needed to make sure I was awake each morning in time to get to the clinic for my shift.

Was it morning already? I felt as if I hadn't slept in days. My head was pounding, and a wince overtook me as the weak light filtered into my room and behind my eyes. It burrowed deep into the back of my skull. What had Roe and I gotten up to last night?

A nice hot shower would clear the fog. Roe had mentioned drinks at his place. At least I remembered that. And the unfortunate encounter with Gary, the desert rat, at the tavern. But the later part of the evening was blurred and foggy—more of a remembered dream or a fleeting nightmare than actual clear recollections.

Visions of a ghoulish chase and the feeling of drowning mixed with flashes of Roe and some other. A dark-haired, dark-eyed man. It must have been the stress of the past week catching up with me and the trauma from our trek through the desert mingling with memories of the stranger from the tavern. All of it colliding in a fractionated miasma in my subconscious. Nothing more than a dream born of terrible things while under the influence of whatever Roe and I enjoyed last night.

Or. . . A really sinister thought occurred. Had Gary slipped something into my drink at the bar? I had been away for several minutes while my beer sat unattended. It might be hard to get a substance that could cause memory loss, but it certainly wasn't impossible. If so, thank the heavens and earth I'd left when I did and had the good fortune to bump into Roe on my way home. Otherwise lecherous sneers and foul conversation could have been the least of my worries.

Nausea pooled in my gut and a monster of a headache danced in my brain. I felt simultaneously hung over and relieved but couldn't remember drinking or getting home safely. What I was certain of was I would either shave Roe bald while he slept or bake him cookies, depending on what he told me had happened during our escapades the previous night.

The one thing I was definitely thankful for was Hale's absence. If he'd been with us, I probably would have made a complete and total fool of myself—hanging on him and begging him to take me somewhere to be alone. At least I didn't *think* he'd been there. I was sure he had night shift duties, but I had the nagging feeling someone else had been involved. I just didn't know who.

Another thing I was thankful for was the rooftop water tanks with their coils of black tubing that pulled the light from the sky to heat the indoor plumbing in our building. Water rushed over my head, loosening some of the bunched muscles in my neck and shoulders. Grabbing a handful of citrus and ginger shampoo and working it into my hair, I desperately hoped it would work its magic and invigorate my addled brain.

As the soap drifted down the drain, part of my tension flowed out with it. Then I winced when the suds hit a scrape on my knee and again when I scrubbed over an enormous bruise on my hip. Vowing to myself to come straight home from clinic that night and climb into bed early, I toweled off and faced the tiny mirror above the sink. The reflection staring back looked terrible. Squinting, I leaned forward and wiped steam from the glass, my tired eyes opening wide. Only the tiniest bit panicked, I hunted around until my hands fell on my glasses. Slamming them into place, I cursed when I was momentarily blinded again by the condensation forming over the lenses. I jerked open the door and stumbled out to the even smaller mirror attached to the chest of drawers on the other side of my bed.

Even though I'd never really been a vain person, I still cringed at the six by six reflection staring back at me. Bags big enough to haul grain hung below my eyes—the frames of my tortoise shell glasses doing little to mask the dusky hue. My complexion—normally a warm terracotta—had transformed to a waxy, woozy beige. It was a perfect match for my dry chapped lips, which just happened to be ringed by a set of ugly bruises.

Hoping to catch Roe before needing to be in the clinic, I threw on a relatively clean pair of cargo pants and matching smock. I was corralling my hair into what might pass as a bun, when I walked into my small living space and found Roe making coffee.

"Damn, Specs. You look worse than me." He smiled and raised his hand to draw attention to the vibrant discoloration blossoming along his left cheek and temple. When I gasped, he added almost as an afterthought, "Feels like I took a hit to the back of my head too."

As I rushed over, he ducked down and let me feel along his crown and down the occipital bone. Sure enough, a large goose egg hematoma was taking up residence on the back of his scalp. He grimaced as my fingers prodded the boggy tissue.

"What the hell happened last night?" I cried.

"You don't remember?" he scoffed.

"No. Do you?"

"Unfortunately, yes. Yes, I do." He handed me a mug of glorious black coffee, and I blew on the surface waiting for him to tell me. He shook his head at whatever it was he was remembering.

In an effort to get him started, I told him what I did remember. "I was at the tavern. Had a beer and a sandwich. There was this obnoxious guy Gary. I think the bastard might have slipped me something." He raised his eyebrows and frowned. "Then running into you outside and heading home. That's it."

He blew out a long breath and sipped at his own mug, wincing slightly before blowing on the surface to cool it. "You have zero recollection of the man—or men I should say—who attacked us?"

"Attacked us? No." I was incredulous, but a flash of rank breath and the thirst for air tugging at my chest made me pause. "Well, maybe. But I thought it was a dream."

"Nope. Not a dream, Shrimpboat. Gross, dirty, shaggy little scrapper toppled us outside. Those bruises on your face are from him. We made it inside, and this other *charming* fellow—thankfully not nearly as dirty and shaggy—showed up and *these* bruises"—he pointed to his face—"are courtesy of him. I've also got some fairly spectacular black and purple spots from the fall off the bike. I will, however, spare you looking at those."

"The man from the tavern?" I remembered out loud. "He followed us and I recognized him. For all that is good and holy, I thought I dreamed all of it. But I still can't remember it all. Did you fight him off or something?"

"I wish I could say I had, but he cold cocked me and the lights went out. I woke up snoozing on your couch with you tucked safely in bed." He looked at me and added wryly, "That's the second time I've been rendered unconscious in the last handful of months. I fear I'm sensing a pattern."

His words had me scrambling up to check my apartment and the locks on my door, only returning when Roe yelled, "Auri, relax. I already checked. He's gone. In fact, I don't know how he did it, but the bastard even took the courtesy of locking your door before he took off."

"Maybe I hit my head too?" I rubbed at the back of my neck, unease filling me. "What crimes did we commit in a past life to deserve this?"

"No clue, Little-bit. But I think we need to let Asher and Gen know what happened before someone decides to pay us a return visit."

Roe walked with me to the clinic, and I filled him in on the conversation I'd had with Gen the previous day. He agreed it wasn't a forgone conclusion one of our mystery men from the night before was responsible for the other attacks, but it did seem quite coincidental if not. We made plans to meet up after work to walk home together, and he also made me promise, just as Geneva had, not go out alone by myself particularly after dark. We intended to track down one of our escorts as soon as possible to let them know what had happened, and I was opening my mouth to suggest he inform his brother as well when he cut me off.

"Don't worry, Goldie-Locks. Hale is top of my list to chat with."

Giving my best friend a hug, I left him on the first floor and tromped up the stairwell to start my morning rounds. As tired as I was, it was going to be the sort of day I had to kick-start by sheer force of will.

My determination began to dissipate as I dropped my bag containing my pens, stethoscope, pocket reference guide, and most importantly, snacks. The staples of my life bloomed in a starburst across the tiles. On my hands and knees, grabbing my supplies, I heard voices coming from the assistants' station.

"Well, obviously, they're both pretty easy on the eyes. Utterly doable. But Roe flirts with everyone. It'd be almost too easy, you know?" The tittering high-pitched voice sounded like one of the new assistants.

"Mmm-hmm" came the noncommittal reply.

The high-pitched voice continued, "But Hale. He's another story. I've always been drawn to the strong silent type. It's like the universe has destined it—me being single and him being delectable. Couple more shifts together and just you wait. We'll be banging in the supply closet."

"Well . . . that's not really such a good idea." That sounded like it might be Janet, one of the level-headed senior assistants.

Shoving my books and granola into my satchel, I strolled around the corner to stand just behind the desk. Janet—the one who knew banging Hale in the closet was a bad idea—saw me and her eyes widened. Young and chipper had her back to me and didn't get the hint. "Obviously Roe's with Aurelia, but he's probably cheating on her the way he acts around here. Definitely too easy. It's the big Belstrohm for me."

I entered around the side of the station, and Janet forced a smile on her face and nodded down to a stack of fresh linen she'd picked up from the counter. "Well, I've got what I came for. See you later."

The chipper little gossip paled when she saw me. She'd only been working here for the past two weeks—newer to the clinic than the doable Belstrohm brothers and myself. A snippet of conversation from the previous night tickled my neocortex and amygdala. This was probably Gary's sister. The one not *bright enough* to be anything more than an assistant. While I was aggravated by the conversation I'd just overheard, I had to feel a little sorry for her, growing up with a brother like that. Besides, other than being unprofessional, she had no way of knowing what my relationships with Roe and Hale were like.

It took me a moment to remember her name was Cookie. Not her nickname but her actual birth-given name. Not sure how I could have forgotten it to begin with.

To her credit, she faltered for only a beat before she plastered the peppy expression back on her face. "You're not as early as usual this morning." It was an unnecessary observation and did nothing to further endear her to me. "Practitioner Duncan has already come and gone for the morning. She got sign out from Practitioner *Hale* Belstrohm"—I tried not to frown at the way she blushed when she differentiated Hale from Roe—"and told me to let you know everything is under control with her patients. Anything important is in their chart notes."

She eyed me conspiratorially then leaned forward and whispered, "She seemed a little disappointed you weren't here by the time she left."

"Well, let's just say my morning hasn't been typical. I'll discuss it with her when I see her." I smiled, but my words held a bite, telling the young assistant the conversation was over. "Has my new admit shown up yet?"

"No." Cookie's pep had taken a hit, but she rallied. "We've got your orders but no sign of the patient."

"How about Sandy? Is she working today?" I'd hoped to chat with her and let her know I couldn't share information about Clarice unless the girl's father gave me express authorization to make Sandy a part of the care team. The young woman's privacy was important. If either she or her father chose not to allow Sandy to be involved, it was a decision I would have to uphold.

"She took the day off. Nora is in charge today."

I nodded and grabbed a stack of charts. "And Hale? Did he leave already as well?"

"I believe he might still be on the first floor. I can go get him if you need to get a sign out from him?" Her hopeful tone matched the eagerness in her eyes.

"No. Don't worry about it." If he was still on the first floor, Roe could fill him in. Plus, despite how petty it made me, I was the tiniest bit satisfied the young assistant wouldn't get to chat with the doable big Belstrohm again this morning. As soon as the thought arose, I squashed it back down. I refused to be the jealous type. Hale could talk to me or her or any other woman in Devil's Meadows and beyond. I would be fine with it.

"I'll go ahead and check in on Diego first then. When Clarice and her father arrive, will you please grab me?"

If the heavens were in my favor, Sandy would help ensure the Donahues arrived earlier today than they had yesterday. It was my turn to work the first floor that afternoon and I had no interest in doing my full history and physical along with all the charting on the girl after I was done down there. Pulling a late-nighter was not high on my list of ways I wanted to spend the evening.

Checking in on Diego, I was pleased to see how well he was doing. He was alert and animated, breathing easily as he played with a set of wooden blocks. The tower he was building was almost as tall as himself. I sat on the floor next to him and listened to his chest while he stacked block on top of block. Only faint wheezes and crackles plagued his lungs today, and I elected not to sit and hold his hand for an extra dose of healing.

A cute kid with a heartbreaking smile and a loving family, he was tiny but a trooper both physically and emotionally. His grandmother made it a point to bring me steaming piles of cheese tamales whenever she got the chance. Diego's mom remained a constant sentinel at her son's bedside, even though she had other children at home. I tried to pop in

47

when she was out getting something to eat or taking a few precious minutes for herself. It was easy for her to believe I simply enjoyed keeping him company while she was gone, and that made me feel more than a little guilty. None of his family members had any idea what I was really doing when I sat with him. It was important they didn't suspect anything unusual. Using tiny measures of healing energy on him—mini miracles I'd come to call them—I was clearing the inflammation and secretions from his lungs little by little. Even these small doses were helpful, but it was also perilous. They could get me into tremendous trouble. If anyone in the clinic got wind of what I was doing, the threat of Medicus Corpus removing me from my position, or worse—tossing me in jail—was apparently quite real.

My mind was still a smidge hazy, and again I frowned at my lack of memories from the previous evening. After speaking with Roe, I had been able to piece it all together, but rather than a crisp visual of what had transpired, I was left with memories that were dreamlike and vague. Chunks of recollection interspersed with thick black holes where no narrative remained.

The missing bits distracted me, and by the time I finished with the assessments and orders on all of my patients and made it back to the assistants' station, Clarice and her father—accompanied by a grim-looking Sandy—were just getting settled in her space. I glanced at the clock and grabbed the folder that served as Clarice's chart. Cookie was busy chatting them up while tucking the sheets in under the narrow bed Clarice would be occupying for the next couple—if not more—days. It was tucked into an out-of-the-way corner next to a window with a lovely view of the run-down building next door.

"Good morning, Clarice." I gave a brief nod in the direction of her father. "Mr. Donahue."

"Good morning to you as well," the weary man replied. Neither he nor his daughter looked as if they had gotten much sleep the night before.

"Once you get settled in, the assistant is going to be drawing some additional blood samples, but it won't be much."

It was Sandy who answered. "Whatever is necessary."

"Actually, Sandy, it needs to be up to Clarice and Conrad."

"Of course. I know that. It's just. . ." Her normally jovial face was lined with concern.

"Sandy mentioned you might not want her to be involved in Clarice's treatment, but if it's all the same to you, I think we'd all be comfortable having her involved," Conrad said.

I smiled at both Sandy and her brother, glad they had broached the subject before I'd had to. "And what do you think of that, Clarice?"

"Sure. Whatever." The accompanying eyeroll was in a league of its own.

Her mood from the day before obviously hadn't improved. I wasn't sure I could blame her. When I was her age, the last thing I would have wanted was to be ill and cooped up in a clinic for who knew how many days.

We discussed the paperwork and additional evaluations I would be ordering. Clarice still looked pale and fragile, but her large eyes were all sparks one moment and ice the next. "Do you have any actual treatment planned, or am I just going to be stuck here getting poked and prodded?"

"It's hard to say. I need to figure out what exactly is causing your symptoms before I throw random medications at you. I make no promises, but I suspect it will be relatively quick, and if all goes well, we can start some therapy tonight with the hopes of you going home in the next day or two."

As I left them to finish getting settled and for Cookie to draw the blood tests I wanted, I mulled things over in my mind. Something didn't feel right. Clearly both Sandy and her brother Conrad were really concerned about Clarice, but the teen gave the impression this was all just a big inconvenience for her. Was I missing something important? Still frustrated by the fog hanging in my brain, I was concerned my mind might be overlooking something obvious in this case too.

Almost involuntarily, my hand rose to my collarbone and fiddled with the golden pendant hanging there. The small orb had been a gift from my mother on my eighteenth birthday. I'd kept it tucked safely away on my journey from Renfield but now wore it on a thin chain around my neck—only rarely taking it off. I even slept and showered with it on. While I didn't consider toying with it a nervous habit, I was aware that I reached for it at times of deep concentration or when I was fidgety and distractible. Somehow stroking my namesake globe was soothing and centering for me, but today it had the unwanted side effect of reminding me how much I missed my folks and the relatively quiet life I'd left behind.

Pushing my longing to see my parents again to the back of my mind, I tried to chalk the girl's attitude up to teenage angst.

6

ROE

My day was an inverse to Shrimpboat's schedule. My duties included covering the first floor for a few hours before I tackled my third floor patients in the afternoon. Plus, I had to work in time to track down one of our escorts as I'd promised Auri I would. Hale could wait until the end of my shift since he was probably passed out at home recovering from his night in the clinic anyway.

As luck would have it, I didn't need to go far to find Asher and give him the rundown on what had happened the night before. He showed up at the clinic in search of some antacids just after I'd started my shift. My growing suspicion was he might be developing an ulcer from all the coffee and worry bubbling around in his gut. I was pleasantly surprised when he agreed to let me look into it, rather than brushing it off as I had expected him to.

After the exam, he was buttoning his shirt when I told him about the two men Auri and I had encountered the night before.

"And this second man told you he was an escort?"

"No." I shook my head. "He said he was called something different where he came from—wherever the hell that is—but that it was similar to an escort."

"And you believed him?" His tone was skeptical.

"I wanted to believe him. Don't look at me like that. You didn't see the other one perched on top of Auri. I was frazzled and wasn't thinking straight and then he sucker punched me soooo"—I drew out the word and tilted my head—"probably not a good guy. But then we woke up in her place safe and sound and he was gone. Soooo, maybe not a bad guy. You tell me. Someone to worry about or just an asshole?"

Asher chuffed a laugh. "Not sure. All the settlements in this area have escorts, but we are employed by Medicus Corpus. We don't *run* the settlement or hubs; that's left up to the councils or leaders to figure out. Some have hired thugs, others community watch or what have you. Medicus pays us to take care of you lot and the supplies and facilities. The rest is up to whoever. *Here*, that whoever is the settlement council. Same as in Renfield. So maybe this guy is just some backwoods glory hound looking to play the part or maybe he's a legit law enforcer. Whatever the case, if he's away from home, it doesn't matter. He's got no power, no jurisdiction, here. And if he's messing with you and Aurelia . . . well then . . . that's *my* jurisdiction."

"And the other piece of human waste?" The memory of him crowded over Goldie-Locks sent a shiver down my spine.

"That's the real concern, isn't it?" Asher was sitting on the cot and sliding on his boots but stopped and glanced around us.

Lowering my voice, I said, "Specs told me about the killings. You think it could be related?"

"A smart man would work under that assumption until proven otherwise, don't you think?"

"I do."

"That's because you're a smart man." He laced up his boots, stood, and rubbed the back of his neck. "You tell anyone I said that, Doc, and I'll deny it to the end."

A slight grin spread over my face. "I wouldn't expect anything less."

The older man sighed. "What are you doing after work tonight?"

"Walking Tiny Badass home."

"Good answer." He thought for a moment. "And your brother?"

"Mmmm . . . I *think* he's off tonight. It's hard to keep track. We live two doors down from each other, but I rarely see him with this schedule."

"It's not an easy job, but you are all handling it well. I'll also deny saying that if you were wondering." He shouldered his bag. "Geneva keeps talking about needing to catch up with you all. I think she's gone soft since our trek." His words held no bite. Watching the woman he loved stepping right up to death's door and knocking on it loudly had been life changing for him as well as her. Without the wonder-working of Holdan and Auri, things would have ended very differently for her and therefore him as well. "How about I meet you here later and join you on a nice evening stroll back to our place for a little catch-up. Your moody brother can tag along if he's not in fact working tonight."

Slinging my stethoscope over my shoulder, I gave him a tiny salute. "Sounds like a plan."

It was later in the afternoon when I saw him again.

Like several of the other building in Devil's Meadows, the clinic roof was covered in large solar panels enabling the interior to be furnished with solar-fed, battery-powered equipment. This included lights, small refrigeration units, and swamp coolers among other things. During daylight hours, it made sense to allow the natural light to flood the space, thereby saving the batteries and allowing them to fully charge. The unfortunate consequence of doing this while simultaneously running the evaporative coolers was often a hot sticky building—particularly on the upper floors.

I'd stepped outside for a little dose of sizzling fresh air and was watching a grey lizard scurry up the side of the building. It was obviously a juvenile since it was no bigger than some of the roaches I'd seen inhabiting the same wall. It moved at lightning speed, and when it disappeared out of view, I turned and startled as I caught sight of someone across the road.

The dark eyes, below the even darker hair, stared right at me. He stood between two ridiculously tall palm trees—their shaggy desiccated fronds hanging just above his head. He made no move to hide or look away when he noticed *me* notice him. My hand trailed up to the still tender bruises on my face, and my temper flared. I was trotting across the road before I knew what I was doing. Maybe he needed to experience what a fair fight felt like.

The bastard just gazed at me, gave an apologetic shrug, and turned away. By the time I made it the forty yards to where he'd been, he was gone. I checked around the outside of the other buildings, between the scattered groups of palms and sagebrush and even in the drainage ditch running along the back of the clinic. No sign of him. After fifteen minutes, all I had to show for my effort was a sweat-drenched shirt and a severe case of swamp-ass.

7

AURELIA

Having completed what I could, I hustled downstairs to enjoy a few minutes outside before my shift on the first floor began. Perhaps the hot desert sunshine would sizzle away the fog shrouding my mind. The day was typical for summer in the desert—hot and blindingly bright. Not a stray wisp of cloud in sight. The last time I'd seen rain had been on the perilous journey to Devil's Meadows, and that particular downpour had almost been the end of me, Roe, and Hale. The ground here was just as dry and parched, and I worried when the rain did finally come, it would sweep through the valley at a treacherous pace.

The mercury continued to climb, and within a handful of minutes I was sweating through my shirt. Using a hand to shield my eyes, I looked up at the twenty-some odd feet of green paint looming over me. The staff and snake emblazoned on the fading white stucco. Medicus Corpus was my new family. Devil's Meadows my new home.

Heading back into the building, I embraced the buzz of activity on the first floor. The assistants were moving patients from the waiting area to a variety of open cots or simple chairs further into the exam space. Glancing around, I caught sight of the two older practitioners—Jassika Duncan and Theo Wong. They were each busy with patients. If they noticed my entrance, they didn't acknowledge it.

I still had a few minutes, so I grabbed my coffee mug and headed to the lounge. A freshly brewed pot stood waiting. I filled my mug to the brim and sat down to look at the first chart in my pile. It was a simple medication to be refilled. Deeper in the stack were updates and questions from patients which needed replies, but nothing overly taxing. I jotted a few messages and reminders to myself of things to have the assistants follow up on or recommendations I could give to my patients when I saw them.

Lying toward the bottom of my stack of charts was a note from Nora—the person who kept me sane and organized when I was working the first floor. Her neat handwriting was almost as familiar as my own at this point, and I'd only been here a couple of months.

Message from Valilier(???) Robichaud. Stopped by to meet with you this morning but I informed him you were unavailable. He will attempt to contact you this evening and wanted me to stress the importance of having an escort if leaving after dark???
PS: What is a Valilier?
—N

The message made no sense.

I didn't know a Valilier Robichaud and had no idea why he would want to contact me. And, to answer Nora's question, I had zero idea what a *valilier* was. Maybe he was a friend of Gen's with the "having an escort home" bit.

"Nora," I called as I read through the note again. The door was open and usually she was within earshot, her desk being just outside the lounge. "You out there?"

I looked up in time to see her lean her chair back enough to let me view her face and shoulders in the open doorway. "Right here, Mija. What's up?"

Despite being at least a decade older than me, Nora exuded a youthful energy that made me utterly jealous. Long chestnut hair framed her face, and she had the best eyebrows I had ever seen. They were so perfect I often joked she drew them on. As amazing as they were, however, they were nothing compared to the intricate black lines and swirls covering both of her arms from wrist to well above the short sleeves of her smock top. I hadn't seen them in their entirety, but Nora had informed me the black ink decorated her skin all the way over her shoulders and into a wing pattern over both of her scapula. Apparently her husband's brother had studied the ancient art of tattooing with a needle and thin wooden dowel. He would add little portions of the intricate design at various important times in Nora's life—her marriage, the birth of her children, and milestone birthdays. She had offered his services to me on more than one occasion, and I assured her I'd think about it.

"Hey, you gorgeous woman. What does this message mean?" I held up the scrap of paper with her handwriting on it. "Who is Valilier Robichaud, and what does he want with me?"

"Huh. I figured you'd know." A quizzical frown crossed her face. "He stopped by first thing this morning looking for you. Made it sound like you would know exactly who he was and why he needed to talk to you. Being the responsible clinic assistant that I am"—she placed a hand to her chest and smiled indulgently—"I informed him you were unavailable. Honestly, I just didn't feel like dragging myself upstairs when I figured you were busy with your patients and were just going to send me back down here to tell him as much."

"Thanks, I think. Was Roe wandering around down here when he stopped by?"

"Mmmnn. I don't think I'd seen him yet actually. Can't really remember though."

"Well then, you would have wasted your time looking for me anyway. I got in late, and if Roe wasn't here yet, neither was I."

Nora nodded. "He seemed annoyed I wouldn't fetch you and made me promise to give you a message telling you to go straight home tonight and to expect a visit from him. Seems like he knows where you live." She raised her eyebrows and got the gleam in her eye that told me whatever she said next was probably going to make me blush.

"Between you and me, I wouldn't mind if he knew where I lived. The jawbone on that man. Whoa! And his backside wasn't bad either. Are you sure you don't know who he is?"

"Nora!" I couldn't contain the laugh bubbling up. "You are a happily married woman, remember?"

She scoffed and waved her hand dismissively. "Mija, it never hurts to look as long as I don't touch!"

Still laughing, I shook my head. "Whatever you say, gorgeous. But honestly, I have absolutely no clue what this is about." The smile died on my face. "Did he sound serious? Like am I in trouble or something?"

We didn't have valiliers in Devil's Meadows or my home settlement of Renfield. At least not that I was aware of. Could he be with Medicus? Had someone realized what I'd been doing with Holdan and the patients here? My mini miracles. Was this going to be my last day providing medical care to those in need? Would I wake tomorrow in a cell?

Nora must have sensed my anxiety because she rubbed her hand on my shoulder. "Awwww, Mija,

I'm sure it's nothing. I'm really sorry I didn't get more info. If it helps, he sounded really pleasant and just wanted to make sure you got home safely tonight."

"Of course. You're probably right. Hey, do me a favor though. If he shows up here again, come grab me, would you? I'll be down here all afternoon and then just need to check upstairs for a minute before I go home tonight."

"Of course." She smiled half-heartedly. "Now you better get to work. Old Mrs. Roilers is here, and she refuses to let anyone other than you tell her there's nothing wrong with her again today."

Mrs. Emma Roilers was the type of patient who normally gravitated toward Roe for care, not me. He was the one who was patient and kind with the elderly. They trusted him when they often treated me like I was an adolescent playing dress-up and pretending to know what I was doing. But for some unknown reason, she'd decided I was the only person she would see when she came to the clinic, and if I didn't happen to be there that day, she'd simply ask when I would be in and come back during my hours on the first floor. I didn't really mind. She was a sweet older woman who'd lost her husband the year before to a stroke.

I rubbed my temples as I headed out into the main floor. After tending to Mrs. Roilers (who in reality was lonely and just wanted someone to talk to), a child with an abscessed tooth, a middle-aged man with a broken toe, two intoxicated teens (who claimed they didn't know each other but probably did), a young mother with elevated blood pressure, and a quiet middle-aged man with one vicious-looking sunburn, I finally had time to sit. My head was pounding and my stomach growling by that point.

Glancing at the clock, I figured I could easily pop back upstairs, check on Clarice, then get on my way home with Roe. Whoever the mysterious valilier was, he would either be there or not. I was hoping for not.

All thoughts of an early bedtime slipped my mind as I looked at Clarice's chart. Her blood work all looked completely normal with the exception of a higher than usual blood count, but her vital signs through the afternoon were confounding. It looked for all the world as if she were being starved of oxygen despite appearing to breathe easily. I examined her again and couldn't find a trace of what would be causing this. Certainly I was overlooking something.

I checked her over once again and sensed something was different. If I could just put my finger on it. . .

It wasn't until I'd explained everything to the girl and her father and was leaving the bedside that I realized what it was. Clarice had been pleasant and smiling through the entire exchange. In fact, I might have gone so far as to say she was giddy with the news that I couldn't explain her symptoms. She was rejoicing in my failure.

Filing the thought away with a hundred other bits of information in my brain, I said goodnight and went in search of Roe to walk home with me.

It wasn't Roe who was waiting for me downstairs. It was Holdan.

"Ms. Morris." He tipped his head at me. "Heading home? I thought we might practice a bit."

"Oh? I wish I could." It wasn't a lie. I'd been making steady progress with my wonder-working, thanks in large part to Holdan and his knowledge of the art.

"But?" he prompted.

"But I've had sort of an off-putting twenty-four hours. I need some sleep, but before I can rest my weary head, I need to talk to Asher and Geneva."

"Do tell?" He started to walk and looked at me in invitation to join him.

"I will, but I need to wait here for Roe. We're supposed to walk home together."

"And here I was thinking it was the elder Mr. Belstrohm you fancied."

I opened my mouth to tell him he was right but snapped it shut instead. He smirked but didn't push the matter.

I felt color flood my cheeks but rather than confirm or deny anything, I gave Holdan the brief version of the previous night's events. He didn't seem particularly interested in any of it but listened anyway. When I was done, he nodded. Then, as if I'd done no more than tell him what I'd had for lunch, he changed the topic entirely.

"You've been practicing though? With your wee little patients?"

"As much as I'm able. I was hoping to sneak you in soon so we could work on a few things."

"That had been my intention this evening, but to be frank, Ms. Morris, I hardly think it's necessary anymore."

I frowned. "Why would you think that?"

"Your skills are sufficient to continue on your own for now. And I'd rather not offend anyone in the clinic. I'm still waiting for a decision from Medicus, you know."

I did know he'd sent a request weeks ago and had yet to hear back. It could take ages for mail to reach its destination, and then more time would be needed for the higher ups to come to a conclusion about Holdan and his time away from practice. When I'd asked him if he'd appealed to the school in Renfield, he'd informed me he'd written to his own training institution. That particular school was an even further distance from DM by tram. It was likely he'd be waiting for several more weeks, if not months.

The last thing he needed was to get caught doing something expressly forbidden by Medicus Corpus. Something like practicing thaumaturgy on patients in their care. I understood that but still felt a little disappointed by his decision.

"Oh, don't look so glum, dear. Perhaps we can work out something in the future. Something away from the prying eyes of the clinic staff."

I tilted my head and studied him. "But the clinic is where the sick people are."

"It's where *most* of the sick people are, true. I had a little something else in mind, however."

"Are you going to tell me what that something might be?"

"All in due time, Ms. Morris. All in due time. For now, rest assured, I intend to utilize *my* time wisely." He wasn't smiling exactly, but something close to it. At a noise from behind us, he looked up, and the ghost of a smile vanished to be replaced by a look of boredom. "Ah, your companion. Do try to have a pleasant evening."

"Listerman," Roe said as he approached and nodded. Holdan tipped an invisible cap to us and sauntered off in the opposite direction from home.

"Charming as always," Roe observed once we were out of earshot.

I couldn't disagree, so I just nodded. Roe placed my arm through his, and we headed back to our building, dust flying up with each step we took.

8

ROE

Auri sat cross-legged on the ground leaning up against a simple canvas-covered sofa, the stripped bone of a roasted chicken leg balanced on one knee, her palm on the other. Hale sat on the sofa behind her, a long leg on either side of her shoulders. Both listened intently as Asher and Gen ran through the details of the other attacks as they knew them.

It wasn't much more than what Gen had previously shared. Apparently there were no new leads in the case or, probably more accurately, nothing new the settlement council wanted revealed. The young women ranged in age from seventeen to thirty-one. Everyone in the hub knew almost everyone else in at least the slightest sense of recognition, but none of the victims were particularly friendly or associated with one another. The only things that seemed to link the attacks were that all had happened after nightfall, and all three of the women were of slight stature—none of them taller than five foot two. All three had last been seen alone, coming or going about their regular routines in the hub settlement. One a teacher, one a farrier's apprentice, and one a woman who made her living in a brothel.

My eyes flashed to where Auri sat. Young woman—check. Slight build—check. After dark—check. The only anomaly was that she hadn't been alone. I'd been with Little-bit when she'd been accosted. Despite what we'd talked about earlier, the more I thought about it, the less likely this seemed to be mere coincidence. My brother—who I'd updated on the way here—seemed to be thinking the same thing. The more Gen and Asher talked, the less and less space Auri had to herself. He'd be fused to her back soon if he didn't stop hunching closer with each new detail.

Auri—universe love her—didn't seem to mind.

Lost in my thoughts, I jumped when a loud banging came at the door.

"Ah no. Please tell me you didn't invite Listerman." I groaned at Gen.

"You know I owe him my life, don't you?"

"You owe Tiny Badass there your life," I retorted, pointing at Auri and causing Specs to pipe up.

"We've been over this a thousand times, Roe. It was both of us. Just as much Holdan as it was me."

Holdan. I still struggled with the man's real name. Some part of me would always think of him as Hollis, and that was precisely what the psycho Nanette had wanted. To erase any bit of identity Holdan Listerman had. I had to get used to who he was in name and in life, if for no other reason than to shove a knife in the dead woman's plan.

"The answer is no, Roe. I didn't invite him, even though I probably should have. We aren't really expecting anyone else." Geneva cocked an eyebrow at her husband.

"I'm on it," Asher announced as he walked to the door and looked through the peephole. Without speaking, he tossed his head to the side, some ultra secret signal only Gen seemed to understand. She rose from her spot on the floor and placed herself between the door and the rest of us.

Asher stepped to the side of the door frame and spoke. "State your name and your business here." His voice was back to that commanding authoritative tone he rarely used with us anymore. Obviously not someone he knew well from the hub then.

An equally clear and controlled voice came back after just a moment's hesitation—the door muffling it slightly. "Valilier Campbell Robichaud. I was told I could find a Ms. Aurelia Morris here this evening."

"Who the hell told him that?" Hale asked and then answered his own question. "Listerman."

Geneva obviously couldn't see the look on my face with her back to me but spoke anyway. "So maybe I did invite him, but he declined."

"Figures," I muttered to no one in particular.

Asher gave us all—his wife included—the *please shut up now* look and we quieted.

"Well, Valilier Robichaud. At this time, I am not convinced I can confirm that Ms. Morris is indeed here."

"That is unfortunate as I really need to speak with her. I left a message for her this morning at the clinic. Perhaps she didn't receive it?" The tone in his voice suggested he knew damn well she received it but had chosen to ignore the request to meet her at her home.

"I cannot confirm that information at this time either," Asher responded.

"Look, Asher Almstedt—I assume that's who I'm conversing with through the door—this is important to Ms. Morris's safety. You of all people should appreciate that."

65

No one used Asher—or Geneva's—surname. They just knew who Asher and Gen were. Almstedt. It sounded so formal I almost laughed.

Asher—clearly not as amused as I was—seemed to think it through for several long moments. The man on the other side was patient for a stretch but then said in exasperation, "I can stand out here all night."

Our escort sighed. "I'm checking you for weapons, so if you've got them, might as well leave them outside."

"No weapons."

Asher slid the deadbolt back slowly and stepped with the door as it swung inward. He nodded at the dark-haired, dark-eyed man who stood on the other side with his hands raised palms forward.

Of course I should have expected this. "For all that is good in the Universe." The words slipped out as I took in the man who'd knocked me out the night before.

"You." Auri rose from her place on the floor—the chicken bone clattering to rest by my boot—and stomped forward as if to confront him. I needn't have worried as both Hale and Gen moved quickly to flank her and prevent her from actually acting on what ever she had planned.

"Ms. Morris. Can I call you Aurelia?" His voice smooth, smile charming. "You seem a touch surprised to see me." The bastard looked around at the rest of us as Asher made good on his warning and patted him down. The charm melted and reformed as surprise when he took in the posture of the room—or at least the portion of it he could see from the far side of the threshold. Did he really think he would just stroll in here and not have to answer for his actions?

Color flared in Auri's cheeks. "I've seen you before."

"Yes." He looked even more confused. "Last night in fact."

"At the tavern."

He nodded. "Yes. And after." He looked around again. "When I assisted you."

I laughed. "Is that what we're calling it? Assistance?"

"I did assist you." He looked at me then back to Auri. "I'm sorry about your friend, but I did what needed to be done to ensure your safety."

When she didn't say anything, he continued, "I'm sorry. Do you not remember me giving you aid?"

"I don't remember much. I assume I have you to thank for that." One hand raised to push her glasses up her nose and the other went to her throat and played with the golden orb dangling there.

"No, actually. I don't think you do." He glanced around the room again, still lurking outside the door. "Look. I'm sorry I frightened you and your friend last night, but I can explain all of this—or at least most of it— if you'll allow me to."

"If my face recalls correctly, you did more than frighten us." I stared at the man, and he stared back. Still not an ounce of regret evident in his eyes, despite his words.

"If you're looking for an invitation into my home, I'm afraid I'll need some sort of credentials or identification," Asher informed him. "We have no 'valiliers' in Devil's Meadows so that title means nothing to me."

I didn't think that was strictly true. He must have had an inkling of the title or the man never would have made it past the threshold.

"In my pocket." He pointed to his left hip, a questioning expression again on his face.

"Go ahead," Asher replied to the unasked question.

The stranger pulled out a small leather wallet and handed over a thick card of some sort. Asher studied it a moment and handed it back.

"Long way from home, Mr. Robichaud. Or do you prefer Valilier Robichaud?"

"I am. It's been a bit of a journey. And Campbell is just fine with me."

"Well, we all know a little about long journeys. Why don't you come on in and we can talk."

I looked from Campbell Robichaud to Asher and then Hale. My brother's face mirrored what I felt. Why the hell was Asher letting this horse pile in for a little chat?

Obviously sensing our unease, Asher said, "Relax, you two. Even if he isn't who he claims to be, I'm sure the five of us can keep him from sucker punching anyone again."

Gen stepped to the small kitchen and brought back one of the two sturdy wooden chairs she and Asher kept at the table there. Setting it a good distance away from the other furniture in the room, she gestured for him to sit. The valilier did so and rested his elbows on his knees. Despite the semblance of a relaxed posture, his body remained tense and his dark eyes alert.

Hale sat back down on the sofa but shifted all the way to one side and Aurelia sat down next to him. I swooped down and grabbed the chicken bone, tossing it in a refuse bin and squeezing in on her other side. Gen resumed her place in the easy chair, and Asher leaned against the wall at her side. He may have invited this man into his home, but he certainly wasn't going to relax until the stranger left again.

Campbell looked around the room and then spoke to Auri. "I realize you think I handled myself poorly last night, and your friend here must have filled you in on the situation if you don't remember it."

"Roe," I said. "The friend's name is Roe Belstrohm."

"Of course. And this is your brother Hale. Geneva and Asher Almstedt." He tilted his head to each of us in turn as he said our names.

"Someone's done his homework," Hale said.

He leveled those dark eyes on my brother and said calmly, "Only an incompetent ass would come into the home of two Medicus Corpus escorts to discuss dark subjects without first doing his homework. I am far from incompetent."

He was competent with a right hook. I'd give him that.

Hale frowned in thought but nodded the slightest bit.

"Seems you have us all at a disadvantage," Auri offered. "You know about us, but we know nothing about you. Why do you keep popping up?"

"It isn't my intention to frighten you, but I have increasing reason to believe you, Ms. Morris, may continue to be in very real danger. The man who attacked you last night—I've been . . . investigating him for a while now. He's actually the reason I've traveled to Devil's Meadows."

I didn't like the way he said investigating. It made me feel like he wasn't giving us the truth. Or at least not all of it.

Geneva finally spoke. "There've been a few other attacks in recent days. Do you believe this same man might be responsible for those as well?"

He blew out a long, slow breath and looked up at the ceiling. Nodding, he answered, "Yes. It's possible. More than possible. Likely. I can't share too much information at this time, but I strongly advise you to stay inside, particularly at night. Can you avoid going in to work for a few days?"

Auri huffed. "You've obviously never been in a clinic the size of ours. Someone needs to tend to the patients, even on weekends."

"Then I advise you only let her go to the clinic and back. Keep someone with her at all times," he directed at Asher.

"Sorry to burst your bubble, but Asher doesn't own me," Specs said evenly as she stared death at the man.

"I didn't mean—"

Auri cut him off. "It doesn't matter what you did or didn't mean. I can't stay inside or at home. I have my shifts at the clinic. And I'm supposed to go with Jassika next week to see to the settlement at the dam."

I'd forgotten about that. Auri had volunteered to go with Jassika for an outreach visit to the settlers who tended the river not far from Devil's Meadows. It's where our drinking water came from. The river was stopped by a massive old concrete dam that used to provide hydroelectric power to the surrounding cities, but since the Grand Divagation, it was completely useless in that regard. Settlers still tended the machinery inside to allow outflow and prevent the river from running dry on the far side. They also had the task of maintaining the intake straw and pump that sent clean drinking water via an aqueduct to the hub. There weren't enough of them to warrant their own Medicus practitioner, so every couple of months a small team of two from DM headed down there with an escort to make sure they were all doing well medically. In emergencies, it was unfortunately up to them to make the journey to us.

When Jassika had asked if any of us had wanted to go, I almost volunteered. Until the older practitioner mentioned she was going to be the lead and she only needed one other medical person with her. The idea of spending three days worth of travel and medical care with only Jassika and one of the escorts sounded about as fun as crotch lice. Naturally, I changed my mind and declined to volunteer, but Specs had jumped on the opportunity. It was no secret she admired the old battle ax, but I had to wonder if she wasn't going to use the time to pump Jassika for information regarding Medicus.

Campbell Robichaud drew me from thoughts of Jassika, Auri, and Medicus. "No one can cover for you?"

"No. We're stretched thin as it is, and even if they could, I wouldn't ask them to."

"I see." The speculative cast of his eyes said he most definitely did not see but was not inclined to argue the point.

"I can tell you don't like my answer, but it's the only one I've got, Valilier Robichaud." Specs puffed out her cheeks and muttered, "That's a mouth full."

"Campbell. It's just easier." A small furrow appeared between the man's brows. "You mentioned going to the dam. What exactly will that entail?"

Asher answered for her. "Three day trip. Doc here and one of the other more seasoned practitioners, along with Gen will set out for the dam settlement half a night's walk from here. Provide whatever care those folk need and then head on back up three nights later."

I wasn't sure why Asher was giving this guy so much info about the excursion and made to say so, but the valilier spoke first.

"Just the three of them?"

"Well, I'm trying to arrange for a tram master to drive the wagon, but if we can't get somebody, Gen is more than capable." There was no question the statement was more than information. It was a warning. Gen would kill him and leave him on the

71

side of the road for the carrion birds should he be stupid enough to try something.

There were of course other escorts in DM, but they were less experienced and spent most of their time standing sentry at the clinic or guarding supplies as they came in at the tram depot. Gen wasn't dumb, and if she thought it necessary, she could always assign one of them as part of the team for the trip.

"In case you hadn't noticed, traveling at night is going to be a problem," Campbell said.

"And in case you hadn't noticed," I retorted, "it's a hundred and ten degrees in the shade during the day."

He slowly turned those dark eyes on me. My guess was he generally had people listening to his every word. We weren't those kind of people.

"Would you rather your lovely friend here be the next on the killer's list?"

"Roe's right," Gen said. "It's just too hot to travel that distance during the day. We might be able to push the departure back to say one in the morning, but that's about it. I'm very well trained. I'll make sure nothing happens to my favorite girl."

He looked like he wanted to argue but held his tongue.

"Well then, if you can't tell us anymore about who you suspect or how we can help, I'd say we're done here." Asher moved toward the door to escort the man out.

The valilier pursed his lips but gave a brief nod and followed him to the door. He hesitated before crossing the threshold.

"I wish I could tell you more. Right now, suffice it to say, I know this man very well. Not his identity, but his actions. He's driven by something none of you could possibly understand. He's smart and he is brazen and he will not stop until he is sated. Or until he is dead. Ms. Morris, please. Stay indoors at night if you can."

9

HALE

Just over two months. We'd had just over two months to get accustomed to a new settlement, new people, a harsh climate, and an even harsher occupation. A new life entirely. We had to throw ourselves into our Medicus duties and nestle in for the rest of a long life of service to these people all the while keeping the enormity of Holdan and Aurelia's secret.

Only two miserable months and already Auri was being targeted from multiple sides.

It was laughable to believe Nanette had been the biggest foe we could face, when the reality was, enemies lay behind so many corners. It was bad enough when I found Jassika and the powers that be for Medicus Corpus were out to catch Auri using her thaumaturgy—her wonder-working. It was ridiculous. She was only trying to help a few sick kids for piss sake.

Now it seemed she had a very real and very imminent threat looming over her. Someone out there had targeted her for their own twisted reason. We had no cause to believe it was tied to the miracles, but I couldn't shake the thought that the two were related. I'd nearly come unglued when Roe filled me in on the events of the previous day. If he hadn't been there. If he wasn't as fiercely protective of her as he was. If he'd been a moment too slow or a bit weaker. If. . .

A shudder ran through me as I thought about all those ifs and what could have happened to this wonderful person I was finally getting to know and appreciate. Based on what Campbell Robichaud had to say, whoever it was that had been targeting and killing the young women of Devil's Meadows had his sights set on Aurelia. Surely he would have mentioned the wonder-working if it was important. Miracles or no, I was going to do whatever it took to ensure she remained safe.

The problem was the independent spirit and dogged determination to do what she thought was good for others and not necessarily what was good for herself. If I could find a few minutes to talk with her, to help her understand how important it was she at least listened to the warnings Robichaud was giving her, maybe I could help her see it didn't need to be an end to her independence, but simply a layer of protection to have someone with her while she ventured out through the streets of DM.

And then there were the letters. It was possible Auri was well on the way to sabotaging herself.

I know she thought she was being safe when she wrote to Lita and Jonaten, but if Jassika Duncan was to be believed, someone was on to what Auri and Listerman were doing. I'd meant to speak to her this evening about it, but with all the other bombs being dropped, I just didn't want to add more to the barrage.

Holdan Listerman should probably be made aware of these developments as he was the one practicing with her to strengthen and control her miracles, all the while petitioning Medicus to let him serve as a practitioner again after his long absence. If anyone found out, his hopes of practicing medicine would evaporate faster than a tear in the desert wind.

Lying in bed and unable to sleep, I couldn't get my mind to let go of the image of Aurelia in trouble. It conjured dozens of scenarios—none of them good. I decided to go out for a run. Stretching my legs and releasing some endorphins might be enough to get me to still my racing mind.

As I exited the first floor of our building, I stopped to make sure the glass door swung all the way shut and the lock clicked home. Breathing in the dry air, I listened as the night insects chirped and buzzed to one another as I did basic warm-up stretches.

Movement to my left drew my attention. Trotting lazily up the road, nose to the ground, was a healthy looking coyote. Its coat was shaggy and patchy, but it clearly had seen no shortage of bunnies and quail to dine on. As it moved closer to the building, my eyes caught on something—or someone—I'd previously missed. Dimly lit by the natural starshine, the figure of a man sat casually on a low bench facing the door. He was so still, at first I thought he might be asleep. Then he dipped his head in acknowledgment, and I recognized the face of Campbell Robichaud.

All thoughts of a relaxing midnight run faded. I used my brass key to unlock the door and went back inside.

Thankfully, Auri had realized the peril she might be in. Her door was locked up tight. No snoozing on the couch for me.

That was the first night I slept on the ground outside Aurelia's door.

10

AURELIA

It had been a handful of days since the valilier—
Campbell—had hit us with the ton of bricks that was
currently my life.

The air smelled like mud. It must have finally
rained the night before because large puddles lined
the walkways and the road was covered with piles of
pebbles and chunks of gravel—the occasional palm
frond or tumbleweed scattered in for good measure.
A single tall silver and steel cloud bunched up to the
south of the valley.

It was shocking and more than a little
disappointing I'd slept through the storm. My fatigue
was thick, and I hated it.

Despite this, the walk to the clinic was almost
enjoyable. Maybe it was the hint of moisture in the
air or because Diego was going home that day. With
any luck, maybe Clarice would be turning a corner
and heading home too. Hale somehow had scored the
day off, so Roe had the pleasure of walking with me.
He was unusually quiet.

"Thinking about something?" I asked. "Or
someone?"

He gave me a little half smile and wrapped his
arm around my shoulder. "Thinking about lots of

77

somethings and a few someones actually. But you are on the top of my list, Shrimpboat."

I huffed at the nickname. "I never asked. What did you think of Valilier Robichaud?"

"Clearly he is an unmitigated ass."

I nodded. "Mmm-hmm."

"You disagree?"

"I don't agree or disagree. He might be an ass, but I think he's telling the truth. He's trying to catch the killer. Doesn't explain why he decked you though."

"Gen says I can be stubborn. Her theory is it was the only way to get me to shut up long enough to get you inside somewhere safe."

It made sense even if it was obviously a little too rash. And violent.

"Well, your beautiful face is still quite beautiful. Meet me later to walk home?" He was beautiful. I'd always thought so. The same green eyes and blond hair as his brother, but it was his smile that knocked folks down. The past few months, that smile had been strained and tight, but every now and then, I got to see the real thing.

He raised an eyebrow. "*You're* taking this whole needs to be chaperoned thing remarkably well."

"I don't think I have much of a choice. Plus, it guarantees I get to spend time with my favorite guys."

He got the wicked gleam in his eye I knew all too well. "I'll make sure tomorrow Listerman is on the docket for chaperone duty." I reached out to pinch his side, but he danced away from me at the entrance to the clinic. "See you tonight, Tiny Badass."

Sandy and Janet were working the fourth floor that day. They had their heads together, and Sandy had tear streaks on her adorable face.

"Good morning, ladies. What's wrong?" I asked the pair.

"Clarice doesn't look so hot this morning, Aurelia," Janet said. "Maybe you can start your rounds with her today?"

"Absolutely. Did something happen?"

"Not that we know of," Janet replied. "The night assistants said everything was quiet, but she seems weaker than she was yesterday."

Sandy looked like she wanted to say something but was hesitant.

"Tell me what you're thinking, Sandy." I tried to keep my tone soft but the words firm.

"I don't know. I think maybe you should talk to her alone. I get the sense she's hiding something from her dad and me." Her eyes flicked to me and back toward the corner housing her niece's cot.

"And. . .? It seems like maybe there's more," I said.

"Sandy, you have to tell her," Janet encouraged.

The cherubic assistant sighed and wiped at her eyes again. "And I don't know. . . She's just. . ." I could see her struggling to find the right words. "She's just not her."

"Well, she's been ill. It can change someone's entire demeanor. With adolescents it can be really exaggerated."

"Aurelia." She leveled a look at me. "I know that." She waved her hand casually around the floor and the dozen cots set up around us. Some occupied, some empty.

"Sorry." I sounded as contrite as I felt.

"Yes, she's sick and I understand that. But there's something else. She acts almost inappropriate. What teen do you know gets happier the sicker she gets? Go talk to her this morning. She looks like she's been run over by a cart full of manure, but she

79

was happy as a lark when I came in this morning. Excited and smiley. She's always been independent and spirited, but this new person? She gives me the chills."

"What does your brother think?"

"He doesn't know what to think. Conrad's been blaming the illness, obviously, but the other day, he told me he was considering getting a shaman in here to exercise the demon in Clarice's soul."

Understanding washed through me. Parents often wanted to blame something bigger when things got bad.

"Well, maybe he can wait on the shaman until we've had a chance to sort through this a bit more. Last thing we need is to frighten all the rest of the kids and families."

Sandy leveled a look at me and shook her head. Her voice was dry and serious when she spoke. "Don't bet on it. Even though he seems so calm and reserved, Conrad's always been a little fanatical. He even went through a period of believing in thaumaturgy. If you aren't fast enough, he'll have a wonder-worker in here eventually."

Telling them the wonder-worker would actually need to know what the illness was to be able to fix it clearly wasn't an option.

"I saw this wagon once—a couple of years ago—when I lived further down south of Jave," Janet interjected. "Had this woman who claimed she could cure any manner of illness. She was mesmerizing, and folks flocked to her and that odious wagon. But I knew better. She felt wrong, and her promises were nothing more than steaming piles of dung."

My heart rate picked up, and my skin went clammy. It had to have been Nanette. Had Janet seen me with Holdan, and would she recognize him?

"Oh." I forced a smile. "I don't think that'll be necessary." If the women noticed my reaction to either Conrad Donahue's possible belief in miracles or the fact that Janet had likely seen a corrupt version of a thaumaturgist who was now very much dead, they would hope I was just a new practitioner who was doubting my own ability to cure one of my patients.

I excused myself after promising to spend a little time with Clarice alone. It would be prudent to see if I could get her to divulge any information she hadn't already willingly shared.

As I made my way to Diego's bedside, my spirits lifted; here was one kiddo who was going to go home today, thanks in part to my medical knowledge and my wonder-working.

As always, he was a beam of sunshine in an otherwise gloomy setting. I did a ridiculous little dance on my way over and then popped my stethoscope into his ears and asked him what he heard.

"Nothing." He giggled at me as I raised my eyebrows questioningly.

"You had to hear *something*," I said. "Let me try."

He took several exaggerated breaths in and out, whooshing air through his pursed lips like he was the wolf trying to blow down a house in one of Roe's stories.

"Well, I hear lungs that are ready to. Go. Home." I punctuated each of the last words with a sharp little clap.

"Yeah?" he asked.

"Oh yeah!" I replied. Then, while he interrupted at least a dozen times, I ran through the list of medications and treatments he would need over the coming days with his mother. She agreed to get him back into the clinic in a week's time to see me or sooner if it seemed he was moving in the wrong direction.

After answering her questions, I turned to Diego and asked if he had any questions for me. A comical thinking expression furrowed his tiny brow before he popped his eyes open like something just occurred to him. "Yes! I have a question!"

"Mr. Diego, what precisely is your question?" All serious voice and professional posture directed at him.

"Why does that new girl over there"—he pointed toward Clarice—"get two special people to help her? Can I have a special other person too, next time I'm here?"

"Well, I certainly hope it's awhile before you're here again, but do you need more special people helping you? Don't I and your mom do a good enough job?" I winked at him.

Diego's mother batted her hand at him and sighed. "He says the new patient has a boy practitioner who comes to see her every night, but only when the assistants aren't looking." She smiled apologetically. "He has a vivid imagination."

"He sure does." I frowned a bit but noticed her looking expectantly at me. "Well, stop by if anything comes up. I'm so pleased he's able to finally get back to a regular routine. That both of you are. And Diego"—I waited until he was looking at me—"make sure you listen to your mom and take your medicine the way you are supposed to. Okay?"

His nod was overly dramatic and exaggerated, but it made me smile as I wandered over to the curtained-off space containing Clarice's cot. The girl was sleeping with her face toward the wall, her father slumped in an uncomfortable-looking chair near her feet. I retrieved my stethoscope from around my neck and murmured to my patient, "just doing a quick check," before listening to her heart and lungs. Everything sounded normal, but her heart rate was noticeably elevated. I expected her to wake while I did my exam, but she only mumbled in her sleep and shifted over onto her side even further. Hadn't Sandy said the girl was awake and cheerful when Sandy and Conrad arrived that morning? That couldn't have been more than an hour or two prior.

What was I missing? I reached around to feel her neck and palpate the length of her clavicles, looking for any suspicious lumps or masses. She shifted again, and I noticed the bruising. In a delicate ring around her neck, a faint blue-red necklace of tiny lacy broken blood vessels marred her otherwise pristine skin. As I bent lower to have a closer look, my stethoscope brushed against her, causing her to shift in her sleep, revealing her face in the watery light. The same pattern of faint traumatic marbling decorated the skin around her mouth. A quick cursory check of her extremities failed to reveal any other areas similar in appearance.

It had to be important, but my mind couldn't or wouldn't conjure any physical ailment that would produce a pattern of bruising consistent with what Clarice was showing. And I was certain those marks hadn't been there on my initial history and physical exam when I admitted her to the clinic—or any of the other times I'd examined her. As I pondered, I caught myself not reaching for my orb pendant but rubbing the tender skin around my own mouth.

I needed to know what had happened since I last saw her. With a gentle but louder voice, I woke the sleeping girl.

"Clarice? Good morning. Clarice? Sorry to wake you, but I was stopping in to check and see how you're doing. How'd you sleep last night?" I was aware of my voice reflexively changing to my most comforting tone, the one I used with scared kiddos and terrified parents.

Clarice groaned and yawned as she rolled flat on her back. "Mmmnnn. Better than Dad. I keep telling him not to stay here, but he'll only leave for a few hours at a time." She sounded slightly disgruntled but then smiled. "My night last night was good though. Really good."

"That's wonderful to hear. You were pretty conked out just now. Are you sure you got enough rest?"

She gave me a noncommittal shrug.

Her father stirred and looked at me with bleary eyes. "Morning, Practitioner Morris."

I smiled and nodded before turning back to Clarice. "So it seems nothing is showing up on your testing, and my detective skills aren't being too helpful. Is there anything else you could tell me that might help me figure out what's been making you feel so tired? Like for example, how you came to have the bruises on your neck and mouth?"

"Bruises? What bruises?" Her father was up and out of his chair quicker than a startled quail. Internally I groaned and cursed myself for the fool I was. Why on earth did I mention it in front of him?

Clarice's reaction was as instantaneous as her dad's. Her hands came up to cover her neck, and she curled her face into her chest, turning on her side in a fetal position. It gave her the appearance of being both younger and smaller than she already was. "I don't know what you're talking about." Her voice was barely audible, muffled as it was by her body and the bunched clinic sheet.

"Oh no you don't," her father scolded, trying in vain to forcibly pull the girl's hands away from her throat.

"Dad! Stop. I'm exhausted. I just need to sleep. You can look later."

"Really, Mr. Donahue. It's not urgent." I tried to put myself between father and daughter. Eventually Sandy came to my rescue, helping to usher Conrad away from the side of the bed. He

84

didn't look happy, but at least he allowed me to walk with him away from the cot and into a quiet alcove near the stairs.

"I know you're concerned. I'm concerned about Clarice as well. Not much of this makes sense to me."

Mr. Donahue nodded and wiped at the liquid slipping from his eyes. "I am just so tired. Tired of this place, and I don't just mean the clinic. I'm tired of Devil's Meadows and tired of Clarice being sick. I'm tired of my sister acting like I'm a lunatic because I believe something more might be needed to help her. It's not that I don't trust you, it's just I don't trust anyone anymore. Not even myself or my daughter."

I waited for him to continue, but he exhaled and picked at a loose thread on the hem of his shirt.

"Is there something you think she isn't telling us?"

"No. Yes. Maybe." He smiled bitterly. "For a while I thought maybe she was doing some sort of drug—that peyote—or something. Then I thought she was depressed. Hell, *I'm depressed*. That runs in families, right? She recently broke things off with a boy she'd been seeing. Maybe that's what triggered it?"

I thought about all the questions he was asking and all the layers of information he was adding to her history. Stuff I hadn't gotten from either of them the other times we'd spoken. Trying to tackle them as best I could, I nodded. "Depression can run in families, yes, and it can cause all sorts of physical symptoms. But I'd rather we make sure there isn't more to this than just her mental health. More testing should be done, but we also should start some mild therapy sessions. See if she might benefit from a little more talking and less prodding. Tomorrow I'm going to be leaving the hub for a few days. If you want, I can have another more experienced practitioner take over while I'm away, or I can let Clarice go home. Medically she seems stable. The change might be good for her. And for you. Being stuck inside these four walls can be a bit much for just about anyone."

Conrad Donahue studied his hands for a moment. "I'll ask Clarice what she wants to do. She ought to have some choices in this whole thing. You'll be here for a while still today?"

"Yes sir. I'm going to speak with one of the other practitioners this afternoon and bounce some ideas off him. Maybe he'll pick up on whatever I'm missing. I'll be back in an hour or two and you can let me know what you both have decided."

As it turned out, I got a two for one deal when I went in search of Theo Wong. Theo had been in Devil's Meadows for almost as long as Jassika Duncan. Where Jassika was cool icy water, Theo was snapping fire—in the best way possible. He was crazy smart but also a life-loving ball of kinetic energy. I had been hoping he could use some of that energy to help me run through a differential list of possible diagnoses for Clarice's aliment. I found him on the second floor, discussing a tricky tooth extraction with Jassika. It didn't take long for them to finish up their chat, and to my immense relief, they both agreed to run through the case with me. Surely one of them would know what the universe was throwing at the teen.

The three of us must have come up with a dozen different possibilities and just as quickly discounted them all. After twenty minutes of this, we lulled into a thoughtful silence.

Theo leaned back and stared at the ceiling, snapping his fingers in the fidgety way he did when he was trying to stay focused but his body wanted to move. "Metabolic . . . genetic . . . something inherent to her that's always been there but is now revealing

86

itself perhaps. Triggered maybe—by hormones or stress."

Jassika nodded but then reiterated what she'd been going back to for the entire conversation, "I still think it's likely above her shoulders. Some sort of transference or psychosomatic complaint. Devil's Meadows isn't exactly a balm for poor mental health."

"I don't disagree, but I promised her father I'd rule out everything else before we chalked it all up to anxiety or depression." I turned and looked at Theo. "How do I even go about testing for genetic or metabolic disorders? We don't have that kind of lab equipment here, do we?"

He looked at me a sardonic scowl. "Of course we don't. You do it the *old*, old-fashioned way. History and physical. Get the story and you'll get the answer."

I flashed back to the very first time I'd met Theo, my second day in Devil's Meadows. We'd been working the first floor together, and it had been an uncharacteristically slow shift. In my foolishness, I had assumed every day in the clinic would be the same. Sadly I was mistaken, and I hadn't had a quiet shift since.

As we sat sipping tea and playing a good game of getting to know each other, Theo had asked me what my favorite bit of medical history was.

"I honestly don't think I've ever thought about it," I replied.

"Never thought about it? That is simply ludicrous! Med history is fascinating. And I'm not talking about all of the stuff we lost during the Great Divagation. I mean the real stuff. Hundreds of years ago stuff."

I was itching to pick his brain then and there about the Divagation and what he knew about it all. Could he tell me about the fall and the loss? Something in me thought he would, but that same something instinctively told me not to go there. The last thing I needed was to trigger any sort of suspicion I was questioning my place in the world. It was imperative I lie low for a while and feel things out first.

"Well, I suppose the whole history of vaccination development is pretty cool. Even though we don't use them anymore, the idea of a few people coming up with inoculations using barnyard animals is pretty ingenious."

He smirked and tilted his head to the side. "Yes, I suppose so, but I was leaning more toward the entertaining stuff."

"Entertaining stuff?"

He popped up and paced in a tight circle, dragging his hand along the top of his chair as he did so.

"I am talking monsters." There was a joyful little gleam in his eyes.

"Monsters?" I frowned. "I'm not aware of any medical history of monsters."

"Sure you are. Werewolves, vampires, and zombies?"

I shook my head, sure confusion was radiating from behind my glasses.

"Medicine can be extremely entertaining if you look at it through history's eyes. The classic symptoms of the rare condition porphyria can include skin involvement leading to blistering when exposed to direct sunlight for extended periods. Dark or black staining of the teeth. Increased hair growth accompanied by personality and mental status changes—including I might add, hallucinations. Acute chest and abdominal pain. Severe anemia which may or may not lead to an increasing appetite for rare meat. Have some of these signs or symptoms—the appetite for rare meat or blood, burning skin, etcetera, and you are a vampire—

although others think that myth is related to the plague or tuberculosis. But if you are extremely hairy and out howling at the moon at night because you are going insane—you are a. . .?" He stopped pacing and stared at me expectantly.

"Werewolf?" Uncertainty and laughter laced my voice.

"Yep-O!" He smiled radiantly, and the pacing started once again, his words tumbling out just as quickly as his feet moved along the worn tiles. "We as clinicians—and more importantly as human beings— have a way of trying to explain or find an answer for every perplexing thing we see. What we now know to be a terrible medical condition was once thought to be the spawn of some devil or demon. Interesting how perceptions change, don't you think? Maybe we can discuss the plague or progeria or zombies tomorrow." He stopped moving long enough to look around at the empty space. "Now where the hell are all the patients? I'm gonna go bonkers if I have to sit still all day."

Theo officially joined the ranks of my favorite mentors that afternoon. Now he wanted me to "get the story" to diagnose Clarice.

"I'll give it one more go at getting her to open up to me, but if she doesn't, it's going to have to wait a few days," I informed him.

"And why is that? Got something better to do?" He raised his eyebrows mockingly.

"I'm planning on sending her home tonight." The two older practitioners looked confused. "I'm going with Jassika tomorrow to the dam settlement by the river."

Jassika's frown cleared. "Oh right. I've been meaning to chat with you about that."

"What about it?" I had a sinking feeling Asher had spoken with Jassika and I was no longer going to be getting out of town as I had planned.

"Don't look so concerned. You're still going. Honestly you've only been here a couple of months—wait til the real drudgery of life in the desert sets in." She said it with a small knowing smile. A smile that said a lifetime in the desert was going to wear me down just as it was taking her—one thin layer at a time. "But I will be staying here. Asher asked if I didn't mind subbing out for this one. He seems to think there might be some trouble on the road and suggested sending one of the younger brawnier practitioners along instead."

"You mean a man," Theo interjected with mock indignity. "Well, he didn't ask me."

Jassika and I both chuckled before she placated him. "Of course they thought you should be first choice for a dangerous bit of travel, but I informed him I needed you here with me. And no, not a man necessarily, but seeing as the younger brawnier ones all have a Y chromosome, it just worked out that way." Then she turned to me again. "I can take a look at your patient if you like, but sending her home might actually be good for her mental state. Give her a bit of a break and keep you from trying anything beyond the standard of care."

She said it so off-handedly I almost didn't register the words or their possible meaning. *Beyond the standard of care?* Did she mean wonder-working? Did she *know?* My heart rate increased, and a icy sweat flooded my body.

Keeping my voice as natural as possible, I said, "That's what I thought too. So who will be going with me to the river?"

"I believe Geneva will be your escort along with another gentleman I've not had the pleasure of meeting—to lend some extra support. Hale Belstrohm will be the second practitioner. Hope you aren't concerned with the change in arrangements."

She didn't look at me but rather studied a stack of papers in her hand.

Emotions warred within me. Concern over Jassika's statement and its implied meaning. Frustration over my lack of progress with Clarice. But overwhelming the others, a healthy dose of excitement about trekking away from DM for three days with Hale as a traveling companion. I'd be lying if I said I tried to control the grin blossoming across my face. I wasn't concerned with the change at all.

The sky was black velvet dusted with starshine debris. The air around us warm and quiet. So incredibly still, it felt like the four of us were alone in the universe. Only the sound of the wheels creaking and the hollow knocks of horse hooves on the packed ground disturbed the space around us.

Night predators were out there—both of the human and animal varieties. I knew that, but it didn't worry me as we walked past the last vestiges of broken-down homes and low-lying buildings on our way out of the hub. Not many lived out here among the decayed stucco and dried-up land. The desert was reclaiming this space, bit by bit, and dunes of sand half buried long-forgotten spaces—the occasional yucca or desert shrub growing atop ancient roofs and abandoned vehicles.

In my infinite wisdom, I hadn't bothered to sleep at all after discharging Clarice and finishing my work at the clinic. Thinking a nap would only make me feel worse when I had to wake and start the hours-long walk to the dam and river settlement, I instead drank barrels full of tea and chatted with Roe until it was time for us to leave. Regretting that decision, I yawned and rubbed my eyes with the hem of my shirt before sliding my glasses back into place.

Neither Geneva nor Hale seemed particularly phased by any lack of sleep. Holdan—who was apparently the added support Jassika had mentioned—at least had the good grace to share in my misery. Unlike me, however, he had no qualms about looking like a leach and bid me goodnight as he climbed into the back of the wagon to close his eyes on the world.

Our transport was nowhere near the size of the trams we'd taken from Renfield to DM, but it still had plenty of space for Holdan's lanky frame to lie down amid the three days' worth of supplies and our basic medical equipment.

"So, did you play a part in this particular assignment, or did I just get lucky?" I asked Hale as we walked several yards ahead of the horses.

"As much as I wish I could claim otherwise, no."

"Really? Whose idea was it then?"

He hooked a thumb over his shoulder toward where Gen sat at the reins of the wagon. "Since they couldn't secure a tram master for the trip, she suggested to Asher bringing Listerman. Ostensibly as an extra set of eyes, but I think she feels bad for him. Medicus still hasn't responded to any of his queries to rejoin the ranks."

"And you?"

"Also Gen's idea."

Geneva was more observant than any of us gave her credit for, but I couldn't voice that to Hale or he'd know just how happy I was to have him along. He'd probably just clam up and ignore me for the rest of the walk. Instead, I teased, "Brawn and brain on this little expedition?"

"It would appear that way. But since I still haven't gotten my dinner date, I figured it was worth the extra sweat."

Maybe Gen wasn't the only one who saw more than I gave them credit for.

Crossing my arms over my chest, I swayed my shoulder into him and smiled as we continued to walk.

We were about three hours into the journey—roughly halfway to our destination—when the metal bridge came into view. Perhaps a hundred and fifty feet above the roadway, it was flanked on both sides by skeletal behemoth structures resembling the remains of some long-dead technological sentries. Proof again that power once flowed freely through the conducting wires and cables.

It wasn't the ancient towers, however, that had me nervous. It was the huddled group of people on the bridge watching our small group as we climbed the steady incline of the road below. Flames flickered from metal barrels dotted along the length of the bridge, outlining the still forms of the dozen or so people clumped in the middle. Without the fires, I doubt we would have noticed them at all.

"This stretch always makes my hackles rise." Geneva kept her voice low in the still air. "Smell anything funny, Aurelia?"

"No, but you know, I don't always pick up on trouble until it's crashing into me."

"True, but if the scent of lightning was in the air on this clear night, I'd be doubly concerned."

"Who are they?" Hale asked.

"Just a rough group who'd rather not live in the settlement with the others. To be fair, they've never given me trouble, just the heebie jeebies. There are stories though, and they have to count for something."

"Stories like the wine stains?" I asked.

93

On our way from Renfield to DM the trams had been set upon by a small band of desert bandits who all wore matching wine-colored paint on their faces. During this attack Gen had been stabbed and had almost succumbed to her injuries and the resulting infection. I certainly wasn't going to blame her for being a tad on edge when we were clearly so outnumbered.

We were traveling directly below them. Anything could happen.

As we crossed under the bridge, a low mournful voice carried on the hushed dry air above. One of the men was singing, his voice a lovely deep baritone. I didn't recognize the tune, but I didn't need to know the song to feel its message in my core. Longing and loss. Bittersweet and tinged with a knowledge as old as time and sand. Knowing what you once had was gone forever and could only be reclaimed in the afterlife. A funeral dirge for lost love and connected souls.

A chill ran down my spine, and fat drops filled my eyes as the haunting tune followed us out past the bridge and further into the dark of the once again endless desert. Long after the notes could no longer be heard, I carried the feel of them in my heart.

We spent the following hour rounding a series of low rocky hills. Railroad rails followed the curve of the hills to our left and a dark void of what I assumed was more sand and scrub to our right. As the sun was beginning to lighten the horizon, we crested a gentle rise and a wonderous sight opened before my eyes. In the distance, where I had thought only sand and brush existed, a series of dilapidated hovels hinted at a long-dead town. Directly in front of us, though, a vast lake sat nestled deep in the craggy and barren landscape. The flat, salt-crusted expanses of dry lake beds were common enough. This was something else entirely. Not to be confused with the round jewel-like alpine lakes like the ones we'd known back in Renfield, but a jagged expanse of water trapped between the nooks and crannies of the rocky hills that held it. It was a body of water out of place in this terrain.

The golden rays of sunlight claiming their ownership over the land sent daggers of light across its cerulean surface. Rather than illuminating the beauty of a cool blue oasis, they exaggerated the harsh brittle landscape. Despite the alien nature of the water in this desert, I found it captivating and glorious—an unwilling giver of life in the arid and barren bit of the earth.

We were only an hour or so from reaching the hearty people who ensured the life-sustaining liquid made it to our thirsty lips, half a day away in Devil's Meadows.

As if summoned by the sight before us, Holdan groaned and stretched in the back of the wagon, finally awake enough to haul his carcass for the remainder of the journey. He dropped from his resting place as Gen broke the silence.

"The Three Sisters." She pointed to a darker shadow among the still-dim landscape. "Old tunnels up ahead. It'll be dark through the majority of the way, but in general they're pretty safe."

The wagon squeaked and rocked as the horses led the way toward the first of three tunnels carved through rough rock the color of misery. As we approached, my pulse quickened at the thought of what could be hiding deep inside. Hale moved a half step closer to my side, but Geneva had spoken true. We had dim watery light for all of perhaps fifteen feet before the path was plunged into near total darkness. The solar lamp, which had dangled from a pole fastened to the seat next to Gen, cast an amber glow. It extended just to the edge of the wagon. No further.

The batteries were nearly spent, and the waning light wavered and sputtered.

Thankfully the darkness lasted only a handful of minutes, and before long we were emerging into the early dawn light once again.

The second "Sister"—though fractionally longer than the first—passed in much the same way. Hale and Holdan muttered bits of conversation to each other and to me as we walked. Again the road opened up and I could see the sky and surrounding hills as we emerged, squinting against the full light of dawn. A slight breeze had picked up, and the sounds of life in the desert rose with it. The third tunnel was several hundred yards ahead.

"I was hoping to glimpse some bighorns this morning," Gen called over her shoulder. "There's a large herd in these hills. They come down for water but usually head back to higher ground for the night. Maybe we'll get lucky on the way back. It's really quite a sight."

That *would* be something to see.

As we came to the final tunnel, Geneva informed us the dam was just to the other side and the building which sheltered the workers was not more than a half hour ahead at most.

My weary feet and bloodshot eyes were thrilled with the prospect of a nap in my future. The others too seemed more than eager to head into the gloom of the last tunnel and get to our destination. As the sun had risen higher, we were graced with a slightly longer stretch of watery light as we traversed the first portion of the tunnel. Unfortunately, this was the longest of the Three Sisters, so the darkness also stretched farther.

The light at the other end was no more than a thumbnail bobbing in a sea of black when I heard it. A faint desiccated rattle. Dried rice in a tin can.

Gen cursed softly.

"What?" I asked. The rattling grew louder. "What is that?"

"Probably a Mojave green."

"English, Gen," Hale responded.

"A rattlesnake. It'll be more scared of you than you are of it, but. . ." She paused, listening. One of the horses snickered and huffed. "Up to the right, I think. Into the wagon if you're able, you three."

She didn't need to tell me twice—never mind it being more scared of me. Walking behind the wooden cart, I could just make out the rear panels in the flickering light. Within a few strides I was up and in the back, taking up much less space than Holdan had while he napped. Hale hoisted himself easily into the back. Where was Holdan?

Hale must have shared at least a little of my concern. "Listerman? Where the piss are you?"

The rattle was louder, and the horses were jittery in response. Their whinnies and bucking could be heard over the sound of Gen's soft ineffective coos.

"Here," I heard Holdan say.

How and why he had gotten so far behind us, I didn't know. He had fresh legs and should easily have been keeping the pace. "I'm here."

His breathing was ragged and punctuated by the sound of his soles slapping the hard pack as he ran to catch up.

"Easy now. Easy." I wasn't sure if Geneva was speaking to Holdan, the horses, or both.

The staccato rattle was clear—not from the right as Gen first thought, but rather the left—and I sensed more than saw Gen direct the horses toward the right wall. As my ears told me we were even with the now-hissing animal, the horses jogged and Holdan missed his grip on the rear panel, slipping and spitting a curse as he fell and rolled away from the wheels.

The expletive cut off, and I heard him jump to his feet only to step forward with a thump and a brittle cry as the snake ceased its hissing and struck.

11

HALE

Listerman was heavier than he looked.

After hearing him yelp and tumble forward, I reached over the side of the wagon and caught the back of his shirt. He wasn't incapacitated thankfully, so between me hauling and him half assed climbing, he made it into the wagon. We signaled to Gen, and she snapped the tired horses into a trot that got us out of the tunnel within a few minutes.

As soon as my pupils adjusted to the morning light, I sliced open the bottom of his pant leg with a knife.

"I think I stepped on it." He grunted and hissed—not unlike the creature that bit him—when I tore at the fabric to get a better look. Having never seen a venomous snake bite before, I wasn't sure what to expect. I certainly hadn't anticipated it to be this bad this quickly.

Roughly a hand's breadth above the ankle, a pair of circular punctures nested amid already swollen flesh. The leg itself wasn't overly discolored, but the rate in which the area was swelling had me more than a little concerned.

"We should hurry and get him somewhere inside so we can treat it before the venom does more

99

damage." Auri hunkered down next to me, swaying with the movement of the wagon as she focused on the wound.

Gen was pulling the horses to the side of the road but wasn't reining them in to stop. "Aren't you supposed to put a tourniquet on it or something?"

"No," Listerman and I answered in unison. Then I continued. "That only traps the venom in the area around the leg and will lead to more tissue damage. We need to get this boot off though, before your leg swells more," I directed Listerman. "Some ice would be great."

"If that was a Mojave snake, he's at risk for paralysis, Hale," Gen snapped.

"I understand, Geneva. But getting worked up isn't going to keep that from happening. Besides, it really doesn't matter what kind of snake it was at this point. Not like we have antivenom just lying around. We'll need to treat the effects as best we can."

Auri turned to Geneva. "Stop the wagon, Gen."

"Auri, we need to get him inside," our escort replied.

"No, really. Stop." Auri looked around. The sun was coming up and none of the workers were out on this side of the shelters. "We need to stop and take care of this before I have an audience."

Listerman and I groaned at the same time, but likely for very different reasons.

"Auri, no," I said.

"Not up to you, Hale."

"If someone sees you. . ."

"They won't. That is why we are stopping here, Geneva."

To her credit, Gen pulled up on the reins and parked the wagon.

To *my* credit, I kept my mouth shut. Listerman, though, did not. "I won't be able to help you, Ms. Morris. Not when I'm like this."

"I understand. Just let me try."

"Who am I to argue?" He smirked and then turned his head to the side and vomited all over a carton of med supplies.

Gen looked back over her shoulder and surveyed the surrounding hills. "Stay in the wagon if you can, Auri. And be quick. There isn't anyone about yet, but soon they'll notice we've arrived, and I don't have a good reason to hold here."

Aurelia nodded and moved to sit on the floor of the wagon, Listerman's damaged leg cradled in her lap. She took a handful of steadying breaths and placed her palm over the punctures, not squeezing, but resting there. Her patient hissed again, his eyes shut tight and perspiration beading on his forehead. At least his breath was normal, not labored or shallow.

Aurelia continued to breathe in and out in a slow and steady rhythm. Listerman settled. Gen and I waited.

No one spoke, which was for the best. Should anyone approach the cart, they would simply see a pretty young woman holding the ankle of an injured man. If things worked out the way everyone was hoping, by the time she removed her hand, it would be easy to argue Listerman had simply tripped or twisted his ankle on the journey. No one would be any the wiser.

A minute ticked by and Listerman was still pale and diaphoretic. Two minutes ticked by and his brow was still furrowed. Three minutes ticked by and the sweating had stopped and his brow had cleared. From what I could see, the bloated flesh of his leg was reducing. Four minutes and Aurelia was trembling and appeared ill, her skin pasty and slick with a sheen of greasy perspiration. At five minutes, I gently removed her hand from Holdan's smooth healthy dermis. Her eyes fluttered open.

101

"Best not to keep pushing. I don't think Holdan wants you passing out on his account."

"Too right, Belstrohm. I'm much better, Ms. Morris. Thank you for your services." Listerman sat up and inspected his previously poisoned lower extremity.

Aurelia smiled weakly and placed her head on my shoulder. She was out before Gen started the horses back into motion.

12

ROE

The boneyard was one of my favorite spots in all of Devil's Meadows. It was where I went to be alone with my thoughts and to hash out either difficult patients or life's little dramas. The dark corner lot, just a few blocks north of the clinic, was not a graveyard in the literal sense, but it certainly didn't take a brilliant mind to see why locals had given it the boneyard designation. It was haunting and thick with the ghosts of a different time.

It was early morning, just before dawn, and I was due in the clinic soon. Sitting on the ground and resting my head back against a rusted bit of signage, I could look in just about any direction and find myself in a world of muted jewel tones. The glass marquees which were once bright and vibrant now slumbered under dense layers of greasy grime and grit.

The first time I stumbled upon the place, I'd tried to envision what the signs had been like when they were glittering treasures in the desert city, but my mind couldn't quite conjure it. Now they held only the vaguest shadows of their long-lost pageantry—aged monarchs once regal, now sad and alone.

Thinking was why I came here, and I definitely had thinking to do. With Auri and Hale off to the dam for the next three days, I wanted nothing more than a quiet spot to sit and ponder the attack. I was sure it had to be related to the other killings. I was also convinced Valilier Campbell Robichaud knew more than he was letting on. Not that he owed us any explanation of what he did or didn't know, but the idea that he might have valuable knowledge and wasn't sharing it with the people here just didn't sit right with me.

And that made me a hypocrite. We also had valuable knowledge. What Auri and Holdan could do for the people here could be life changing, but we were all too anxious to share it.

Hence, being in the boneyard. I needed to square my thoughts and figure what could be done about it all—Auri, the attacks, Medicus, and Campbell Robichaud.

Speak a demon's name and he shall appear. Or in my case, think a demon's name. The demon in question strolled out from around a tram-sized silver stiletto. The jagged remains of a thousand glass globes dotted its surface and reflected light from the solar torch in Campbell's hand.

"You following me now? Or I guess I should say again?"

He didn't respond immediately, just continued walking up the dirt aisle between the broken bits of a twinkling past. He looked around the backside of a broken giantess dressed in boots and a wide brimmed hat, then turned and slowly approached where I sat in the dust.

"No. Not following you."

"Someone else then?"

"Yes, or I was. Lost the trail back by your clinic and just kept moving in the direction I thought best. And here you are."

104

"Here I am." I hated sounding so clipped and guarded. Charming and pleasant had always been my go to. Until that damn trek through the desert. Things were shifting all around me and I found myself shifting with them. I wasn't a fan.

He looked at me a moment and surprised me by plunking down in the dirt directly across from where I sat. He leaned up against a remarkably intact sign emblazoned with a four-leaf clover—his posture mirroring my own.

"What is all this anyway?" the valilier asked as he looked around.

"As best I can figure, it's the remnants of what DM used to be."

"It really is something. I wonder what it was like when they all worked and lit up the night sky?"

The idea that I had thought the very same thing so many times before twisted and roiled in me. It made no sense whatsoever that I should be angry about something so trivial. Everyone who walked through here likely voiced the same sentiment.

"I guess we'll never know." Sarcasm dripped from me with each word.

He focused on me, head cocked to the side. "I am not your enemy."

"Forgive me for not altogether believing you."

Obviously he didn't have time for the wasted conversation I was giving him. He stood and dusted off the ass of his pants. "Come find me when you change your mind."

Somehow, I thought there was a better chance of snow in the near future.

Yawning, I stretched and stared up at what was left of the fading stars. My body was weary and the day hadn't even begun. Clearly my mind was just as tired because I swore I could see lights moving up and out toward the horizon. Not twinkling stars or an overly bright moon, but strange greenish bronze dotted lights in a triangular pattern. I blinked and scrubbed at my face. When I looked again, they were gone.

Sadly, the changeup that allowed Hale to accompany Auri to the dam settlement meant I had to suffer my own miserable mood alone. With neither of them around to listen to me complain about the endless stream of patients entering the first floor and the long hours and reeking body fluids I was now dedicating my body, mind, and life to, I fell into a bit of a funk.

To add salt to a festering wound, apparently some nasty gastrointestinal bug was running rampant through the settlement, and every vomiting soul and their diarrheal brother ended up in our care. It smelled like norovirus everywhere I turned. Had nobody in this forsaken desert learned how to wash their hands, for piss sake.

I kept a jar of alcohol base with me at all times—my hands cracked and raw from the endless administration of it in an urgent attempt to keep the virus from my body. I *loathed* vomiting. Loathed it.

The front door banged open again and again, dust and dirt blowing in with each patient.

Moving from cot to cot, I plastered a smile on my face and acted like every patient was the most important. And that's what it was—an act. I'd been the star in the theater of my life for so long, it was almost second nature. Most days it was easy, but others? Not so much. Hale knew the real me, and at times I was convinced Auri did too, but for everyone else, the witty smile and easy charm were all they knew.

The patients just kept coming. I had no idea how much longer I could continue the charade. I would provide the care needed until I collapsed on the floor, but being pleasant while doing it was becoming a losing battle.

I felt a tap on my shoulder and turned to find Janet standing there. "If you have any more patients complaining about waiting too long, I just might quit in protest."

She smiled and handed me a thick canvas-covered book. "Not at all. Just wanted to give this back before I forgot. In case you left before me tonight."

I smiled at her. A real—not forced—smile. That was something. "What'd you think?"

"It was good. Not as great as the last one but good."

"Yeah. I completely agree. Not as much carnage and too much romance, but it's still a decent story. I've got yours at home. I'll bring it in tomorrow," I told her.

Janet had a love for reading adventure stories and old fantastical tales just as I did. We'd recently started chatting about them, and it turned out we each had a few the other hadn't read. Once I had more time on my hands, I'd get down to the modest library everyone talked about and check out what they had on their shelves too.

"Keep it as long as you like. I've read it three times already, and it isn't even my favorite."

Thanking her, I tucked the book back into my bag in the lounge and headed out to see my next patient.

"Don't worry about me," the young woman on the narrow bed told me. "Just make sure"—she groaned, turned, and curled her clenched fists into her abdomen—"just make sure Sadie is all right please."

Sadie, the child in question, was no more than two years old. She lay sleeping on the cot with her mother. The toddler's lips were dry and she cried intermittently, but her vital signs weren't too far out of the normal range. Plus, I'd been told by Janet, she'd been wearing a wet diaper when she arrived. So not terribly dehydrated.

"Practitioner Wong is making up more electrolyte solution as we speak. We'll have her hydrated up in no time. You look like you could use some as well, then you'll both be on your way."

She smiled wanly and closed her eyes only to shoot right back up and retch into the small ceramic bowl at the bedside, placed there for just that purpose.

The remainder of the afternoon continued in much the same way. Theo finished the electrolyte solution—a combination of sterilized water, sugar, and just the right amount of salt—and the assistants set about ensuring the patients drank it. Despite our instructions to take only small sips every few minutes, some chugged whole bottles down, just to see it come right back up.

Both Sadie and her mother, a sharp young woman with the ability to follow instructions, were able to drink enough over the course of a few hours—and more importantly, keep it down—to allow me to send them out the door along with a satchel of salt and sugar as well as some ginger and peppermint to mix up and use at home for continued rehydration.

The ill and afflicted continued to flow in. Thankfully, Nora, Janet, and a few other skilled assistants were able to triage them in order of severity, and by the time sundown arrived, the vast majority of them were well on their way to recovery. We only had three patients who needed more than the oral concoction could remedy, and those three ended up with IVs slowly dripping fat bags of saline directly into their thirsty veins. The assistants were able to get these dehydrated bodies moved upstairs using the generator-powered lifts. It was a slow process, but easier than putting them in hand chairs and carrying them up the stairs.

"If I am stuck in the lav all night, I'm going to be livid," Theo informed me when I entered the lounge and dropped into a chair.

The alcohol solution stung as I coated my cracked and bleeding hands in another thick layer. "You and me both."

"At least this is just some shitty—pun fully intended—virus. When I was a much younger man, we had an outbreak of *e. coli*. Got into one of the gardens, and the veg we were feeding everyone was contaminated. Not good. We lost a lot of people in a real brief period of time."

The idea of such an outbreak sounded horrific. I couldn't imagine what it must have been like for the people of the settlement, let alone the practitioners trying to treat them.

"How many?" I asked.

"Too many. Most people were only relatively sick. Stuck in bed, bloody diarrhea. . ." He waved his hand in a nonchalant gesture. "Then we started seeing more and more sepsis, end organ damage, kidney failure. Not enough fluids prepped. No real stock of antibiotics."

He looked lost for a moment, then smiled and snapped back. "But that was a long time ago. No use in me burdening you with it when we have our own poop sandwich to deal with today."

I couldn't disagree. Standing, I stretched my arms high over my head and twisted a few times, satisfied with the resulting series of pops running up my spine. I was halfway out the door when I decided to ask the question that had been brewing in my mind since Auri voiced it as we trudged through the desert a lifetime ago.

"What do you think it was like before?" I had a good rapport with Theo, and he was likely to be more honest with me than anyone in all of Medicus.

"Before what?" He sounded distracted. Perhaps still lost in the nightmare memory—a pile of dead patients.

"Before the Grand Divagation."

His face snapped to mine and for once there was caution in his eyes. "I don't know." He drew the words out. Wary perhaps of where this was going.

Undaunted, I pushed on. "I mean it had to be better, right? Easier to treat people? Easier to diagnose them?" I sounded like Auri had.

At one time, I didn't think it mattered, but once Specs had suggested it, I couldn't let the idea go.

"Maybe, but I believe we have all we need right here"—he tapped his temple—"to save many, *many* lives. You didn't need fancy medical equipment today to provide comfort and care to a whole bucketload of folks."

"Yeah, but like you said, it was just a virus. Wouldn't you have been able to save more lives all those years ago if you'd had the proper medicines and equipment?"

"Keep your voice down!" He hissed. Theo was the last person I expected to lose his temper so easily.

Raising my hands, I stammered an apology.

He went to the door, glanced outside, then shut it firmly.

"I didn't mean to suggest—"

"Stop. Just zip it for a minute." He leaned against the closed door and shut his eyes. It was the first time he appeared his age. "Look, you can't talk like that around here. Even hinting at the idea that the Divagation shouldn't have happened or that Medicus is deliberately keeping our hands tied will get you nowhere. I certainly won't agree with you."

That last bit was a lie. It was in the way his eyes flashed when he said it. More than that, I hadn't hinted at Medicus tying our hands. Only that things weren't available as they'd once been. Was he projecting his own speculation on the conversation?

"Now what you might want to know is why the whole thing happened in the first place. *That* is a legitimate question, and while it isn't taught in your primary or secondary school, any decent lover of history could give you a few answers."

And Theo loved history.

"You know about the wars of course."

I nodded.

"People can be horrific to one another. Particularly when resources—land, food, energy—are at stake."

Again I nodded. This wasn't anything new.

"Imagine if you can, a world full of wonderful technology. Lights turning on to the sound of your voice. Machines that could think, act, and feel more real than reality itself. Computers that could not only see inside a person's body but also tell you which chemical cocktail to give if they found an ailment or illness hidden there.

"Too many people with too much information, making their own diagnosis and then demanding their own kind of treatments. Others ripping apart whole ecosystems and killing off entire species just because it was convenient or because they could. Traveling not just across a vast city but the entire world itself in a day. Imagine fighting over all of that and having information available at the snap of a finger."

The noise from the patients and staff outside seemed to melt away as his words hung in the air.

He hadn't asked a question, but I answered just the same. "Too much, too fast, too accessible, and too damn easy."

He rubbed at his temples. "It must have been a complete and total trash fire. I'm glad I wasn't around to see it."

I nodded a third time.

"So then they had the peace accords. This is where the lessons were meant to be learned and the previous evils righted and all the other bat guano people tell each other to make their idea seem like the right thing.

"The brilliant minds got together and came up with a plan. Shut it all off. Simple enough. Shut it down. Everything. The power flow, the information flow, the humanity flow. All of it. Make people work for it all again. Make it feel less necessary to fight and more necessary to survive.

"Now supposedly it wasn't done overnight with just the flip of a switch. No way really it could have been. But it wasn't a years' long gentle transition either. Six months they said. Six months they gave people to prepare. But really how do you prepare for something like that? You don't.

"First, the travel was cut off. Then the information streams. And then the power grids. The things we have now, the solar generators and individual solar-powered devices were all still available, but no more mass access to unlimited supplies. And when the power was gone, so was the large-scale manufacturing—not just medications and machines related to medicine—all of it. The manufacturing. The climate control. Mass transit. Food processing. Sewage processing. All of the little things that were comfortable and easy. All the other commodities, just gone. The war was over but the real fight had just begun."

"Why though?" I asked. "I get wanting to reel things in, but why so extreme?"

"That I can't answer. Not sure anyone kept any sort of record of those discussions and talks leading up to the day the Divagation happened."

"It must have been madness." I thought about how the folks here in DM sometimes reacted to minor inconveniences. What must it have been like to have your entire life uprooted and turned on its head?

"By all accounts it was. Again, the historical record here is shady. This has all been scraped together from here and there, personal diaries that fell into the right hands, verbal stories passed down in families, things like that. The speculation is that roughly three-quarters of the earth's human population perished during the wars and in the two years during the Divagation and the months following it."

I scoffed, thinking of the mountains of decomposing cadavers that would have remained. "That can't be right."

"Can't it? Forget lack of meds and proper hygiene. The sickness alone would have done in huge numbers. But remember, those people, they weren't like we are now. Many of them never had to do anything for themselves. Some knew how to farm and others how to hunt. But many more couldn't keep their own water clean or their homes warm. I'm sure they fought over resources and out of fear. The wars weren't on a large scale, but I'd wager more than a few minor skirmishes broke out between neighbors."

"And the ones with the plan? What'd you call them? *Brilliant minds*? They were all down with this happening?" I didn't think Theo had that answer either, but still I had to ask.

"Again, it's not my place, or yours, to speculate on that, Practitioner Belstrohm." He gave me an odd look that was hard to read. "But a person might like to believe it didn't really play out the way it was planned. Most people only expect other people to react the way they themselves would. Or how they *believe* they would. Presumably the idea of mass casualties bordering on extinction was far from the thoughts in those brilliant minds, but. . ." He raised his hands and shrugged.

"What about Medicus?"

"Had nothing to do with it." He was dismissive in his quick response.

My doubt must have shown on my face.

"From what I gather, Medicus formed a good twenty years later. Accessing the previous technology wasn't possible, but a group of dedicated people collected what printed information they could and started making small batches of the medications that were possible based on old recipes and formularies. You know, growing penicillin in mold and great heaping bunches of belladonna. It was mostly folks who had practiced medicine before the Divagation and had been trying to help those in their communities during the following years. They knew the skills and procedures would be lost if they weren't handed down, so they eventually started teaching others. And here we are."

It seemed completely ludicrous to me, but we all knew where we were now. And we knew it was miles behind where medicine once was. Maybe Theo was right.

"But if that's the case, why doesn't Medicus want us to do more? Find new treatments and expand our therapies?"

Theo stared at his hands and looked up at me. "That, Roe Belstrohm, is a very good question and one you need to be very careful in asking."

114

13

AURELIA

Holdan was well when I woke up. More than well actually.

The sight that greeted me as I exited the small room we'd been given for our lodging was nothing short of breathtaking.

The building itself sat just to the west of the concrete dam. It was quite possibly the largest structure I'd ever laid eyes on, and I had a curious sense of unbalance as I took in the massive grey wall and the miles of pale blue water growing out behind it—the lake. The near side was a canyon chasm with a thin ribbon of water snaking its way from the bottom of the dam and around a slow bend far out in the distance.

While I'd slept off the effects of the miracle and the preceding six hours of walking, he had apparently taken it upon himself to assist Hale and Geneva with the initial introductions and setup of the makeshift clinic. More than that—he was helping Hale with some patient care.

A relatively well-maintained road ran across the top of the dam. Just outside our building, a stone sculpture stood guard. It might have once been a sphinx or maybe an angel. It was hard to say as

115

the head was missing and what I believed were wings were shattered just above the joint where they left the body.

I found the others gathered with a few of the settlers in the meeting room across the road in a separate structure that seemed to grow from the grey concrete of the dam itself. The windows of the space looked out over the drop on the river side of the dam. The view was both beautiful and terrifying.

Hale looked up when I entered. A smile of what I hoped was relief crossed his chiseled face. The moment was brief though, as he turned back to whatever it was Holdan was doing next to him.

I stepped closer without saying anything. From what I could gather, Hale was supervising Holdan as the latter finished a series of sutures on a small incision on the posterior neck of a woman.

Raising an eyebrow, I asked a silent question.

"Simple epidermal cyst," Hale said by way of explanation.

Simple it might be, but if Medicus got word of Holdan practicing before he had been given express permission from them to do so, things would most definitely get complicated for him. Not to mention what they would think about Gen and Hale letting it occur. The way Holdan had been pushing for an answer and getting nowhere lately, I supposed it was a chance he was willing to take, but that didn't explain the others' willingness to go along with it.

At least he was using Medicus Corpus–approved techniques and not his other *special* skills.

"Feeling better, Ms. Morris?" he asked as I plunked down next to him and watched him tie off the last of the silk knots.

Careful not to speak too freely with settlers about, I replied, "Much better. Thanks. I guess the journey tired me more than I expected."

"You still need to build up your stamina. It'll come," he said casually. He'd been telling me the effects of the wonder-working on my body would lessen with time, and to a certain extent that was true. Nothing had been as bad as that first time I'd worked a major wonder while saving Geneva in the desert, but I still felt weak and shaky after each healing.

Holdan cleaned and dressed the wound, appearing every bit the competent Medicus practitioner he once was and wished to be again.

Hale had brought my kit when they set up and I wasted no more time jumping in to help, as a few of the other settlers filtered in requesting minor treatments. They were hardy folks and didn't require much. I realized later the work they did probably had a lot to do with them remaining fit and healthier than many of the settlers I'd met during my time in Devil's Meadows.

As the afternoon melted into evening, a middle-aged man with legs like tree trunks and skin roughly the same color and texture as my boots appeared at the entrance to the meeting hall. He wore his thick salt and pepper hair to his shoulders. Gen introduced him as Josef, and apparently he was what the settlement termed a foreman—a leader in the work done down inside the depths of the dam as well as in the daily running of life for the settlers.

Josef invited us to a gathering that night for dinner and entertainment as well as a tour of the dam itself the following day. Both sounded exciting to me. As it turned out, I was right. Both would turn out to be thrilling, but for very different reasons.

After returning to our assigned accommodation to wash up and change out of our clinical clothes, we returned to the same open meeting room for the evening meal. While we'd been away, the room had been transformed from a

117

makeshift clinic into a cozy communal dining hall. Several small tables had been set with four to six places apiece, and one larger banquet style table rested against the far wall beneath the windows. It was laden with heaping plates of roasted corn, stewed root vegetables, and firm beans in a spicy sauce. A large platter of decent-sized fish and several loaves of dense flat bread were piled beside carafes of room temperature water and a jug of dark brown beer. Dozens of candles were interspersed among the food and centered on each of the smaller tables. Josef rose from his place at one of these to welcome us back.

"Aw, Joe. You all always go to too much trouble," Geneva said as she looked around. "I keep telling you, none of this is necessary."

"And I keep telling you, Geneva, we get so few courteous visitors here, it's nice to socialize on occasion."

Josef had his silver and black hair pulled back in a leather tie low on his neck. Combined with the deep crow's-feet around his eyes, it gave him a gravity I hadn't appreciated earlier in the day. If he knew what he was doing down there in the depths of the dam—and I had no reason to suspect otherwise—it made sense to have him in charge. His quiet confidence reminded me quite a bit of Asher.

He smiled warmly, the crow's-feet digging deeper into his bronzed skin, and led us to the serving table.

We piled heaps of warm food on our plates and sat where he indicated. Holdan and I were at his table, Hale and Gen one table over.

The veg and corn were simple and delicious. I prodded at the fish with my fork and it flaked apart, but I hesitated in taking a bite. Fish in the desert just seemed a bit suspect.

"Trout," Josef said as I stabbed at it for possibly the third time. "From the lake." He tilted his chin toward the far end of the room, opposite the windows overlooking the gorge.

"Of course." I smiled but felt the heat rising in my cheeks. I had no intention of insulting anyone, but I was sure I'd done just that.

Taking a dainty bite, my smile widened. I might have even made an *mmmmm* sound. It wasn't just flaky. It was light and delicately flavored with lemon and olives. I heard a deep chuckle that could only be Hale. He was probably watching me make a fool of myself and savoring it just as I was savoring the food.

I would have shot him a nasty look had Holdan not chosen the exact moment to teasingly scold me as well. "No need to sound so surprised, Ms. Morris. The poor dead souls in the bottom of the lake have gone to great efforts to flavor the stock here quite well."

Sifting through all my interactions with the man, I couldn't recall a single instance of him joking about anything. Let alone something like this. "Dead souls? As in dead bodies?"

I noticed he didn't have any fish on his plate.

"Hmm. I see you've heard the legends then?" Josef half commented, half asked.

"Is that all they are? Legends? I was led to believe it was a matter of historical record."

I'd grown accustomed to Holdan and his clipped superior tone. Despite how he sounded, Josef didn't seem to take offense. His lips tipped up at the corners as he watched us with calm eyes.

When he spoke, he didn't direct his comments to Holdan exclusively, but to the room at large. "History or legend. Doesn't matter much what you call it. Eventually it's all the same."

"I'm afraid I'm still in the dark," I interjected.

119

The woman who sat to my right smiled benignly. She was considerably younger than Josef. Not much older than me, I'd guess. Still, I felt she must have been his wife or lover. I'd watched them interact through the short time we'd been here and they seemed comfortable and connected.

"Pay no attention to your friend there," she told me. "Even if what they say is true, those poor souls are long gone. Their flesh taken by the lake generations past, and their bones long buried beneath the silt and the sand at the bottom."

I smiled a bit, but my hand trembled as I put down my fork. "I appreciate that, but I'm not so sure it puts me at ease."

"Josef," she said sternly, "put this sweet lady out of her misery so she can finish her dinner in peace. She needn't be worried about ghosts in the night or flesh in her fish."

"Yes, Yana, love." His smile at the woman was one of both long-suffering commitments and dearest adoration. Definitely a couple then. "You see, Ms. Morris—"

Leaning forward, I cut him off. "Aurelia, please. Holdan is the only one who calls me Ms. Morris."

"Right then, Aurelia. This dam is a manmade wonder of engineering. Born of intense labor, courageous vision, and the sweat from thousands of backs." I nodded. "And before the dam was built, there was no lake here at all, only just the winding curves and bends of the mighty river you see coming out the other side."

I glanced to the windows even though I knew exactly what he meant.

"Just as with any great river and the life water it flows, there were once tiny towns dotting the banks of the great beast. When it came time for the dam to be built, the space between these rocky walls was chosen based on the short distance from one side to the other. The builders worked for a number of years to pour all of the concrete you feel beneath your feet. Some of them even died in the process. But it isn't the workers your friend was mentioning. It was the town's folk who watched the great grey monster grow taller over their shoulders."

A chair squeaked, and I glanced over my shoulder to find Hale pulling his seat up next to mine to hear the story better.

"The water downstream was still being piped through a tunnel to the other side—you'll see what I'm talking about tomorrow when we go in—so the lake didn't exist even as the wall grew higher.

"Some say those town folks were told time and again—over years mind you—that the water would come when the tunnel was closed and they either didn't care or didn't believe it to be true. Others claim they were never informed and had no idea what was to come. I think that's a load of dung taller than my head. How could they not see what was happening? Hell, some of the men from that town worked on the crew building the thing. Either way, they never left. Not as the grey monster went up and not after the tunnel with the flow through was closed.

"The river rose and filled in the lake and some folks will tell you the people of that small town let the water rise right on over them. I personally don't believe that either. I believe they'd moved on long before and the town was all empty homes and boarded-up shops. Either way, it would have been a slow fill, rising by a few feet per day. Not some instant swell swallowing them up."

He cleared his throat and smiled. "So you see, there is a town down there. Buried under more metric tons of water than I can count. And if there were people in that town? Well, this dam has been here for a few hundred years, so I'm sure the fish are just fine to eat."

Yana clapped in an affectionate way, and Josef sighed and took a long deep draw on his mug of beer. "Now finish on up. We've got dancing to do."

The music wasn't loud by any means, but it had a presence in the small space that demanded attention. Josef sat casually on a straight back chair, picking and strumming the perfectly tuned strings of a well-worn guitar. It was a rich sound, perfectly balanced with the soft lyrics Yana sang. They had quite a repertoire, and clearly the settlers here had favorites. As they finished one song, another was called out for them to start.

For the first couple of songs, I just sat and listened to the lovely harmony of the voice and the strings. When the third song started, a cool firm hand grabbed mine and I was more than a little surprised to find Holdan pulling me to my feet.

"Come on, Ms. Morris. Let's see how well you fixed this leg of mine." And then we were whirling and spinning to the upbeat tempo of a song I'd never heard before.

To my surprise, Holdan was a wonderful dancer. To my even greater surprise, I enjoyed spinning around the room with him. It was no secret I wasn't the most coordinated or agile person on the planet, so dancing had never been a strong suit. I tended to be more of the 'sit in a corner and enjoy the music while trying not to move' type. But as the man I'd once feared and loathed in equal measures led me with grace and confidence, I gradually began to relax and found myself smiling.

When the song ended to a round of jubilant applause, Gen drifted over and claimed the next dance. I was a tinge disappointed but refused to let it show. Instead, I slipped back against the wall and watched the few couples who were making the most of the candlelight and song. Before long, the melody faded and clapping once again erupted in the tiny space.

Yana announced they would be taking a brief break. No one seemed to mind, most likely knowing the duo would be back for more harmonies before the night ended.

"Enjoy your dance?" Hale asked as he sidled up next to me.

"I did."

He snorted somewhere between disbelieving and annoyed.

"Well, I did whether you believe me or not."

"Oh, I believe you, just surprised is all."

"There's nothing to be surprised about. I'm not his biggest fan either, but the last few weeks, I've come to realize, he isn't as terrible as we all were led to believe. Some days I think that was Nanette's biggest crime."

Hale frowned and shrugged. "I never said he was terrible. I just thought you didn't like activities that required coordination." One corner of his lip rose as he eyed me from the side.

I punched him in the arm and winced, shaking out my hand. His grin widened, and his eyebrows flicked up. "That make you feel better?"

"Yes, actually it did."

"Good. I get the next dance."

My cheeks flushed as I nodded. Hopefully I wouldn't make a complete and utter fool of myself. I'd never seen Hale dance, but he was good at just about anything that involved any amount of athleticism, so this would probably be no different.

I didn't have much time to think about it, as Josef and Yana set down their mugs and took up their places once more by the windows. Rather than strumming out an upbeat tempo, however, Josef simply sat with his guitar on his knee and stared

123

adoringly at Yana. She began to sing a slow sweet song sans accompaniment. Her voice was the clear ring of a bell in the hushed room. It was an old song I'd heard before—a rich tune of love and reunion. No one moved, mesmerized as we were by the spell she poured into the cramped space. If I'd been asked in that moment, I would have said Yana was the true wonder-worker, casting her magic over anyone with ears and a soul.

After the first stanza, Josef began to strum along. The thrall was broken, and he nodded in acknowledgment of the crime he willingly committed. "Sorry, folks. Time to dance."

The tempo picked up only a fraction, and a few couples embraced and began a slow two step mixed with sways and stutters. Hale didn't wait for my reaction, just swept me into the circle of his arms as we joined the others in the slow swaying shuffle.

"I'm sure you were hoping for something livelier." All trace of teasing was gone from his voice.

"No, this is fine." I tilted my head back to look up at him, refusing to simply stare into the center of his chest for the next few minutes.

"Not going to lie, I was hoping for a bit more than fine, but I'll take what I can get."

Shaking my head was all the response I could muster.

We danced for a few more minutes, slowing circling the room. It wasn't an awkward feeling exactly, but I did think I should say something to distract myself from being this close to him. The last thing either of us needed was for me to actually drool on his shoes.

"So what do you think of the place so far?" I asked.

"The dam? It's pretty impressive." His words rustled against my hair.

"Yes. It is, but I meant more DM in general. Is it what you expected?"

"Hard to say. My expectations were pretty limited. I didn't spend much time thinking about where we were going to end up. I was just so focused on getting through school and keeping an eye on Roe. I was happy to go anywhere."

"I don't think I ever told you before. But he's lucky to have you for a brother. And the people of Devil's Meadows are lucky to have you as a surgeon." My neck was tight from tilting back, but I couldn't look away from his thoughtful green eyes.

He nodded by way of reply.

I continued, "During the initial days on the road, we didn't get off on the right foot, but I feel lucky to have you here too." I pulled my hand free from his and moved to push my glasses back up on my nose, but Hale beat me to it, gently sliding them back into position. I didn't say anything. Didn't know what to say as he stared down at me and used the same hand to tuck a stray hair behind my ear.

"You shouldn't feel lucky, Aurelia."

"Why not?" My voice was barely above a whisper.

"I'm nothing special." He moved a fraction of an inch closer, and I noticed we'd stop our circular progress around the room. We just stood to the side, swaying in our own little bubble.

My heart fluttered and my palms grew warm. Hale's head dipped toward me, and I rose up on my toes as the music ended and applause once more clacked through the room. Hale straightened and looked around then began to clap politely with the others. It took a good ten seconds to compose myself and wipe the disappointment from my face before I turned and applauded our hosts.

We stayed for another set of songs before retiring to our assigned sleeping area. We were in for a long haul the following day and all needed some rest.

I danced with Holdan again as well as Geneva and a couple of men from the settlement. I didn't dance a second time with Hale.

The following morning came and went in much the same way all of my days did. Up to my eyeballs in other people's complaints. Ointments, elixirs, pills, and instructions were traded for tales of muscle pain, inflamed hemorrhoids, swollen feet, and crusting rashes. Just as the day before, we didn't see many overweight patients and very few with illnesses stemming from inactivity. It was quite the opposite. Overuse injuries and signs of hard work ailed them. There were a few settlers who stopped in just to get a general once over—no complaints or questions. It felt too easy with these patients, but secretly I praised these lovely souls for just being well.

Josef and a man I'd danced with the previous evening who had introduced himself as Jonesy, arrived after lunch. We packed up our limited equipment and set off to descend into the belly of the dam.

If I thought it was intimidating from the outside, it was nothing compared to what I felt as we descended flight after flight of stairs further down the concrete structure. Phantom moans and groans reminded me of the crushing volume of water just to the other side of the dank dark wall. Jonesy explained as we walked down and down and down that the dam didn't actually serve any purpose these days other than keeping the settlements down river from getting flooded should it let loose. The equipment, which once generated power for millions of lives, was no longer serviceable, and even if it were, the power lines connecting it to Devil's Meadows and other communities further downstream had been dismantled during the Grand Divagation.

"So's ya see, it just needs to be drained. Like yer bladder or whatnot. Can't have it overflowing," Jonesy explained as we rested on a small landing approximately halfway down. "The water comes through, but it isn't turning nothing. Just going straight on through. It's our job make sure it keeps flowin.'"

Jonesy was easily older than my father, but he took the stairs like a much younger man. I understood why most of the settlers here were so fit. My quads were already feeling the strain, and we were just going *down*. The thought of climbing all the way back up had me wanting to vomit already.

Of course Gen and Hale both looked like this was a walk though heavenly pastures. Even Holdan didn't seem phased by the exertion. I shuddered to think what state I'd be in if I hadn't been trying to improve my stamina with my daily exercise. I'd thank Geneva for her advice later.

Catching my breath, I took in the metal rungs of the ladders running near the stairs as well as the various gears, wheels, and spigots. They must have all had a purpose at one time, and perhaps they still did, but the rust and corrosion I saw had me doubting it.

We were beginning to walk again when a loud clanging started somewhere up above. Josef frowned and looked at Jonesy.

"The outlet valves been giving you trouble again?" he asked.

"No, sir. Checked on 'em myself yesterday. That sounded higher up toward the top. Not sure what could be causing it."

The clanging came again, this time interspersed with shorter softer taps in a series of stops and starts. *Tap-tap-tap. Clang. Clang. Clang. Tap-tap-tap.* Then silence.

Geneva looked thoughtful as both Josef and Jonesy frowned at the noise.

"Are we to understand this isn't the typical sounds the pipes in here make?" Holdan asked Josef.

"We're fairly accustomed to the moans and groans," Josef explained. "Even though the concrete is several meters thick and cured long ago, it still has a tendency to transfer the odd sound now and then. Nah, this is something different."

"Perhaps the ghosts of those long-drowned townsfolk then?" When Hale whispered the words in my ear, a shiver ran down my spine. From the words or his voice, I couldn't be sure.

"Not funny," I mumbled. A soft laugh rumbled in his chest.

Tap-tap-tap. Clang. Clang. Clang. Tap-tap-tap. The sound echoed down through the narrow space. For reasons I couldn't explain, it unsettled me.

We continued to walk lower, headed for the base and the area where the workers could turn the valves needed to adjust the outflow from the lake. Jonesy was a step or two below me. It was easy for Hale to speak over me from his place two steps behind and above. "So, Jonesy, who assigned you all to work this thing?"

"What do ya mean, who assigned it?"

"Well, someone must have asked you all to keep the dam in order, right? If the settlements each make their own rules and govern themselves, it would seem after the Divagation the dam would have just fallen into disrepair. How'd you all end up being the stewards of the place?"

"No one asked us and no one assigned us this work either. We've just always been here. My pops and my grandpop and his grandpop before all the way back to when things fell apart. They were smart enough to know it needed to be managed and so they managed it. Josef's family too and on down the line."

"You just stayed out of the goodness of your soul?" I asked.

"Well, yeah. Plus, where else would I go?"

"Anywhere, I suppose," I said.

He scoffed and waved the hand not holding the rail. "No sense in leaving and having to try to find something better. We got a good thing here. A'course, every now and then one of the young men or women decide to try their luck in Devil's Meadows or farther afield, and no shame in that. Some come back to us, some don't. And every now and then we get a traveler through who decides they need some honest work and settles in and stays awhile."

When Hale asked how they could possibly sustain themselves here without any other trade, Jonesy went on to explain there was a trade of sorts. Just as DM sent them Medicus practitioners to see after their needs—along with other goods—in exchange for the clean drinking water they were able to pump from the lake, other settlements down river also saw the value in maintaining the dam. Over time each settlement worked out a trade with the workers here. The areas along the river either needed the water or feared having their settlements flooded should something happen to the dam. Some sent shipments of food up monthly. Others had caravans of traders work out deals to provide various sundries. And a few simply paid in shipments of coins, which the dam workers used to keep a sort of basic economy running. It was all fairly simple and straightforward. The workers started out keeping things running because it had been the right thing to do but now made a lucrative living off it.

We were finally to the base platform, and I craned my neck back as far as it would go to take in the height of the structure. A weird feeling of vertigo washed through me at the sight, and I had to close my eyes for a moment.

"Pretty damn impressive, isn't it?" Hale asked me.

I nodded and returned to staring at the grey walls surrounding me.

The clanging and tapping sounded a few more times, never seeming to grow any quieter despite the distance we'd covered since the first time we heard it. It almost seemed to be following us down into the bowels of the place. Once I thought it, the idea that someone was following wouldn't leave me.

Josef and Jonesy—even Gen—seemed uneasy each time the sound reached us as well. As Josef continued to explain the various areas inside—which ones were still used, which ones weren't, and how they were maintained—Jonesy disappeared back up the stairs, only to join us roughly fifteen minutes later.

After the eight or ninth set of noises, I mentioned my worry to Geneva. "Do you think it's the pipes or do you think someone might be making that racket?"

"If it's pipes, they seem pretty consistent with the pattern."

"You think someone is in here with us?" I couldn't control the tremor in my voice.

"I'm sure there are. They keep a half dozen bodies inside to work the valves most shifts. I asked Josef about it, but he says today's crew is all accounted for."

Presumably that was where Jonesy had ventured off to. He was checking on the crew and perhaps even the noise itself.

"At any rate, I think it's best we start heading back up. There really isn't much else to see." If my legs could have cried at Geneva's words, they would have. The idea of climbing all seven hundred steps back up was unappealing at best. She gave me a sympathetic pat. "You three go on ahead, I'll let Josef know we're going up."

Both Holdan and Hale were more than happy to set back up and while I knew Hale wouldn't bat an eyelash at the climb, I was more than a little surprised when Holdan was able to take the stairs quick enough to get a good bit ahead of us.

"Let him go," Hale said when I suggested we call him back to wait for us. "I wanted to talk to you about something anyway, and I just haven't felt like the time has been right."

"Okay." If my heart hadn't already been beating a million miles an hour, it would have then. Maybe he was going to tell me what I'd been waiting months to hear. That I hadn't read into things. That he wanted to be more to me than my best friend's brother. As it turned out, I was thinking about the brief kiss we'd shared and he was thinking about something entirely different.

"I don't want you to read more into this than there is"—never a good start—"but I found a letter in your apartment awhile back, and it has me worried."

My mind raced to think what letter he could possibly mean. The only letters I'd gotten recently were from my parents and . . . Lita. He'd found a letter from Lita obviously. Which one?

I stumbled as I tried to look back at him but caught myself on the railing and continued my climb.

"I'm not really sure how you just found a letter that was addressed to me in my own apartment, but I'll let that go for now. Why you think it's any business of yours to be worried I'd like to hear." My tone was as cool as it could be when I could barely catch my breath.

"It's my business because I can't stand the thought of you getting caught. It wasn't like I was snooping through your things, Aurelia. It was lying

131

right out on the sofa for anyone to see. Anyone to read. Don't you get how bad that could be for you?"

"For me. Not for you, Hale. And that letter didn't say anything incriminating. It was one friend to another saying she might try to come visit with her ill child. I'm a Medicus Corpus practitioner, Hale. It would make all the sense in the world for her to bring Jonaten here."

"Not when they have their own practitioners in that settlement, it doesn't. And I hate to say it, Aurelia, but not when you couldn't cure him the first time."

"I thought the old stone cold asshole Hale had changed his ways, but it seems I was mistaken about that too."

"Too? What else do you think you were mistaken about?"

I was happy he was climbing behind me. I didn't want him to see my face. The sweating and panting were bad enough, but I could feel my cheeks crumbling toward tears, and I could keep that to myself.

"Aurelia."

I kept trudging up the stairs one slow step at a time.

"Come on. Auri. Stop."

Wasn't going to happen.

He reached his long arm up and grabbed my wrist. I yanked it free and spun around, my arms pinwheeling to keep from falling down the concrete steps as I did so.

"What?"

"I'm not trying to be an ass." He studied me for a beat. "I'm not. Really. I didn't think reading the letter was a big deal. I realize now it was. I was wrong, and I'm sorry for that. But the rest of it? I'm worried, and I won't apologize for that."

"There's nothing to worry about. No one knows what I've been doing. I've been careful."

"Really? Then why is it, do you suppose, Jassika stopped me the other day and told me to relay a message. *She* knows what you're doing, and she says Medicus might be on to you too. She's warning you to stop."

I scoffed. "She can't know anything. I've been ultra careful. Holdan has too, I'm sure. He wants to get back into Medicus and wouldn't risk it. You must be mistaken about what she meant." But part of me knew. That offhanded comment before we'd left. *Beyond the standard of care.*

"Auri, listen to me. Her exact words were *'Tell her to mind herself very carefully.'* That sounds pretty serious. We can't risk you getting caught."

I wanted to argue. Despite signing up voluntarily for this position, I was already getting weary of other people telling me how to live my life. When to work. When to sleep. Who to try to help and how. Now Hale was adding himself to the list. Maybe it was better when he disliked me. At least then I wouldn't keep getting my hopes up something was about to change just to have him treat me like his kid brother's little friend again.

"You know," I began but immediately shut my mouth when the banging noise echoed again. It was louder too. Really loud. Maybe just a flight or two above us. Holdan had to be close to whatever it was.

Tap-tap-tap. CLANG. CLANG. CLANG. *Tap-tap-tap.*

"Holdan? Can you see what it is?" I called. No answer. "Holdan?"

Silence filled the space, and then the banging began in earnest. No pattern or rhythm just violent pounding sounds.

"Listerman?" Hale yelled as he came even to my step and passed around me. I followed him to the

133

next small landing, but he was moving quicker than I ever could.

My legs were shaking and my breath was sawing in and out. I wanted to believe it was all from the exertion, but I knew the noise and cramped space was likely playing just as big of a role.

"Damn it, Listerman. Can you hear me?" Hale was yelling up the stairs. He looked back toward me and said, "Stay here. I'm just going to run up the next couple of flights and see what the piss is going on."

He ran easily upward, the soles of his boots barely making a sound as his agile figure took the steps two at a time. I looked over the rail and saw Geneva had barely started the upward climb. Jonesy and Josef were still on the concrete base and appeared to be in a deep discussion over something.

Whatever or whoever was making such a noise gave one last loud CLANG. The sound echoed off the walls of concrete and then the world fell silent. I couldn't even hear Hale as he continued to ascend the steps. Time ticked by. Perhaps a minute. Perhaps two.

I'd gotten my breath back and decided waiting here wasn't doing anyone any good. There was only one route and it was up. Whether Hale found the source of the noise and figured out where Holdan had gotten to or not, me waiting for Gen was ridiculous. She'd easily catch me on the upward climb.

I made it another two flights before I smelled it. The scent of lightning laced the air. Thick ozone trapped here in the depths of a concrete dam. Trouble was coming, and I had no idea from where.

I pushed my legs faster but already they were tired and worn. Then I heard it. Rasping ragged breaths that seemed to come from all around me.

"Holdan?" I called softly. "Is that you?"

134

Nothing.

"Hale?" A little louder.

No response. I craned my head back to look up the stairs but couldn't see either of my friends up there. Grasping the railing, I bent at the waist to look down. I could see Geneva making her way up the steps, but that breathing couldn't be coming from her.

Was it possible the banging was all a distraction? A way to separate us? Valilier Robichaud had warned me I was in danger. Was my attacker waiting to get me alone?

Tap-tap-tap. Clang. Clang. Clang. Tap-tap-tap.

Distant once again but still from above.

I pushed on, and the sounds of ragged respirations grew louder. I could hear it all around me. Feel it on my neck. My heart rate picked up even faster, my gelatinous legs shaking even more. I tried to calm myself. To bring my heart and my anxious mind under control, but it was little use.

One long slow exhale of ragged breath just behind me and this time I could swear I not only heard and felt the breath but smelled the sour stink drag across my face.

All thought left me except the need to get up out of this concrete mausoleum before I was just as dead as those poor souls buried under tons of water on the far side of the concrete wall.

I ran as fast as my short legs could take me up the stairs.

Up and up I went. I didn't look back, didn't look anywhere but at my feet and the endless steps in front of me. We'd gone down seven hundred steps and it felt like I had run back up twice as many before I slammed into a body on one of the top landings.

135

"Ms. Morris. Are you quite all right?" Holdan grasped my arms and held me upright when I thought my legs would collapse beneath me.

I shook my head from side to side. Too winded to speak but needing to convey that no . . . no I was not all right.

"Auri." Hale stepped around a concrete pillar he had been behind. "What is it?"

I couldn't speak. Just kept shaking my head. Tears streamed down my face as I pointed to the steps.

Hale held one elbow and Holdan the other as they both looked downward.

"Nothing there, Ms. Morris." Holdan stepped back and looked at me quizzically.

I finally had enough air in my lungs to speak. "There was someone down there. Chasing me."

Hale started forward. "Chasing you? Up the stairs?"

"Yes." I panted. "I think. He was breathing heavy on me."

"Breathing on you?" Holdan didn't sound convinced.

To be fair, I sounded confused and pathetic even in my own ears.

"I'll go check it out." Hale was heading toward the steps when another loud clang reverberated over the small landing. "Shit. Just a minute."

He stepped back around the concrete pillar, and I could just make out the outline of a metal door hidden there. It had a turn wheel on the outside that both Hale and Holdan had to grip to get moving. After a few grunts and some serious straining on their part, the wheel spun and the door swung open, revealing a pair of frightened and weeping teens.

After a brief explanation, it became clear they'd come down here earlier in the day and decided to use the privacy of the space. Unfortunately the door had swung shut, trapping them inside. They'd been using a metal wrench to bang on the door, hoping someone would hear and let them out.

It explained the noise, but not the ozone smell and not the rancid breath I'd felt on my neck.

Hale was on his way down to investigate further when Geneva made it to the landing. She listened to my story and said, "It's no use going back down, Hale. There isn't anybody down there. I would have passed them on the way."

No one said anything as I shook my head.

The others waited for Josef and Jonesy at the stairwell entrance. Alone in my confusion, I walked back to our bunks and tried to convince myself I wasn't losing my mind.

14

HALE

The sun was a bright and brilliant bastard. As the rays beat down upon my head, they did absolutely nothing to improve my mood.

For every step I took closer to Aurelia, something came along to send me another leap back. I'd messed up, and while the chasm didn't seem too vast to bridge, I was getting frustrated with myself for causing it at all.

The issue with the letter had seemed insignificant at the time, but obviously I'd really screwed up. My head told me I'd done what I thought best, but my gut was strongly disagreeing. It was all new territory for me.

Up until that point, I'd spent my life trying to protect the person I cared about the most in the world—Roe. And while my relationship with Aurelia was a completely different set of circumstances, the drive to protect her felt just as strong. It had been growing for a while now and even though I couldn't pinpoint exactly where along the road to Devil's Meadows it had started, it had definitely hit full force when I watched her go limp performing the miracle on Geneva.

Part of me thought it was seeing her so vulnerable that had made me kiss her when she woke. Another part argued it was because she shared such a close bond with my brother and my jealousy was the cause for my actions. But I wasn't some naive kid. If what I felt was real, my feelings would not only linger but grow. I'd decided to be patient and let things settle for us all in Devil's Meadows before I pushed further forward.

I'd been partially right. Despite not getting to spend much time together lately, my feelings for her were continuing to grow stronger. The only problem was I hadn't planned on her not reciprocating. Maybe waiting had been a huge mistake.

And then she found out I'd read her mail.

When Aurelia had run up those stairs the day before, like the devil and all his demons were after her, I was ready to do whatever it took to keep her safe. But once she'd calmed down and realized it was likely just a trick of the acoustics inside the concrete structure, she walked away. Not only was I *not* the person she looked to for comfort, it was as if I was no more to her than Listerman.

Sweat raced down my temples and was forming a thick band of wet material at the collar of my shirt. I was having trouble finding the motivation to rise from the spot I'd claimed by the creepy broken angle, but if I stayed out much longer, the sun would cook my skin to jerky. Already I could feel the tiny pricks of pain up and down my exposed arms. Mixed with the stinging perspiration, it was becoming more and more unpleasant. It was evident I'd need to go inside and face the awkward silence that had sat heavily between Auri and me all morning.

I just needed a minute more. Taking a calming breath, I rested my head against the statue's pedestal and closed my eyes.

139

The biting bits of pain in my arms grew more intense and traveled up to my neck and down to my lower legs—which made no sense at all as my ankles and calves were covered with my cargo pants and heavy socks.

Opening my eyes, I leaped to my feet when I saw the damned anthill and the trail of minuscule marauders marching their happy asses all over me. At least a dozen thick red bodies were weaving through the hair of my arms. Several others were visible on my shirt and pants, and I could feel even more methodically climbing upward from my boots.

Dancing from one stomping foot to the other, I ran my hands down my arms and across the back of my neck before shaking the rest from the front of my shirt. They were persistent little bastards though, and the more I moved, the harder they seemed to cling to me with their tiny jaws. I actually had one clinging to my thumb with its mandibular pincers. No amount of shaking was doing the trick so I finally squeezed it between my fingers and pulled it free.

I'd just brushed the last from my upper body when a sharp sting came above my knee. Letting them get any further north was not an option.

No one else was fool enough to be out in the sweltering heat, so I did what needed to be done. The belt was off and my pants were around my ankles when Aurelia decided she needed to be out of doors. Thank the heavens I had declined to drop my shorts as well as my cargos. It must have been quite the sight—me hopping around like a lunatic with my pants around my ankles.

She first looked shocked, then concerned, and finally amused. It was the laughter on her face that had me flushed with irritation.

"Not seeing anything to laugh at," I bit out.

"Really?" she teased. "The mighty Hale Belstrohm hopping about like a deranged jackrabbit seems a tiny bit comical to me."

"Not when the jackrabbit is being eaten alive. The least you could is help me."

Jogging over, she pushed her glasses up. Her lips twisted to the side, and she brushed her hands down the back of my shirt and over my hamstrings.

"You ought to just take them all the way off." I flushed until I noticed her gesturing toward the crumples cargos tangled up with my boots. "We can wash out the wee monsters so you don't get any more bites. You're just as likely to end up on your butt as not with them like that."

We moved away from the mound I'd inadvertently sat on. Aurelia knelt down to unlace my boots, and I nearly jumped out of my skin. It was a precarious position, but she only told me to hold still. When the laces were free, she stood and stepped back, giving me room to toe off the leather footwear and remove my pants completely.

Auri motioned toward the building we'd been sleeping in and I followed, pulling off my shirt as we entered and dropping it along with my cargos into a pile by the door.

"I've got some salve in my bag," she told me as she moved toward her cot. "It's just a mix of aloe and sage, but it should take out some of the sting."

Dropping onto one of the benches, I watched as she rummaged around in the canvas totes and returned with a small mason jar filled with a thick white goop.

She made a gimme gesture with her fingers. "Arms first."

When I complied, Auri began dotting the red raised bites with the slave and gingerly massaged it into my skin. It didn't do much for the pain, but the movement of her fingers was soothing nonetheless.

141

"I'm not a fan of you not talking to me," I said.

"I'm talking to you."

"Only because I sat in a pile of ants."

"Well, you weren't talking to me either this morning." She looked up from my arm to meet my eyes.

"Because you're mad and I'm trying to respect your space."

"I'm not mad, Hale." She looked back down at the bites. "I just . . . I was, I don't know. Disappointed? That you read my mail even though it was sitting out. And the thing with Jassika. Why didn't she come to me herself? Does everyone think I can't handle myself? That I need either Roe or you to keep me sheltered and in line?"

"I've never thought I could keep you in line. And Roe cares about you. You know that. After everything you two have been through together, of course he's bound to want to protect you." She sighed and her fingers stopped their ministrations. "Jassika, well, I can't speak for her, nor do I want to. You know she isn't my favorite, but she could be a real threat to you if you aren't careful."

She started dabbing again. "I just want to help them. The kids. Their parents. I finally feel like I have this gift that could make a real difference, you know?"

"You've always made a real difference, Aurelia. Whether you have this wonder-working in your veins or not." I placed my hand below her chin and tilted her eyes up toward mine. "I mean it. Your patients love you. But I understand when you say you want to do more. I'd feel the same in your position."

She started touching the angry swollen lumps, this time on my legs. She wasn't dipping her fingers in the jar of salve. Despite this, with each light touch, the sting and burn of the bites was lessening.

"You don't have to do that."

"I know. But I want to. Hold still."

Every muscle in my body obeyed, and I sat motionless as she worked a dozen minor miracles over my legs and arms. When she reached the spot on my collarbone, she hesitated. Then, instead of placing her fingertips on the bite there, she pressed her lips to it. The air left my lungs in a long slow exhale. Bending forward from where she stood, she worked her way up to the three other spots along my neck and to a last one I didn't even register I had, on my jaw.

When she was done, her lips just a breath away from my ear, she muttered, "Better?"

I managed a slight nod.

"Good." And her lips were on mine. Soft and warm and the slightest bit hesitant. I let her kiss me and didn't dare move, worried it would shatter the magic of the moment. I'd been thinking about this for far too long and wanted to enjoy every second of it.

She pulled back and looked at me with confusion.

"Was that . . . should I not have . . . I mean. . ." She wouldn't look at me. "Was that wrong?"

"No." My voice was hoarse. "It was very very right."

Unable to control myself a moment longer, I wrapped my arms around her, one diving into the thick curls at the base of her neck, the other cradling her face. Then I was kissing her like I would never get enough. She smiled against my lips, and I finally drew a breath. Her glasses were askew, and she pulled them free and set them next to me on the bed.

I pulled her into my lap and studied the flecks of gold in her irises. She was as lovely as her name indicated. Before I knew it, I had her lips beneath mine once more.

"I've been wanting to do that for weeks now, but I thought the first time was a fluke," she admitted when I finally gave her a chance to breathe, much less talk.

"That's because I'm an idiot. I should have said something or done something a long time ago. I just wanted you to get settled and not feel pressured."

"I don't think the words idiot and Hale Belstrohm have ever been in the same sentence before."

"You obviously never listen to Roe then."

She smiled and looked down. "I was worried, you know. I'm not exactly the kind of woman a man like you typically goes for." *A man like me?*

Taken aback, I asked, "Are you kidding me?"

"Not at all. I'm short and brainy and—"

"Please don't insult me further. You are kind and dedicated and brilliant and beautiful. Just because you're intelligent and wear glasses doesn't mean anything. I'm not that shallow."

She smiled and it lit up her entire face—the entire room. My heart tugged in my chest. "Thank you." It was simple, and I appreciated that she could take the compliment without arguing further.

I realized then how this would look to anyone who wandered in. Me in just my shorts and her perched on my lap.

"As much as I would love to take this even further, we should probably save that for when we can really be alone."

The crestfallen look on her face was enough to have me kissing her again, but much more briefly. She found her glasses and I found some clothes.

When we walked out into the bright sunshine, the sun didn't seem quite so brutal.

15

AURELIA

We returned to DM the next day. And while I felt like so much had changed in the few short days we'd been away, the reality was most everything remained the same. If Geneva and Holdan noticed a difference in the relationship between Hale and me, they didn't let on.

As we rolled into the settlement, a lightness rested in me that I hadn't felt in months. We made quick work of unloading our supplies at the clinic. Holdan left with Geneva to return the wagon and horses to the tram masters who oversaw the Medicus stables, then met up with us as we walked back toward home. Unfortunately, the lightness I'd experienced dissipated when I saw Asher standing in the courtyard outside the building he and Geneva called home.

Hands behind his back and feet spread wide, he looked every bit the intimidating escort I recalled from our early days on the road from Renfield. Only when Gen smiled and waved did his face soften a fraction. She wrapped her arms around his waist and gave him a brief peck on the cheek. He kissed the top of her head and looked to the rest of us.

"We need to talk. All three of you."

145

After dumping our personal belongings, we met up at the benches outside. Asher leaned back in his seat, arms crossed over his chest and thunder in his eyes. He didn't look at any of us but seemed instead to focus on a tumbleweed taking a leisurely bouncing stroll through the landscape.

"I thought we were all in agreement that we were going to keep certain aspects of your talents to ourselves."

I frowned but agreed. "We did."

He nodded. "And as part of that agreement, it was made clear just how unacceptable Medicus Corpus—not only your employer, but for all intents and purposes around here, the law of the land—would view this. It was not to be discussed, correct?"

Again, I agreed.

"And it was also made clear, that should the information get out, it wouldn't necessarily be bad for just the both of you, but for the escorts who are tasked with seeing you safe and Medicus's interests protected."

"Of course," Hale snapped. "Where exactly are you going with this, Asher?"

But of course both Hale and I knew where. Hadn't he just told me Jassika was on to something? He'd warned me about my letters to Lita, and I'd argued he was wrong. Well, maybe Hale wasn't wrong. Maybe I had gotten myself into trouble.

"I'll tell you where, Doc." His face darkened and his nostrils flared just a little. "Two days ago, I received word from the folks a few steps up the food chain that they had received word things here at the Devil's Meadows Medicus Corpus clinic may not be entirely on the up and up. Seems that maybe someone might be practicing medicine outside the prescribed Medicus standard of care."

"But how—" I started.

146

"It doesn't matter how." The words flashed forth so violently I flinched. It didn't stop him from continuing, but at least he calmed his tone. "The letter didn't name you specifically, but it did say they'd received information that, and I quote, 'a new member of the practice team appears to be utilizing techniques not sanctioned by Medicus Corpus for the diagnosis and treatment of patients in their care.' The letter went on to say they would be reaching out to senior members of the practitioner team to gain insight and if needed they plan to come and investigate in person."

"Interesting." Holdan's voice was crisp. "I don't suppose they mentioned my petitions then?"

"As a matter of fact they did. Your request has been received and is on hold until further inquiries can be made into your claims of where you've been for the last seven years."

"To be fair, I expected nothing more, but still I'll admit it's a tad disappointing." He brushed at a dirty spot on his vest and only managed to make it worse.

"It may be more than disappointing. According to the other Belstrohm brother, it seems maybe you've been assisting Aurelia here in additional training?"

"Not anymore. We agreed I was doing fine on my own." I hated that I sounded like I was making excuses.

"Stop and think for a minute before you continue along that vein. In fact, stop and think about this entire situation. What have you been doing and how could you possibly think it was advisable to continue?"

"I've been doing what I have always tried to do. I'm healing people."

"Oh, Doc." Asher's voice, tired and worn, exuded disappointment. "Please tell me you haven't actually been using your wonder-working while inside the clinic."

"So what if I have! It's the whole point of being in Medicus, isn't it? To heal people? So what if I use a little extra if a sick person really needs it! I've been careful. I only ever use it when no one's around. When it's just me and my patient."

"There's always someone around, Auri." Gen's voice was gentle, but I could tell she was worried as well. "Always. There may not be another escort or practitioner watching your every move, but the housekeepers, the assistants, even the patients. They all have eyes and ears."

"Don't say that. Maybe it isn't even someone in the clinic. What about Jude and Jake? Or Phoebe. Wade? Any one of them could have said something."

The other group of practitioners and escorts we'd traveled with from Renfield had certainly known something extraordinary had happened on the long trek to DM. In fact, Jude and Jake had known all about me and Holdan performing a miracle on Geneva. I didn't actually believe one of them had ratted us out though. I was just so rattled by the entirety of this conversation, I was grasping at straws.

I pushed my glasses up and tilted my head back. Hale, already standing at my side, wrapped his arm around my shoulder and pulled me in closer to him. "We'll figure it all out," he said into my hair.

"You are absolutely right," Asher acknowledged. "It could be any one of them. But I'll wager you feel just as I do. It's pretty unlikely. I'll send word to Jake to see if he might know anything about it."

"And how is your mail any more secure than mine?" I wanted to pull the words back as soon as they'd left my lips. It didn't help that I could actually *feel* Hale wince as I said them.

"And what mail would that be, Doc?"

I looked up at Hale and then to Gen and Asher. Even Holdan looked interested.

"Doc?"

I opened my mouth but couldn't actually think of what to say. Exhaling, I fidgeted with the pendant at my throat.

"The mail I've been exchanging with Lita." Both Asher and Geneva looked slightly perplexed, but Holdan's face broke into a wide grin.

"Well done, Ms. Morris."

"I'm not following," Asher said.

I could see the moment Geneva realized what I meant. The clouded confusion on her face cleared and then she was grimacing as if I'd said something particularly repulsive.

"You didn't tell her?" she said. More of a plea than a question.

"No, not exactly. I simply wrote to see how Jonaten was doing. She replied that he was better for a time but now seems to be relapsing. I suggested I might have some new techniques to try and that if they could possibly make the trek, I'd be happy to assist with his care."

"Are we talking about the child in the farming settlement?" Asher asked.

"Indeed we are," Holdan replied merrily.

"For the love of sin." Asher looked as if he might actually need to hit something. "Right. What a swine cluster this is. Okay, Doc. Listen to me. Please. No more. No more letters. No more wonder-working. No more sneaking around with Holdan offering little bits of help. Not until I can see which way the wind is going to blow on this thing. Listerman, you too. Not a toe out of line, understood? Not if you ever want a chance of practicing medicine again.

"I'll get word to Jake. See what he knows, and in the meantime, I'll reply to the bastards who are trying to ruin all our lives. Put them off for a bit if I can. If we're lucky, they'll think it was some unfounded report and leave us be."

I nodded my understanding but felt numb deep inside. What use was having this gift if all it did was bring just as much grief as it did peace?

Hale held me to his side as we walked back inside. Holdan smirked as he left us at the entrance. Off for a drink he'd said.

Hale dropped his arm when he saw Roe was waiting by my door. My best friend immediately set up camp on my sofa, wanting to share all he'd learned from Theo and the little he'd learned from Campbell. When he spoke about the valilier, I noticed a shine in his eye that made me wonder how he really felt about the man. In all reality, it was probably just my own happiness at the budding relationship with Hale clouding my thoughts—wishing the same happiness for my best friend. He seemed less excited when we filled him in on the dressing down I'd just gotten from Asher.

Over the next handful of days, things swung back into the same routine, the three of us sometimes seeing each other at work, sometimes not. One of the Belstrohms, Asher, or Gen showing up to walk me to and from my shifts at the clinic. If I was lucky to have Hale on the same shift as me, I'd wait for him to walk me home and spend a few extra minutes together before one of us would inevitably fall asleep on the sofa. He had this great way of brushing my hair with his fingers that melted all tension and worry from my mind and sent me into the most blissful oblivion after a long day. I'm sure I drooled in his lap at least once.

The night of the attack, I'd had the day off, but Hale had a full schedule of minor surgical procedures to attend to. He'd promised to come straight to my place for dinner, and I was planning on asking him to stay the night.

Hope of rain had been a constant since we'd arrived in the desert hub settlement. Now we were getting it.

Monsoon season in the desert was upon us. Thunder rumbled in the distance and the occasional bright flash of lightning strobed through the windows of my apartment. I looked out the small pane next to me, watching the storm clouds far off to the south, and hoped the rain would wash away the dry depression from the air. It was soothing in its chaotic beauty. The scent of electricity filling my nose was unsettling at first, but as soon as the bolts danced in the sky, I knew it was only a thunderstorm and began to relax.

If Hale didn't show up soon, I was going to be asleep on the couch—lulled by flashes of light and the pattering of drops against the glass—before he arrived. The clinic was going to either kill us all slowly or make sure we never had time to dream of anything other than serving the settlement. I'd never really minded before if Hale was busy stitching up a lacerated ear or removing a gallbladder. He was a gifted surgeon and dedicated to his craft. At the moment, however, I wanted his gifted hands here with me and not in the cracks and crevices of some crusty old hub resident.

My planned dinner of warm cheese, cold roasted quail smothered in local raw honey, and prickly pear jam on bread sat untouched on the table. The least I could do was wait for him to arrive to dig in. I wasn't a savage.

Or maybe I was. Dipping my finger through the gooey mess of sweet and savory wasn't going to spoil the whole meal. I was wiping the sticky evidence from my hand after nearly swooning over the delicious taste, when a loud urgent knock came from the front door. Under normal circumstances, either Hale or Roe would have just strolled on in, but at Gen and Asher's behest, I'd been locking my door the minute I entered my apartment.

"Hold on, Handsome! I was just, eh, getting dinner together," I called as I placed the towel back on its hanger and hurried the short distance from the kitchen to the entry.

Flipping the bolt with one hand and pushing my glasses up with the other, I smiled and turned the knob. It wasn't the gorgeous green eyes and striking face of Hale on the other side of the threshold. It was a monster. Maybe he'd once been a man, but the filthy, frothing, ragged thing staring hungrily at me was a nightmare made flesh.

The storm had tricked me into ignoring the warning smell of ozone and letting down my guard.

In my shock, my brain barely had time to register the haggard features of the lunatic coming at me before I was simultaneously trying to step back and slam the door shut.

Never agile, my clumsiness certainly didn't serve me well in the moment. The door easily bounced off his outstretched arms, and my feet stumbled more than stepped. He shot forward, delivering a quick blow to my left temple. My momentum sent me slamming into a small table against the wall. I hit the ground hard, my face next to my shoes. Then he was on me.

He smelled of rotten meat, unwashed clothing, and the dusty desert night.

The olfactory nerves in our brains provide one of the strongest associations to memory, and when his stench and foul breath hit me, my mind immediately pulled up a memory of being pushed off a bike and onto the ground outside. This had happened before.

I curled in tighter, making the small target of my body smaller yet. I dropped my chin to my chest and used my arms to shield my face. The motion caused the creature's—for in the moment he was certainly more creature than man—open mouth to slam into my forearm. I had the vague sense of blood trickling from where his teeth skated across my flesh. He wasn't interested in biting, though. Rather, he was desperately trying to pull my hands from my face.

I thought I heard him giggling, as if the struggle was merely a happy game of rough and tumble between children, instead of a vicious attack. He let up for a moment, and I had a brief flash of hope that he had tired of the game and was going to leave me be. The flicker of hope was crushed before it had fully formed as with uncanny strength, he reached into my hair with one hand and yanked, tilting my head back, while using the other to wrench at my left wrist. The hand holding my hair pulled tighter, and I clawed at him. It was exactly what he wanted, for no sooner had I moved my arms than he was driving his face down onto mine—mouth gaping like a fish out of water—to cover my own. The elemental revulsion I felt might have saved my life. My body jerked with such force, the monster on top of me lost his grip on my hair, and his mouth slid down onto my cheek rather than covering my mouth. He was forced to readjust his hold on me, which gave me the chance I needed. My shorter legs were already folded between us, and I kicked out as hard as I could, hitting him somewhere in the midsection. Not as good as getting him in the balls, but it was enough to drive the breath out of him in a whoosh.

Scrambling away, I made it to my hands and knees in the center of the room.

"Little harlot," he screamed. Spittle flew from his lips in streams.

Somewhere in the struggle, my glasses had come off. A bulky blurred shape crouched between me and the door. I needed to keep my head and think. Screaming seemed my best option. Surely some of the other residents of the building would hear something and at the very least go to fetch an escort.

I pushed up to my feet, and he rose with me.

"Help me!" Despite my best intentions, saying the words made tears spring to my eyes, and my voice cracked.

He chuckled, with no mirth or joy in the sound. "You can yell all you like, little healing harlot. By the time anyone arrives, I'll be long gone."

"You don't need to hurt me. You can take whatever medicines or money you want."

"No medicine can help me. You should know that. Only *you* can help me."

I nodded, latching onto the idea. People needed my help every day. "Okay. Let me help you. Let me heal you."

"Yes," he said. "Yes. You can heal me."

Holding shaking hands up in front of my chest, part in defense and part in supplication, I repeated the words. "I can. Let me heal you." Would they register with him?

No. Apparently not.

He sprang. His breath preceded him. It was horrid. If I lived through this, I would always remember the stench of his breath. Fetid and sour. Blowing down onto my upturned face as he first knocked me back then pinned me to the floor.

"No." My head thrashed back and forth.

"No." I bucked and twisted.

"No." I screamed. And then his mouth was on mine.

It couldn't have been more than five seconds, but it seemed to stretch out. Minutes. Hours. Days,

154

longer. A slurping suction and my breath leaving as he pulled and tugged the air from my body. But it wasn't just the air. Tiny bits of energy—magic and miracles—flowed along with the oxygen and carbon dioxide he was drawing from me. My soul clutched and clawed at those bits, desperate to hold onto them in the face of the thief robbing me.

I was drowning, I was dying. Under the weight of the body on top of me and the injustice of the theft, my mind crashed within the confines of my skull. I wanted to scream, but even if my mouth could get the sound out, my lungs were empty. Black lights danced behind my eyes.

Another crash. This one not inside my head. A crash at the front door and then a roar. "Son of a bitch."

I knew that voice.

A deep thud and a lightening off my chest and face.

"Stay down." This voice was also vaguely familiar. Was he talking to me?

My eyes fluttered open, and I turned to see a blurry version of Hale smashing his fist into the face of the creature who only moments ago was stealing my life and quite possibly my miracles. He showed the creature little mercy, standing to kick him in the ribs and kidneys. My attacker lay in a fetal position—not unlike the one I'd been in only moments before—on the ground several feet from me.

The second voice in my apartment belonged to Campbell Robichaud. They must have arrived at the same time. Struggling to catch my breath, I watched as Campbell hauled Hale off before he killed the thing that had nearly killed me.

"We need to get some answers out of him before you end him," he told Hale, although he didn't sound happy about it.

155

Hale in turn looked like he would be happy to end Campbell *and* the monster both and worry about answers later.

"Hale," I croaked, and murder flooded from his face to be replaced by an entirely different emotion. He was at my side within a breath and scooped me up easily and softly, burying my face against his shaking chest.

I couldn't see Campbell from this position, but I sensed his movements and heard the sharp intake of breath as he rolled the monster over. A hissing, wheezing breath escaped my assailant then a small breathless chuckle.

"Hey there, Campbell. Happy to see me?" When he got no reply, he added, "Hmm. I'll take that as a no."

Hours later, in the dark and quiet, Hale told me he'd never seen someone take a beating like that and then move so quickly. Before Campbell could react, the lunatic popped up and vanished out the door.

16

ROE

"I'd wondered for so long what had happened to Desmond," Campbell told me. "When his brother skipped out, I assumed he broke a little and wanted some time to heal. They were always so close. Never in my darkest nightmares would I think it was him I've been trailing all this way. All this time."

We'd returned to the boneyard—Valilier Campbell Robichaud and I.

Hale had run up to my room to inform me he was moving Auri into his apartment for the time being—the locks on her door had been rendered nearly useless from all the banging and abuse the jam had taken. I'd flown down the stairs to check on my tough and tiny best friend for myself. When I'd arrived, both Auri and Campbell looked pretty shaken. Specs had some mild bruising on her face and her breathing was quick and shallow. It calmed fractionally when Hale and I entered her apartment. By the time either she or Campbell were up to talking, we all knew the assailant would be long gone.

So Hale had moved Auri and an armload of her things upstairs, and Campbell and I had gone for a walk. I still didn't like or trust the man, but he looked like he could use someone to talk to and Auri deserved some answers. It was the least I could do to try and kill two birds with one stone.

The rain had stopped, but I could still hear distant rumblings of thunder from far out over the western mountains where flashes of white occasionally illuminated the inky sky. The air was heavy but not oppressive.

We sat in my favorite spot, between the four-leaf clover and the giantess in the boots.

"Did Asher tell you anything? About me? Where I come from?" He didn't look at me as he spoke—instead studied the spiraling pattern his finger was drawing in the dust between his bent knees.

"Nah." I shook my head. "Not a word."

"East and north. The Avions. Do you know them?"

I shook my head again but realized he wouldn't see me, so I told him it sounded vaguely familiar but that was all.

"It's a beautiful area. Full of expansive lakes and endless green fields." He stopped talking but continued to run his finger in the spiral in the dirt. First clockwise, then reverse. He stopped his dust doodling and looked up at me. "Desmond is my partner."

"Your partner?" I wasn't sure what I was expecting, but it certainly wasn't that.

He nodded but one side of his lip twitched up. "Like Geneva and Asher," he explained.

I knew what a partner was for piss sake, but he quickly amended, "Like Geneva and Asher are escort partners. Shit, I'm making a mess of this. Desmond is my valilier partner. We work together."

I made an "O" with my mouth but didn't say anything.

He sighed and started doodling in the dirt again. "Or we were partners. I've known him more

158

than half my life and now this. He's the murdering arse I've been tracking."

"I don't understand any of this. You realize that, right?" I didn't care if that piece of human waste was his partner, or his brother, or even his lover. I wanted answers to what was happening here.

"I should have gotten there sooner" was his only reply.

It was an odd thing to say and seemed to imply he knew an attack on Little-bit was coming.

"Wait a minute." I popped to my feet. "Gotten where sooner? Are you saying you knew Auri was at risk tonight?"

"I thought she might be in trouble." The words were slow and measured. He didn't even bother to look at me as I stalked over and stood towering over him, fists clenching and unclenching at my sides. "But honestly, I didn't think he would strike so close to dusk."

"And you didn't say anything?"

"You can sit back down. Let me tell you what I know, and then if you want to get a few good shots in, I'll let you." He sounded so calm. Almost dejected. He wasn't going to get off quite that easily though.

I didn't sit, but I did back up a step. "Did you have something to do with Specs getting targeted?"

"Did I specifically help him target her? Of course not. Although, objectively I can see why you might suspect something. Oh for shit's sake, sit down."

He was right, either I was going to hit him or I wasn't. Glaring, I hunkered down against the old neon sign, still on the balls of my feet but not looming over him.

"Tell me."

"I've been tracking a killer for the last eighteen months. I've traveled an insanely long distance to put an end to these attacks, and up until tonight, I had no idea the person I was after was my best friend."

The waves of anger and frustration rolling off him had me half convinced he was telling the truth.

"Continue." I twirled my hand in what was probably kind of an asshole move, but such is life. I still needed answers.

"I'll tell you everything. But the truth might not really be what you're looking for. It's complicated."

Staring into the depths of his dark brown eyes, I waited.

He blew out a long breath. "Really complicated."

"Believe it or not, I can handle complicated."

The ghost of a smile touched his face. "Yeah, well . . . here goes.

"As we spoke about the other night, valiliers aren't exactly the same thing as your escorts. We don't work for Medicus directly. We're employed by the settlements in the Avions. More or less to keep the peace."

"So you're a law enforcer?"

"Yes and no. Sometimes I feel more like a student of animal behavior—a wrangler."

A frown pulled at the corners of my mouth.

"We do the normal things—arrests, citations, even the occasional punishment or execution." My eyes widened at the casualness of his tone, particularly on the last word. "But not with the usual settlers. In the Avions, we have what you might call a special population. A large number of the people there carry a specifically inheritable genetic condition that manifests in early adulthood and leads into a slow spiral of illness. Terrible headaches, heat intolerance, excessive sensitivity to certain stimuli. You medical folk call it photophobia and phonophobia."

"Sensitivity to light and noise?" I clarified. Sometimes folks used a medical word in entirely the wrong way.

"Yes, but it's intense. Daylight makes the headaches worse. There's also pallor, fatigue, slower metabolisms, and . . . insanity. Madness runs in our blood."

In all of my studying with Medicus and in all the reading I'd done over the years, I'd never heard of such an illness and told him as much.

He nodded. "It isn't something we tend to share with those from outside our settlements. Not good for trade and the like if folks think they're dealing with a bunch of psychotic madmen."

"Just madmen? No madwomen?" Nanette might have been related in some way.

"It doesn't affect them."

So Nanette was just a sadistic manipulator. That made sense. Several genetic disorders were linked to X or Y chromosomes. This could be one of them. If it actually existed.

"So let's say I believe you. Why travel all that way to retrieve one lone guy with a few delusions?"

"It's more than just delusions, Roe."

"Well then, you aren't doing a very good job of explaining."

"No. I suppose I'm not." He hesitated, and I could see the wheels spinning, either deciding what to tell me or how to tell it, I wasn't sure.

"I'm fairly certain this will sound bad no matter how I put it, so I may as well be direct. I saw your friend in the tavern the other night with her over-the-top admirer." Gary. "Something about her sparked something in me, and I decided to follow her home. More than a decision really. Call it a *compulsion*. A *compulsion* to follow her. I can tell you, I have *never* felt compelled to follow *any* woman before. I saw the attack, but at the time, I didn't realize it was Desmond who'd hit her. I never saw his face.

"Over the last eighteen months, I've seen other victims. Most of them were nothing more than dead bodies by the time I got there. But there have been a few lucky ones who were able to fight him off and get away. As far as I know, he never returned for those other women. But the compulsion I felt from Aurelia—I knew he'd come back. She isn't like the other survivors. It's why I tried to warn her—warn you all—not to allow her be an easy target."

I loved Goldie-Locks to the end of the earth and back, but why was it always Auri? Why was he compelled to follow *her?* I thought I might know, but there was a better chance of an ice cube staying frozen on a DM summer day than there was of me saying anything to Campbell about my suspicion. It was time to play a different angle.

"Not in the mood for fantastical stories. I've got a shelf full of those at home."

"It's no story."

"If you say so."

"What makes you think I'm making this up?"

"The compulsion bit for starters. The clear half truths and the fact you know her attacker but despite your close bond and tracking him for going on two years, you have failed to stop him. Take your pick." I sat back and stretched my legs out in front of me.

He scrubbed at his face. "You remember the attack but she doesn't. Does that seem normal to you?"

"I remember you knocking me out. You can add that to my previous list."

"Yeah, at some point you are just going to need to get past that." He folded his arms across his chest and studied me. "You're a smart guy. Think

162

about this. Why would you remember the attack and she wouldn't?"

"I don't know," I bit out at him. "Stress response or something similar. Maybe a minor concussion."

"Maybe. Did she have other signs of concussion?"

"No.

"Get stressed easily? Act out or overly dramatic for the hell of it?"

"No. But she isn't regularly tackled and nearly suffocated either."

"Suffocated? Interesting." He said it almost to himself, and before I could ask what he was thinking, he continued. "Fair point. But let's just pretend for a moment . . . maybe there's something more."

I didn't like where this might be going, but there didn't seem to be any reasonable way to steer the conversation. "Not sure what good pretending will be."

"Let's pretend there is something else you aren't telling me," he responded.

"What's to tell? You're the one who danced into town and is obviously withholding information while innocent young women are dying on the streets."

"Would it help if I told you a very specific component of the madness of our people involves a drive and a hunger you cannot name? A longing for energy that only comes from a specific source that cannot be found. A coldness that cannot be driven out by the heat of the noonday sunlight or near the warmth of the fire. A source to end the starvation that one may roam the world looking for and never find. Not in a lifetime. Would any of that help get you to loosen your tongue and help me to help you and Aurelia?"

Definitely did not like where this was going. When he spoke like this, it reminded me so much of those harrowing days I'd spent with Holdan Listerman—then known only to me as Hollis—and that bitch Nanette.

"Honestly, Valilier Robichaud, I'm not sure what it is you are suggesting, but this conversation has gone far enough. You're starting to make me think the only lunatic in DM right now is you. It's time to go home and check in on Auri and Hale."

I pushed myself to my feet and walked toward the path leading me out of the boneyard.

He frowned, the furrow deepening between his intense black-brown eyes. "Fine, Practitioner Belstrohm. You win. But don't think for a minute I don't know what you're doing. Your friend is special. I can smell it on her. And if I can, so can Desmond. He hasn't yet had his fill."

"Is that a threat?" My voice was icy in the hot night air. I was back to standing over him again.

Not easily intimidated, he casually stood and got within six inches of my face. "No. As I've been trying to tell you all—it's a warning."

"Then how about you enlighten me. His fill of what exactly?"

He stepped around me and onto the path. "The same thing we all want. His fill of her miracles."

Despite its designation as a hub settlement, Devil's Meadows was obviously a mere shade of the vibrant thriving city it must have once been. As I walked back toward our housing complex, I looked at the remnants of the hulking buildings just to the south of us. Monstrous concrete structures stood crumbling in a long row for several miles.

When I'd asked Asher about them weeks ago, he'd told me they were mostly abandoned. It had been too difficult to maintain the towering edifices over the years, and without sufficient power to drive the lighting and elevators, it didn't make any practical sense to try. He suspected the random loner or group of survivalists might be inhabiting them, but for the most part, unless they were on the scavenging teams, the settlers left the dangerous structures well enough alone.

I was staring at the dark shadows of the distant architecture as I walked back to our housing complex and only noticed the furtive outline of a man heading toward the open sewage tunnel gate when I was nearly upon him. It was no surprise when Holdan Listerman raised his head and hurried farther into the tunnel.

He had to have seen me but gave no sign— just continued on his way. Likely he didn't think I would follow, and on most nights he would have been correct. It had already been a bastard of a night, so throwing caution to the wind, I hurried in after him.

The sewage system didn't really get used for much anymore, but the rain water from the monsoon storms ran though these tunnels and into natural washes on the east side of the valley. A trickle of runoff from the earlier storm wound through the tunnel but certainly not enough to pose any sort of threat.

Listerman made no effort to hide himself, and the bobbing light of his handheld solar torch was easy enough to follow. If he wasn't hiding, I saw no reason to conceal my own progress and clicked the button on my light. The last thing I needed was to trip and fall over whatever piles of debris might be lurking here.

The ground was a smooth flat concrete for the most part. Every now and again, a chunk was missing or a slab of garbage marred the surface, but

165

it was easy enough to navigate. I was surprised at how clean and preserved the way was. Coming around a bend, I realized why.

Holdan stood not a hundred yards up, and he wasn't alone. A woman held her arm out to him, and he had her hand cradled in both of his own, examining something on her palm.

A makeshift town built of tents and old furniture clogged the storm channel. My light bounced from one wall to the other, but in reality it wasn't needed at all. A series of hanging lamps ran for the length of tunnel I could see, suspended by thick coils of rope and repurposed wires. It wasn't exactly brightly lit, but it was far from total darkness. Flicking off my torch, I shoved it in my back pocket and slowly approached the scene.

"Mr. Belstrohm. If you value your life, you might want to stop where you're at." Listerman didn't turn to address me but rather continued to study the woman's hand or whatever she held.

I stopped walking.

Listerman turned the hand this way and that, then seemed satisfied and released it. The woman stepped back almost shyly.

"The folks down here don't relish visitors." He dusted his hand on his pants and turned in my direction.

"And yet here you are," I replied.

"Yes. Here I am." He riffled through the bag on his shoulder and produced a small vial of something. "Wait where you are, and I'll be with you in a moment."

He turned back toward the woman and handed her the vial. She nodded and looked my way then scurried back into the maze of tents and old sofas. At least two dozen other pale faces were studying me from various hidey holes or from behind draped bits of tarp and cloth.

166

A mangy orange and white cat moved from between the stained and crusty cushions of an overturned armchair to run its back and neck over Listerman's legs. Perhaps it felt a kinship to the ginger devil. It yowled and took off running down the passage when he walked toward me.

"What was in the vial?" I asked as he approached. "Selling them fake potions to cure all their ails?"

It wasn't fair I know. Holdan Listerman had proved himself capable of more than just fraud, but I still couldn't make myself trust him completely. Part of me thought he was just fine with that too.

"Just a tincture for her arthritis. Good old standard Medicus Corpus fare, nothing more."

"And Medicus knows you're doing this?"

"Of course they don't. If they knew, I'd be practicing with the rest of you." He sounded tired and resigned but raised his chin and looked at me with every bit of the condescension I associated with him. "And you are supposed to be the smart one."

"Then what are you doing here? Who are these people?"

As if on cue, three men shuffled out from their hiding spots. They were ragged and greasy. Clothing torn and teeth rotting. The one in the front had a beard to his mid chest that might have had small animals nesting in it for all the tangles and knots. It wasn't his clothing or his beard that grabbed my attention however. It was the dark wine patch running from his mop of unkempt hair, over his left eye and down into that raggedy beard.

"Hold up there." I flicked my chin up. "What's on your face, friend?" It looked an awful lot like the "wine stains" the bandits who'd attacked us and nearly killed Geneva wore on their faces.

"I'm not your friend. And if you know what's good for you, you'll get outta here," he shouted at me.

167

Listerman turned and raised his hands in a calming gesture. "Now, now. Mr. Belstrohm didn't mean anything by it. He's here with me and I'm here to help, remember?"

"Get out. You're not wanted here," old greasy haired yelled at me, then turned to Holdan. "You too! Get out. We don't need your help. First you, then that crazed one. Now you're bringing more into our place. Well, it's our place. Not yours. Get out!"

Listerman tried for another minute or two to talk the man down, but he and his friends were shuffling toward us. I realized one in the back had picked up a length of splintered wood—a broken chair leg by the looks of it—and was swinging it gently from side to side in front of him. As he moved under one of the lamps, I noticed he also had a red smear over the side of his face, and this time it was distinctly in the shape of a handprint.

"Come on, Listerman. Time to go." I grabbed his shoulder and turned him back the way we'd come. He hesitated but eventually sighed and followed me out. The shouts to leave and never come back grew louder. We weren't running, but the threats of death and dismemberment certainly helped to push our feet a little faster.

We were nearly to the gated entrance when he finally spoke to me. "Well, there goes any chance I've got at being a useful member of the world again. I should be angry with you, but I suppose it's my own fault. I knew you were following but didn't ask you to stop. I suppose I didn't realize what a *complete* buffoon you could be."

"Ouch. And here I thought we were friends." I laced the words with as much sweetly sick sarcasm as I could muster.

He replied with a tight eye-squinting smile. I supposed I touched a nerve. Good.

168

We continued walking back toward the housing complex.

"You know," he finally said. "There was a time when I wasn't so very different than you."

"I find that extraordinarily hard to believe."

"Of all people, you should know, just because you don't believe something, doesn't mean it isn't true."

The jab hit where he aimed. It was no secret I was the last person to believe Aurelia was capable of performing miracles. Even Hale had bought into her story long before I did. But then again, I was fairly certain, Hale was more than a little enamored with Specs by that point. A fact neither had yet to confirm to my face but was evident nonetheless. I hadn't swallowed the whole thaumaturgy thing until I'd seen Gen spared from the ravages of septic shock with my own eyes. Listerman and Goldie-Locks had saved her with nothing more than their bare hands and whatever energy magic they both possessed.

"Point taken."

"My *point* is, I was once just as you are now. There were of course some minor differences"—he raised an eyebrow at me—"but for all intents and purposes, I was a young, well-liked, skilled Medicus Corpus practitioner, who only ever dreamed of helping the sick and the unfortunate in this hellish world."

"So. What happened? Nanette flip her skirts your way and all good intentions were lost?"

"Laugh all you like, but you saw her and that damned wagon. I was lost to her even before I met the woman. She set her sights on me and I was as good as enslaved. Unlike Ms. Morris, I had no one standing by my side to help reel me back from the brink."

In the desert, night isn't just for humans. As we walked, large hummingbird moths danced

169

through the air overhead and an eerie set of green eyes watched us from behind a spindly half dead bush. His words seemed fitting in the dark desolation.

My curiosity was piqued. "How then? If you were so upstanding, how did she lure you away?"

He looked at me askance. "How much do you know about the other Medicus schools?"

"Only that they exist. Scattered about in various locales. The closest is somewhere to the west. Near the northern coast."

Because of the darkness, I sensed rather than saw him nod.

"It is. I however, trained at a school somewhat farther afield and to the east. Much like you," he said pointedly, "it was in the settlement where I was born and raised. There are at least three others I know of. Of course, when I was studying, I had no notion of these settlements or the Medicus facilities in them, but my travels with Nanette took me farther than I had ever imagined as a boy.

"Those other sites aren't really important, just an example of how naïve I was—how naïve Medicus keeps us all—when I was studying. And, I suppose, of how vast a reach the great Medicus Corpus wields. I worked hard and was dedicated to the life and the career I'd chosen. My parents were proud I was eager to get out into the world and do some good. The day of my Match came, and I was simply thrilled to be assigned to a small settlement in the mountains east of my home. I made the journey, just about ten days it took."

A covey of quail rustled in the brush as we passed.

"It was beautiful. Tall pines, clear mountain lakes. Lovely people who welcomed me. I was replacing one of the two practitioners there. I loved every moment of it—until the winter came."

We were almost back to the housing block, and from there I could see the windows along our side of the structure. Deep black shadows marked many of the windows, including both Aurelia's and mine. There was, however, the flickering of candle flame from the panes of the room I knew to be Hale's. A moment of jealousy flashed through me—aimed at my brother for taking my best friend or at my best friend for stealing time from me with my brother, I couldn't say.

"Couldn't handle the cold?" I asked, just to take my mind off what they might be doing up there. It wasn't a mental image I needed or wanted.

To my surprise, he replied, "Yes."

"Really? It got a little chilly and you decided to run off with a psychotic witch?"

"No. As I told you, Nanette had her sights on me long before I even knew who or what she was. But yes. I decided to run off. Things in the settlement had been going well. I was liked and respected. I worked hard and I helped people. But when the winter came, there was so much snow and the mountain seemed so isolated. I got what they called cabin fever hundreds of years ago. One blisteringly cold day, when I could barely make the trek from my small home to the clinic, I got the idea I would leave as soon as the weather cleared. I endured several more weeks of freezing to my core—a cold so deep it felt like needles piercing my face and hands anytime I was out of doors. The heat here is draining, but the cold. . . It hurts." He looked as haunted as a person could.

"Then we had a break. The sun was out and the snow began to melt. I knew if I stayed, another cold front would come barreling in and I'd be trapped."

Medicus positions were for life. I don't know if the idea of leaving revolted or inspired me.

171

"So you did it? You just left."

"I did. But about an hour's walk in, I came to my senses and turned back. I was sitting in front of my small hearth with a roaring fire going before anyone in the settlement or Medicus even knew I'd been gone."

I frowned. "So you didn't leave? What the piss, Listerman! I thought you were building up to some great escape plan here."

"I left in my heart, Mr. Belstrohm." He tapped his chest. "I continued my work, but in my heart and in my soul, I abandoned those people.

"And when Nanette rolled into the settlement the next spring, not only could she smell the miracles and wonder in me, she could also smell the shame and regret in both my leaving and in my staying. It was easy for her to charm me with lovely tales of helping people with my other gifts and using my thaumaturgy to help countless of the sick that Medicus couldn't or wouldn't let me save. She knew I wanted out and she used that knowledge like the master manipulator she was.

"I never gave up my desire to heal and to help. Just lost sight of the correct way to do it for a brief time. I thought the cold and the loneliness were bad, but I had no inkling of what true misery was. She showed me."

We'd reached the door to our building. There was no use asking him to elaborate further. I knew how the rest went. He'd become enthralled with the witch who wore a beautiful mask. She in turn used him in any way she could, and when bigger and better prey came along, she'd intended to have Holdan Listerman—by then known only as Hollis—capture Aurelia for the same purpose. To give her magic the prestige she so twistedly craved. Not just a powerful wielder of magic but one who could heal the sick and the dying—being elevated to a goddess in the eyes of the people she encountered.

"At any rate, you won't need to worry about me much longer. If I don't get word soon, I think it will be time for me to move on. For a man of my particular talents, there must be greener pastures somewhere."

Part of me would never trust Listerman—not after what he and Nanette had put me through. Certainly not after knowing he might have traded Aurelia's freedom for his own. But as much as I hated it, I did understand him. How often had I felt lonely and trapped in this life I was now living? How often had I hoped for someone to come along and sweep me away? And how often had I questioned whether I'd be willing to reveal myself when that person arrived?

Listerman's room was on the same floor as Aurelia's—just down the hall.

As I made to walk the final flight of stairs up to my own, solar torch in hand, I stopped him on the landing.

"Medicus will take you back, I'm sure. They just like us all to suffer for our craft a little."

Hand on the doorknob, he didn't turn, nor did he look at me when he answered. "Mr. Belstrohm. I hope you are correct."

"Before you go," I called, his back still turned to me. "Two things. One, that guy had a wine stain on his face. I don't know if you ran into his kind in the desert but we did. Gen would probably appreciate it if you steered clear of them. And two, he mentioned a crazed man. It might be good to think on what that means."

He didn't say anything but nodded just a fraction before he opened the door and disappeared.

As much as the horrific events of the previous night should have warranted a break for Aurelia, she'd refused to take the day off. Rather than kicking it at home with her feet up and a warm mug of tea for company, she insisted on coming into work. At least Hale and I were on shift with her for the day and we could all walk home together. After the previous night, I swear my brother might have had a stroke if he couldn't check in on her half a dozen times per hour.

The clinic was settling down for the night. We'd already given sign out to the covering practitioner and were waiting for Goldie-Locks to finish up some last-minute orders before we could go back home and indulge in some cards, popcorn, and maybe even a beer or two. The assistant with the too-tight smock top and exaggerated swing in her hips was eyeing Hale like he was a fat juicy steak. Honestly, if she wasn't careful she was going to slip on her own drool and snap a hip.

Hale—completely oblivious to the sultry looks and flirty hair tosses—was leaning over the counter and looking down at the chart Aurelia was documenting.

"Hey, Cookie," I called. I had to put the poor girl out of her misery and have her focus on a task that didn't involve getting my brother to look at her cleavage. "Can you check to see if we have extra saline bags up here? I think we're running low downstairs and I'm sure they'll be needing them come morning."

"Oh." She looked crestfallen. "Um, sure. I'd be happy to."

She threw one more longing look at Hale and disappeared around the corner heading to the supply room.

"So." I stared at my brother, one of the people I loved most in this world, as he stood watching one of the other few people on that same list. "You two are. . .?"

Specs spun around so quickly her thick dark braid whipped her in the face, causing her glasses to slide and dangle perilously at the end of her nose, revealing wide golden-hazel eyes. She hastily pushed her glasses back in place. I should have known she wasn't as absorbed in her work as she appeared.

"The two of us are, what?" Hale smirked, all but challenging me to say aloud what I'd been suspecting for some time.

"Are you two now a thing?"

"A thing? Well, I guess that depends on what 'a thing' is exactly."

Sometimes I really detested my brother. "For the love of all that is right in the universe. You know what I mean."

"Well, if you mean are we friends? Then the answer is yes." Cool as winter in Renfield.

Little-bit looked simultaneously relieved and disappointed at his response.

"I know you're friends. You yanked that stick out of your ass on the way from Renfield, remember?"

"Oh, so does 'a thing' mean are we dating? Because honestly I don't know that either of us has time to truly date anyone right now, you know." His smirk was now more of a grin.

"Don't be such a—"

"Or by 'a thing' do you mean are we sleeping together?"

Aurelia looked like she was going to vomit. Hale looked equal parts smug and irate.

"Absolutely we've slept together. Countless times. Many of them with you right there with us. In tents, under the stars."

I huffed out a breath. Then I realized he was referring to all those times we'd camped on the long journey from Renfield through the desert and on to

Devil's Meadows. My ire rose as he both avoided the question and taunted me at the same time. Aurelia had been my best friend for almost as long as I could remember. Didn't I have a right to know if she and my brother were moving on to a new phase of life— one that didn't include me?

"Look, ass face. I don't think it's an unreasonable question," I snarked.

Auri looked like she wanted to step in, but to defend me or Hale I didn't know.

"You don't think it unreasonable to ask me about my sex life in public? Fine. But do you think it's unreasonable to ask about Aurelia's?"

"No."

"Roe!" Auri raised her eyebrows at me.

"I mean no, that isn't what I'm asking." I looked between them and blew out a long breath. "I don't care if you're just sleeping together. I mean, I *do* care." I shook my head trying to express what exactly it was I wanted to know. Neither of them spoke. They just quietly waited for me to continue. "I care about what that might mean. I care about you of course, Hale, but Aurelia. I care more about Aurelia."

"Roe." Tiny Badass didn't look so confident now. She looked mortified and confused. "I always thought. . ." She opened and closed her mouth several times. "I always thought you didn't . . . you weren't . . . I never thought you were interested in me in that way."

Leaning his hips up against the table behind him, arms crossed over his chest, Hale didn't look nearly as confused. He just looked pissed. The same moody bastard I was used to.

I chuckled and ducked my head then turned and grabbed both of Auri's hands. "Specs. Relax. You're right. I love you dearly, but not like I want to marry you and have fat babies together love. I love you in the way that I don't want you to get hurt."

"Bastard." Hale exhaled the word more than spoke it.

"I'm not going to get hurt, Roe." She looked at Hale, and a tentative smile emerged. "At least I have no intention of getting hurt. Hale, do you intend to crush my heart under your gigantic feet?"

"Not part of the plan. No." He was actually grinning at her. Hale didn't grin at people.

I grimaced. "Neither of you are going to make this any easier on me are you?"

"Nope," Auri answered quickly.

Hale seemed to cool his temper. He walked over and placed a hand on my shoulder. "A bit of faith would be nice, little brother." He looked at me for a brief moment and added, "Look. I understand your concern. I'd probably think the same thing, but we are taking this as it comes. I promise not to disappoint you."

I nodded. "Just so we are clear. If you hurt her . . . I will kill you."

He nodded back. "Noted." I would have expected nothing less.

Specs rolled her eyes, shook her head, and went back to finishing up her charting.

If Cookie found the saline I'd sent her to retrieve, I didn't see it. We were gone before she made it back to the desk.

17

AURELIA

A few days later, I was finishing up at the clinic one evening after a particularly rough day. It had been one of those shifts where I just couldn't catch up. Between urgent visits and caring for my tiny fourth floor patients, I swear I'd run up and down the stairs several dozen times. Plus, Clarice had been readmitted two days prior looking decidedly worse than when she'd gone home. Not being any closer to solving the mystery, I'd enlisted Jassika to help me identify the source of her illness. This was risky, knowing I couldn't use my thaumaturgy to help the girl if needed, but I was running out of other ideas.

The sun was sinking toward the western mountains—peach and violet light flowing through the dust-covered window and suffusing my work space in a tranquil glow. If I'd learned anything in my time since leaving Renfield, it was that desert sunsets were some of the most glorious things I'd ever experienced.

Sitting there, lost in thought and absently stroking my golden orb necklace, my mind bounced back and forth from thoughts of Clarice and her mystery illness, to the letter I'd just composed and sent to Lita asking for an update on Jonaten, to my new favorite subject—Hale.

The stack of work in front of me wasn't going to get any smaller if I didn't get to it, but in a moment of weakness, I decided to skim through and find the most important things and leave the rest for the next day. Picking through my stack of documents, my hand stilled when it came to a folded piece of dirty scrap paper. It wasn't addressed to Practitioner Morris as most of my notes and memos were, and not even to Aurelia or Mija as Nora sometimes informally wrote. Barely legible, the words *You can't hide* were written in shaky script.

Unfolding the sheet, my eyes drifted to the only word written on the inside. *Tonight.*

I dropped it in the pile and recoiled from the stack. The blood left my face in a rush even as my heart rate doubled. If this was Roe's idea of a joke, it wasn't funny. But if it wasn't from him, who would have left it? One of the assistants perhaps, but they had no reason to do such a thing. Hale maybe? Could he be referring to some time spent cuddled up together? Not likely. He wasn't the cryptic weird message type.

There was no logical explanation that didn't involve someone trying to unsettle me. I was worried I knew who that person was. What I didn't know was how he could have gotten the note into my stack.

We'd made arrangements earlier for Holdan to walk me home. He still owed me for the wonder-working after his snake bite, and I was hoping if the other practitioners got used to seeing him around more, they might actually help him out when it came time for Medicus to finally make a decision about letting him practice again. So, after checking with the night team, I made my way downstairs to wait for him by the entrance. People were always coming and going, whether they were practitioners, assistants, patients, or visitors, and I felt perfectly safe standing under the yellow-white glow of the solar lamps placed there. An older man with a bad limp and bloodshot eyes swung the door open and shuffled in, followed by a young man with a screaming toddler in his arms. The child's front teeth were bloody with a decent-sized tear in his bottom lip. I quickly moved aside to let them get to the check-in counter, then turned my eyes back out into the night. Holdan was nowhere to be seen.

After a few minutes, I was ready to give up on him. It wouldn't surprise me if he'd forgotten or just decided it wasn't worth his time. The door swung open again and I recognized the dark hair and intense expression of Campbell Robichaud heading toward me.

"Your friend got tied up," he said by way of greeting. "Roe asked me if I'd come and walk you home."

Interesting. I couldn't imagine what had shifted enough to have Roe trusting this man, but there must have been something. Maybe just the fact he'd helped Hale subdue his old partner, but my bet was there was more. Which meant maybe I should trust him enough to tell him about the note.

Pulling the paper from the side pocket of my cargo pants, I handed it over to him. "This got slipped into my paperwork today. It might be nothing, but it feels like a threat."

He studied it but didn't speak.

"I don't mean to sound paranoid, but does that look like it could be from your friend?"

He nodded. "I can't be certain, but anything is possible."

Even though I could see his tension building as he looked at the paper, I had to ask, "Will you please tell me who this guy is? I know you spoke with Roe, but I haven't been able to pin him down on

180

the details—either because he doesn't know them or because he doesn't want me worried."

Campbell cleared his throat. "I don't want to be distracted while we walk, so your choice. Is there somewhere a little more private we can go, or do you want to wait until we're back at your place?"

He must have read something in my expression. "What?" He twisted his lips and looked down at his shoes, shaking his head. "You still don't trust me? Roe does but you don't."

"If the situation were reversed, and you'd been attacked twice in just a few weeks, would you trust you?"

"Fair. We should talk here then. Maybe I can convince you I'm on your side. And it doesn't have to be super secluded, just out of the main thoroughfare." He said the words with a quiet intensity that made me believe he was telling the truth.

"We can sit in the practitioner lounge." I nodded toward the back of the floor where the door to the lounge stood ajar. The lights were off, indicating no one was using it at the moment.

Once we were settled, Campbell told me everything he'd already shared with Roe. About his home, the people there, their history of mental decline and the drive some of them had to quench an insatiable thirst. He spoke of miracles and wonder and that alone must have been what Roe had heard to trust him at least a little. He also told me about his partner and how close they'd been—almost like family.

"So you can smell it in me?" I squinched up my nose and tried to play it off, but the idea made me a little queasy. Hadn't that been similar to what Holdan had said Nanette did? Smelled the miracle and wonder-working in my veins?

He nodded. "It isn't unpleasant, don't worry."

Being *pleasant smelling* was the least of my concerns.

"Someday remind me to tell you how creepy that statement was." His lip curled up on one side. I continued, "And if you like all of your teeth where they are, never say that in front of Hale. He can be . . . prickly."

"Ah, yes. Thanks for the warning."

Wanting to direct the conversation back to more important matters, I crossed my arms and said, "So you're telling me, the man who attacked me is your partner."

Campbell nodded grimly. "*Was* my partner. Desmond."

"And you haven't spoken to him in several years?" I picked up an orange that'd been left on the table and tossed it back and forth from one hand to the other.

"Not since he disappeared shortly after his kid brother took off. I always assumed he was out looking for Wes. But maybe it had nothing to do with that."

"And this is common in the population where you hail from?"

"Yes."

"What about you?" I studied the orange. Back and forth. Back and forth.

"What *about* me?"

"Should I be concerned?"

"Yes."

For all my fidgeting, he sat relaxed and composed even as he affirmed my fear. I caught the orange and held it between my hands. Looking up from the fruit to the man across from me, I studied him. Digested what he'd divulged.

If he'd been willing to share something so personal, surely he meant well.

"Okay." I nodded.

He frowned and looked back at me. "I'm being serious. For the time being, I'll do everything in my power to protect you and track down Desmond. I don't have any urges or cravings, and I believe I'm thinking clearly, but it could all change in time. It's only right you should know."

"But are you sure it'll happen to you? Genetics can be strong, but how do you know if you'll be affected also."

"Honestly I don't. But as I told Roe, there is a draw to you that I can't explain. It has to be the same tug that's brought Desmond back to you repeatedly."

He spoke slowly, measuring his words and their impact. I could sense he didn't want to cause me more worry. The look on his face though spoke of grief which time had yet to mend. I'd seen the look before on mothers and friends, uncles and lovers. It was the look of anyone who had ever lost a loved one too soon. Desmond might still be walking the earth, but in Campbell's mind he was already dead.

"Has anyone in your family suffered the same fate?"

He shook his head. "I haven't any siblings, and my father is still quite healthy and strong."

"Ah, only child. It explains a lot."

"I'm assuming that wasn't an insult. Not many people have the balls to insult me openly." He cocked an eyebrow in my direction.

"Not an insult, I can assure you, but give me time. I'm sure I will eventually." It was my turn to smile when he looked uncertain. "I'm an only child too. But back to more important things. How about your mother?"

"Also alive and feisty as ever." He kicked back in his chair, getting comfortable and visibly relaxing as we chatted. "And as happy as that makes me, it doesn't really count. It only affects males as far as we can tell."

Interesting. "How about on your mother's side? Do you have any uncles?"

"You ask a lot of questions."

"Yes, I do." I waited.

He smiled again. "No uncles that I know of. Her father died when she was a baby—in an accident—so it's hard to say."

Picking up my pen and a sheet of notepaper, I doodled out a haphazard set of lines, circles, and squares—my version of a basic family tree. "It really would be helpful to know about anyone else on your mother's side. If you think of anyone, distant cousins, grandparents, anyone at all you know of that you're related to by blood with the same malady, let me know."

He assured me he would and stood. Following his lead, I stood and stretched my arms overhead. It was getting late, and I desperately wanted to get home and tuck myself into bed.

"You look beat. Let's get you home."

I gathered my things. "Just what a girl likes to hear."

At the start of our conversation, I wasn't convinced I could trust the man, but somehow over the course of a handful of minutes, the unease had melted away. It was uncanny.

"You can be fatigued and still wear it well. But you don't need my compliments I'm sure."

"I'll take a compliment anywhere I can get one."

"As long as it's not within earshot of Mr. Belstrohm, correct," he teased.

"Exactly." It was odd to be so comfortable with Campbell, but for some strange reason, I felt like I'd known him much longer than I had.

"You have nothing to fear on that account at least." He looked away uncomfortably. Then he grimaced and said, "We should get going."

"I guess Roe was right. It feels like I can trust you."

"Roe told you that?" Surprise laced his words.

"Well, no, not exactly, but if he sent you here to walk me home, he must trust you. He's also a little protective, but much more in an annoying brother sort of way."

He started to say something but was interrupted by a knock on the door frame. As if on instinct, he stepped in front of me.

"Relax." I placed a hand on the back of his shoulder. "I don't think Nora here is a threat."

"Sorry, Mija. Am I interrupting something?" She smiled and actually winked at Campbell. *For the love of all that is good, actually winked at him.* I huffed out a laugh.

"No *ma'am.* We were just leaving," I said pointedly.

"Well, Practitioner Duncan asked me to see if you were still around."

I could think of only one reason Jassika would be looking for me after my shift had ended. "Did Clarice take a turn for the worse?"

"No, but she's been a bit of a handful all evening. We tried to swap her to a location closer to the assistant desk, and she's not having any of it. Duncan wants to send her home tomorrow if she's going to be disturbing the other kids. Just wanted me to give you a heads up."

I pushed up my glasses and sighed. "I'm not going back up there tonight. Let her stay in her current bed, and I'll see her first thing tomorrow morning."

Nora gave me a thumbs up and, throwing one more flirty grin at Campbell, disappeared back through the open door.

"She seems friendly," Campbell noted as we headed toward the front doors.

"Yes." I chuckled, shaking my head. "Yes she is."

Campbell made sure I was delivered to my doorstep—or more accurately, Hale's doorstep—without incident.

The cryptic message proved to be eerie and odd, but otherwise nothing more than that. I was not attacked. No madman looking to suck the miracles from my soul. I slept soundly and woke the next morning to more heat and dust and patients needing me.

Life in Devil's Meadows continued as usual for one more day.

18

AURELIA

The attack came more or less just as we'd expected. It was night and I was alone. At least that was the impression we gave. The idea of using myself as bait had made me shiver. Both Hale and Roe voiced their opposition to the plan. Loudly. But as Geneva pointed out, it was my decision to make, and I wanted nothing more than to allow Campbell to catch his friend and return with him to their home far off in the east.

It was a plan we all came to agree upon more or less. If Campbell had any chance of catching Desmond before he killed again, it needed to be done. My biggest regret was Hale wasn't there. He was working nights again—my shifts actually—and there simply was no way to rearrange the schedule at the last minute. At least Roe was with me. And I had the added comfort of knowing Gen and Asher would do everything in their power to keep me safe.

I was tired of looking over my shoulder everywhere I went. Tired of reading creepy cryptic notes tucked into my work things. Tired of having to be constantly accompanied every time I stepped outside or answered my door. I wanted my life back. If that meant being alone on a crumbling bridge overlooking what once might have been a beautiful fountain and hoping Campbell was faster and smarter than his prey, so be it.

The plan was simply really. Roe had escorted me on a seemingly innocent walk to look at the old architecture. Just after the sun set, he'd left me in my designated position and scrambled into hiding along with Gen, Asher, and Campbell. If all went to plan, Desmond would find me alone, and when he made his move, they would make theirs.

We'd ventured farther south of the main habitable area of the settlement—closer to where the trams came in and out of the hub. The buildings there must have once been magnificent but now were little more than crumbling eyesores. Too big to be maintained in any useful way without the assistance of giant power grids, they'd been left to decay and rot—parts scavenged by those in need and by crews sent in from the settlements. The teams collected anything from wiring to furniture to slabs of wood that could be burned.

I stood in front of one of these monstrosities, isolated and exposed. The facade of the enormous crumbling structure had bits of sculpted concrete made to look like an ancient palace, complete with broken statues and tall white pillars. Between the building and the road, a large concrete pond took up residence. In the full moon's light I could make out the scene before me. The water must have been clean and clear at one time, but now a thick green shag of algae rested below the foot or two of murky foul-smelling water. My feet were planted on the cracked and crumbling bridge elevated around the front edge of the reservoir. Resting my elbow on the balustrade and staring out at the beam of the solar torch in my left hand, I could see water rippling in small circles where night-loving insects alighted on the surface.

It was eerily quiet.

Off in the distance, a series of faint green-white lights danced across the sky. I'd never seen anything like it before. I blinked, and they seemed to bounce over the horizon and out of sight.

My skin rose in goose bumps as a skittering from the road reached my ears and snagged my attention. I swung the light vaguely toward the road but could make out no movement. Telling myself it was one of my friends getting into a more mobile position, I made myself face the stagnant pond.

Again the skittering. Pebbles kicked on the dry road. I opened my mouth to call out to Roe. Then clamped it shut again. It would do none of us any good for me to lose my nerve now and blow the entire thing.

My knees were shaking the third time the noise came. It was closer and I swear I could smell rotten breath on the night breeze. The beam of my light was unsteady—partially from nerves, partially from being in my nondominant hand—as I swung it back and forth. It was just like the dam. My mind was jumping at noises, but my eyes told me nothing was amiss.

"Who's there?" I called. If my voice trembled and I appeared afraid, so be it. It would help to sell the illusion of me alone at night away from safety. Ripe for the picking.

Maybe this plan wasn't the best after all. Would Campbell and Asher really look down on me if I called a halt to the whole thing? I didn't think so.

Just as I decided to give in to my fear, he sprang.

As if made from the night itself, one shadow separated from the others and he was on me. I braced for the hit as best I could, back to the concrete pylon linking sections of the ornamental railing, and crouched to absorb the impact.

Eyes crazed, mouth slack, and if such a thing was possible, filthier than the last time I'd seen him, Desmond grabbed at my head. Thank the heavens I'd braided my hair tight to my scalp or he would have had enough purchase to force my head back and chin up. As it was, it felt as though his intention was to wrench my skull from my vertebral column. Tucking my chin down, I fought to not let my face come up toward his.

The torch fell from my left hand, but I clutched tight to the object in my right. One other time in my life I'd purposefully injured a man. It had been with a scalpel instead of the pouch I held firm to. In his hunger and madness, Desmond didn't seem to notice, but that wouldn't matter if I couldn't actually use the weapon I was clutching.

Within moments, I heard the pounding footsteps of my friends. If Desmond heard them, he made no indication, just continued to wrestle my head back.

I couldn't see how far away the others were. I knew they'd been far enough that Desmond wouldn't sense them in the shadows and realize the trap we'd laid. If I didn't get my chance soon, he might have an opportunity to make a break and get away. Roe held a similar packet of powder in his possession, but if Desmond was as quick as he'd been before, even my friend's athleticism and speed would mean nothing.

Cracking an eye open and struggling against his hold, I scanned to see where they were. Asher and Geneva were still climbing from their hiding spots below the bridge, close in distance but a more laborious task. Roe and Campbell were sprinting from the near side of the road. They'd told me they would be hiding within easy reach and they were. Despite Roe's lankier legs, Campbell matched him stride for stride. Roe wrestled a packet of powder from his pocket on the run. If he got here and I was still in Desmond's clutch, there'd be no way for me to avoid that powder and I'd be in for a nice long nap.

"Let me see that pretty face," Desmond spat out as he pulled hard enough on my braid to bring tears to my eyes.

It was now or never. Bringing up my right hand, I drew in a breath. Raising my face to his, I blew the powder from my palm just like blowing the puff from a dandelion head. Instead of scattering delicate white puffs of seed, my breath pushed a cloud of powder directly into Desmond's eyes and gaping mouth. He jerked backward, still clutching my braid in his grimy fist. I stumbled at the force of his hold and went down with him as he staggered back—the effects of the powder taking hold nearly instantaneously.

My knee banged into the ground, but Roe caught me before I went all the way down.

Campbell, meanwhile, had his knee firmly pinned onto Desmond's chest, a look somewhere between relief and sorrow lining his handsome features. He was breathing hard, but I had a feeling it had more to do with his mental state than with the brief sprint across the road.

Asher and Gen arrived in time to help secure the restraints on his wrists and ankles, then helped carry Desmond to the small wagon they'd left just up the road.

The powder had been Roe's idea. A mix of peyote, oleander, and magic. The magic wasn't really magic at all. It had taken only a few minutes with Holdan to learn that the last ingredient was nothing more than strongly concentrated opium powder. A couple of minutes in the pharmacology lab, and I was able to reproduce the substance Nanette and Holdan—then Hollis—had used to subdue Roe all those weeks ago. It was probably something Hale would find handy when he was doing minor procedures in the clinic.

As the others loaded the sedated form into the back of the wagon, I couldn't help but marvel at how well the whole thing had gone. It seemed almost too easy.

Campbell would take Desmond to one of the hub's holding cells in a building not far from the site of the clinic. He'd be held there for the time it took Campbell to collect the supplies he'd need for the month-long journey back to the Avions. When I'd asked if he'd be able to keep his partner from harming anyone along the way, he'd given me a grim nod and then glanced at Asher.

"What was that look?" I asked Gen.

She smiled sadly. "Asher's going with him. Just to ensure everything is handled properly and we won't have a repeat series of incidents on our hands."

"But that'll take months." I couldn't believe Medicus or Geneva would allow his absence for such a lengthy time.

"Yeah. It will." She chewed absently on her lower lip. "They'll be promoting one of the fellas from clinic guard to my assistant while he's gone."

Desmond groaned and tried to roll to his side, but Roe was having none of it.

"Oh no you don't, you grimy bastard." He blew his own packet of power directly into the bound man's face.

19

HALE

It's not that I loathed nights in the clinic, it was just that the long dark shifts weren't my favorite part of the job. The independence was good and it had a calmer feel—not so many people around giving me their opinion of how to do this, that, or the other. There was the occasional emergent procedure—those nights when I had to do a complicated laceration closure or remove a foreign body from one orifice or another. Even the occasional emergent chest tube or peritoneal tap. Those nights when I was focused on a single patient and problem were more than fine.

But the majority of nights, it was just tending to other practitioners' patients and dealing with urgent first floor walk-ins. In general I was fine being alone, but recently I'd come to treasure the time I got to spend with my brother and of course Aurelia. We could go several days at a crack and only see one another in passing.

But the worst bit was just how incredibly creepy the building itself could feel. I'm not one to scare easily. Never been afraid of the dark. The clinic though had a heavy, oppressive feel to it. The lighting was for shit. We had oil lamps burning in sconces on the walls and the overhead solar lamps scattered about, but these were spaced oddly and kept low to both save on the battery lives and to afford the patients at least an attempt at sleep.

The unfortunate resulting effect was misshapen islands of light—some flickering and others a sickly yellow—floating in a miasma of antiseptic and stool-smelling darkness. Add to this the murmur of snoring patients and the occasional scream of pain, and it could be a real thing to experience.

For unknown reasons, a couple of the practitioners preferred nights and had no qualms about tucking themselves in for a nap when they weren't busy. I hadn't developed a knack for shutting my brain down long enough to drift off, however. Roe said it was because I was wound too tight. He might be right.

Love it or hate, it was my turn to be on for my three-in-a-row. Technically, it was Auri's turn, but we'd all agreed—even the older practitioners who felt the same way I did about the shifts—while her attacker was roaming the settlement, she wasn't doing nights alone at the clinic. And since having two of us here together made no sense and would only add to the day shift's burden, I volunteered to cover her set.

The rat bastard had been caught the night before, and by the grace of the stars in heaven, no one had been hurt in the process. But since it was the last of the three-in-a-row, it just made sense for me to keep the shift. Auri could pay me back—or not—in the future.

Having seen and treated a woman with a urinary tract infection, a man with a ruptured eardrum (courtesy of his overzealous wife, a toothpick, and a nasty little cockroach which found his ear canal to be snuggly and warm), and lastly a decent case of impetigo—the first floor was under

194

control. The only snag had been in trying to explain to Mrs. Roilers that Aurelia wouldn't be in that night but I'd be happy to help her with her sciatica. She looked at me with a face of long suffering and not so politely insinuated I was zero good to her before she left.

I made my way from floor to floor, stopping to check on the healing surgical patients on two, the chronically ill older folks on three, and finally headed for the stairs leading to the little patients staying overnight on four.

The stairway from three to four was particularly dark. The solar light was malfunctioning and I had only my handheld lamp to illuminate the steps. As I exited the door on the floor, everything was relatively quiet save for the soft cooing of a mother and the occasional squawks of her fussy toddler.

The assistant working the desk looked up as I approached. She appeared momentarily flustered but then smiled and stood as I walked to the far side where the standing counter was. I grabbed the stack of charts from their holder and noticed her leaning against it studying me.

Keeping my voice barely above a whisper lest I wake the sleeping children and their parents, I told her not to worry about getting up. I nodded back to the chair she'd recently vacated. "I'm just checking in."

"It's all right, I need to stretch anyway." Her voice was too loud and too eager in the hushed atmosphere. "Is there anything I can assist you with?"

Not looking up from the charts I was reviewing and keeping my voice low in the hope she'd follow suit, I replied, "Nope. I'm all good. Thanks."

"You sure?"

I continued to read the chart in front of me. "Uh-huh."

195

Everything seemed stable and straightforward with the patients of the floor. Vitals were good for the most part, medications had been given, and there didn't seem to be any newly reported problems.

That was until I reached the last of the half dozen folders. It was labeled with the name Clarice Donahue. Auri had been pretty stressed over the teen of late. She'd even mentioned some conflict with Jassika over sending the girl home prematurely. Obviously Aurelia had won that argument and the girl was still in-house. Flipping the folder open, I noticed the flow sheet for the evening was completely blank. Not a temperature, heart, rate, medication, or pain check to be found. I frowned and turned the page over. Blank there too.

"Sorry," I said finally looking up at the assistant. Having ignored my earlier suggestion to relax and sit, she now stood no more than a foot from my left elbow. "What was your name again?"

Irritation flashed across her features but cleared as she smiled and replied, "Cookie."

I stood in bafflement, not sure how to reply. Then, realizing she'd actually given me her name and not some request for a treat, I was able to respond. "Right . . . Cookie, why aren't there any vitals or other notes recorded for this patient? Was she discharged?"

The assistant moved closer and placed her hand on my arm, leaning unnecessarily close to read the blocky name on the chart. Her chest brushed against me, and I stepped back, folding my arms across my own chest. She looked up, bottom lip out in an exaggerated pout, but didn't immediately answer my question.

I raised my eyebrows and dipped my head toward the paper file with bold black lettering DONAHUE, C. across the front, waiting for her to respond.

"No, she's still here."

"Then why isn't anything documented? Have you not checked in on her all night?"

"She's been kind of a foul little brat, so I've left her alone. I'm sure she's stable though. Doesn't really seem like she needs to be here at all."

As if an ill-tempered patient was a singular experience in the clinic.

"Right. Which bed is she?" I asked.

Now instead of pouting she looked equal parts nervous and defiant.

"Over in the corner, behind the privacy screen." Great. The assistant didn't even have a straight visual line to the kid. "Her dad left this afternoon. She's just been sleeping since."

"Right," I said again. My solar torch was flickering, so I grabbed one of the extra oil lamps and lit the wick. I turned toward the corner of the floor but stopped myself and turned back. "And, Cookie, it's important to remember, people count on us to be professionals."

Whether I was referring to skipping out on her duties or getting into someone else's personal space or both, I wasn't sure. But I felt I'd be remiss if I didn't say something.

If the rest of the clinic was creepy, this corner of the fourth floor was downright macabre. Tiny empty cradles and cage-like toddler beds designed to keep their occupants from climbing out were interspersed with cartoony wall drawings and garishly hued paint. In the light of day it might be bright and fun, but in the darkness and flickering light it was the stuff of nightmares. How did these kids sleep here?

A thick pink sheet of material tacked to a tall metal frame served as a movable privacy screen in the far corner. As I walked toward it, I caught movement from behind the material.

197

"It's all right, babe. Go ahead." The voice of a young woman whispered in the dark space as I approached. What kind of shenanigans was this kid up to?

"Clarice," a harsh gravelly voice full of pleading and perhaps sorrow replied. The hairs on the back of my neck rose with the sound.

"Do it," the girl responded, more command than acquiescence. Her words were followed by a choked grunt and then the sound of a deep whistle of air through an open window.

I was just to the corner when I raised the lamp over my head with one hand and moved the framed screen with the other.

Clarice was sitting on the edge of her bed, her body wrapped in the arms of a young man. The embrace initially appeared to be one of passion, the girl's head thrown back, her arms around his waist. But then I noticed her eyes were rolled back so I could see only the whites, and the veins of her neck were taut with strain. Even though their lips weren't touching—a centimeter or two of space between them—the boy's mouth was open as if he would devour her completely.

The noise I'd thought of as the wind was in fact one long inhale from the young man. He was drawing and dragging as if he could fill not only his lungs, but his entire body with one long breath.

"What the hell?" I yelled—now not caring how many babes or parents I woke—as I strode toward the obscene encounter. The boy at least had the good sense to break the connection and jump back from me as I reached for him.

"I'm sorry. I didn't mean to," he stammered as Clarice's body slumped backward onto the narrow bed.

He looked from her to me and back again. "I'm so, so sorry."

Then he was dashing past me. As he dodged between me and the screen, it toppled and crashed into my hand holding the oil lamp. I juggled it in the air. If it hit the ground and shattered, it would be disastrous. It took both of my hands and all of my focus for a brief moment to keep the flames within the lamp. A moment the boy used to scamper past me and out of my reach.

Cookie for her part looked like a rabbit in the presence of a hawk—stone still and eyes wide.

Clarice was lying crumpled on her side. Her breathing was rapid and shallow. Her lips a shade somewhere between grey and gone.

Grabbing her wrist, I felt the thready beats of her pulse. They were too weak and much too irregular. Scooping her up, I did the only thing I could think to do. I yelled at Cookie to bring a lamp, and I ran to the stairwell and down the steps to the first floor.

Banging out the door at the bottom, I shouted instructions to Nora and Janet. Thank the universe for small mercies, they were both working the first floor that night.

My eyes caught on a man I thought might have been Campbell Robichaud, but I couldn't be certain. When I glanced back after laying Clarice on one of the emergency tables, he was gone. Nora had a bag of saline pumping into the IV already placed in Clarice's hand and Janet was pulling over the emergency cart before I knew they were moving.

The girl's breaths were becoming more labored with an agonal quality to them. "Bag and mask please, Janet."

She handed me a fitted face mask attached to a pliant bladder-like bag. I assisted the respiratory effort, trying to time it so as not to fight Clarice's body. Nora cracked open the emergency cart and, trying to anticipate what I might call for next, pulled out several vials of medication. We had all that was available from Medicus, but the tiny glass tubes and bottles didn't seem like nearly enough. If her heart failed, these medications would not save her.

It was controlled chaos. Janet, Nora, and I moving together, around, and on top of one another in an effort to sustain the teen's life.

Above the din, I heard a man's breathless voice as he entered the building. "What was *he* doing here?" he asked no one in particular as he hurried to the stairwell.

He must have noticed the commotion and realized who our patient was. An unearthly wail rang through the first floor.

"No, no, no," the older man—Clarice's father judging by the reaction as well as the close physical resemblance—flew to his daughter's side and nearly collapsed on top of her.

"Sir. Please," Nora said. Calm as water on a still day. "You need to give us space to help her." Again I thanked the heavens and all its stars for Nora being on that night.

"She's my baby," Clarice's father choked out.

"I know. I know. We're doing all we can for her. Please come sit right over here for me." She had the man by the elbow and was leading him to a chair Janet had pulled to the side of our work space. "Please let us do our jobs."

I needed more access to get the medications running, so I asked Janet to place another IV. As soon as it was taped in place, I gave Clarice a dose of a foxglove distillation as well as the only dose of epinephrine we had. We needed more of the lifesaving medication, but it was difficult to produce. Medicus rationed it severely.

My plan was to help her as much as I could in the short term and hope her body and soul would take care of the rest. Feeling her pulse again, I wasn't reassured.

Cookie had gone at some point to fetch one of the other assistants from the second or third floor. Together, they were ushering the other patients away and toward the front of the clinic. The less of an audience and the fewer distractions we had, the better.

There in the peculiar pool of bilious half light, with the sounds of a father's grief playing in the background, we did all we could for the girl. My own words to Aurelia from months before came back to me. *Sometimes our medicine works, and sometimes the universe has other plans.*

Unfortunately that night, the universe won.

20

ROE

Little-bit and I had escaped the clinic for the night and decided on the stroll home that our garden boxes were in dire need of a little care before we turned in for the night, with weeding and the daily watering to be done. Some of the plants needed a prune, and Auri planned to set out a small harvest of leaves overnight to dry.

A person never really thinks of gardening as a suitable pastime when you live in the desert. The air is arid, the wind harsh and unforgiving. I'd seen for myself how the rushing air could strip paint from a building given the time and the inclination. Water comes rarely, and when it does, it's just as liable to drown delicate plants as it is to nourish them.

Only the hardiest and most stubborn succulents naturally grow in this environ. But just as Auri, Hale, and I had been transplanted from a more temperate clime, so too had most of the seeds and saplings now growing in the raised beds outside our housing complex.

It was no secret Specs loved the pharmacology lab, and often, the concoctions she produced were simple medicinal remedies brewed, distilled, or emulsified from the leaves, stems, and roots of the plants we grew or harvested from the settlement's bigger gardens. Occasionally, even the desert itself gave up its strange botanical specimens for us to use.

It wasn't my favorite activity, but it was simple and mundane. At the time, simple and mundane were exactly what we both needed to take our minds off recent events.

Unfortunately, my bespectacled friend had other ideas. We'd barely gotten done with the initial weeding when she began telling me a crazy theory she had regarding the patient who'd been stumping her for the past couple of weeks. If she'd told me her thoughts on the matter three months ago, I would have thought she was having some sort of psychotic break. After witnessing what I had since leaving Renfield, it didn't sound practical, but I couldn't dismiss it out of hand.

I was thinning the overgrown mint bushes when Campbell arrived.

"Just checking in on things," he said casually, looking first at me, then at Auri. She had the same sandy soil on the bridge of her nose that she had all over her hands. Maybe, I thought, she should have the frames tightened. Or better yet, she should ask Holdan to work a miracle on her eyes, then she wouldn't need those thick glasses at all anymore.

Without preamble, Auri asked, "What are the chances of Desmond getting whatever he was trying to get from me from someone else? Someone like one of my patients?"

Campbell frowned. "Has there been a death at the clinic I'm not aware of?"

"No. Thank the stars. I was just wondering if it was possible to attack someone repeatedly and have them survive."

"Well, yes. You're still alive."

She nodded. "Right."

Campbell looked thoughtful. For a split second I assumed he was expecting us to be skeptical of the story he'd told, but I realized he already knew Aurelia could wield miracles and wonder. Maybe he was just processing her theory. As far as I knew, no one had shared with him the story of Hollis and Nanette. He wouldn't know we'd all taken Nanette's lashes then watched as Listerman and Goldie-Locks patched us up.

"Interesting question. Before I answer, do you mind if I ask what makes you suggest it?"

"Well, I mind you acting like we're no brighter than coyote feces," Auri answered, sweet venom lacing each word.

Campbell smiled at this but didn't rise to the bait.

"Look," she said, exasperated. "You show up here with a story about your people craving magic and miracles at the same time I'm attacked—not once, but twice. And"—she raised her index finger lest he dare to interrupt her—"all this happens to coincide with a young woman's illness that can't be explained."

"You're that confident in your abilities that not knowing her diagnosis is out of the question?" He didn't say it meanly, but as if he was genuinely curious. I wondered which abilities he was referring to.

"Yes." She said it simply, no hint of rancor or irritation. "But even if I wasn't, I've had no less than three other practitioners trying to help me figure it out. They are all good at their jobs. Two of them are the most experienced and knowledgeable I've encountered. Someone should have come up with something by this point."

I crossed my arms and leaned against the raised wooden box. The sun had fully set by that time, and the only illumination we had was from the raised solar lamps and the smattering of stars in the cloudless sky.

"None of us are fully convinced of your story," I told him, "but we do have some experience with the strange and unusual. More than just Aurelia's ability to heal. You may not be exactly what you say you are, but if you believe your people are some kind of energy vampires, then so does your murderous buddy Desmond. Based on our previous experience, I'm guessing he's batty enough to have killed the other women in the settlement and likely wouldn't bat an eye at messing with a kid. Am I wrong?"

He pinched the bridge of his nose and shook his head. "The man I knew, the Desmond I trusted my life to, would never harm a soul. But no, I can't say you're wrong. He's not the man he was. This decline . . . it's a bit tough to witness. But"—he held his hand up in a wait gesture when I opened my mouth—"I'm not being sentimental when I say I don't think it's him."

"Because. . .?" I raised my eyebrows and put my hands to the side.

"He looked starved when we last saw him. He perked up quickly after attacking Aurelia, but he still looked frail and malnourished. I've never seen anyone actually draw the wonders out, but I always sort of believed the myths. If the magic is there, it would restore the soul and heal the body. From what I understand, your young patient has been ill for quite some time. Weeks, didn't you say?"

Auri nodded, hand on her chin.

"That would imply, *if* her illness is related to one of my people, she is being slowly drained. Desmond didn't look as if he had even a shred of self-control left. And he isn't restored. He isn't well. If he was well. . ."

"What?" Auri prodded, not a little exasperated.

205

"Let's just say, Hale and I would have been no match for the man he once was. He'd have mopped the floor with the both of us."

I doubted that very much. Campbell might be weaker than he appeared, but he'd never seen Hale get angry.

"I think we're also missing a bigger point," I added.

Valilier Robichaud focused those intense dark eyes on me. "I think we're missing a lot of things."

"Does Clarice even have the power of wonder-working?"

Auri had already thought of this apparently. "I've been asking myself that. Holdan and Campbell seem to think they can sense the miracles in me. Nanette certainly could. But I can't tell the difference. Holdan doesn't give off any particular scent or aura that I can pick up. He says eventually I'll be attuned to it, but for now—nothing."

"For the sake of argument, let's assume she has a touch of the thaumaturgy buried down deep," Campbell said. "We have to be dealing with a third person. Someone not as lustful and crazed. Someone who could be more patient but still drawn to those kernels of magic. My worry is that patience may run out."

"Why do I get the feeling there's something else you aren't telling us?" I asked.

"For the love of the stars, the pair of you ask so many questions." He didn't seem angry, just surprised.

"It's the sign of a good practitioner," Auri explained, as if it were the simplest thing in the world. "Well, except for Hale. He asks hardly any questions at all and he's still amazingly skilled." She wasn't wrong, but the syrupy way she said it made me roll my eyes. Thank the heavens she wasn't looking at me. "You have to ask the right questions and the patient will give you all the answers you need for a diagnosis. So what's the answer to Roe's question?"

"Complicated." A single word he didn't seem inclined to expound upon.

"So if it's not Desmond, who else could it be?" Auri demanded.

"Not only that, but how?" I was picturing the vampires in my timeworn storybooks. Human monsters with pointed fangs, drawing lifeblood from their unwilling victim's necks.

"You saw the how when Desmond went after Aurelia."

"Seeing and understanding aren't the same thing."

"It must be sort of the opposite of what Nanette did." Auri's face was contemplative. She stroked the pendant around her neck, and I knew she was trying to work through the mechanics.

"How do you mean?" Of course Campbell hadn't been there. He wouldn't know what we'd suffered from that woman. The lashes of energy that couldn't be seen but could certainly be felt.

Aurelia gave him the short and incredibly unsavory version of our trek from Renfield to Devil's Meadows. He listened intently. It was clear he was more than adept at his job. He collected bits of information and stored them away for when he'd need to piece them together to solve his puzzle.

"When we—or, well, when I—just before Nanette was killed, and she was lashing the others with her magic, I could feel it rushing and tugging around and away from me. I imagine it could be sort of the same thing."

Campbell nodded and asked a few other questions. Auri gave what few answers she could. In return, he bounced a few of his own speculations back at her. We discussed it as the dusting of stars

207

brightened in the sky. A low hoot filled the air. A small burrowing owl alighted atop a larger than average barrel cactus. The creature's eyes were luminous in the surrounding gloom. I couldn't control the grin tugging at my lips as the pint-sized bird of prey studied us from its perch.

"Hey Auri, it's another tiny badass." She grinned right back, just as I'd expected.

What was somewhat less expected was the throaty chuckle from Campbell. It sent a slight shiver up my spine.

Shortly after we tidied up the garden, Campbell informed us he wanted to check things out at the clinic. Auri, perhaps suspicious of his true motivations, informed him he wouldn't be able to get into the fourth floor without a parent's consent. Depending on who was working the desk, I thought she might be wrong. Some of the assistants took their duties more seriously than others. I could think of one assistant in particular who would likely bend a rule or two for a man with a face and a badge like Valilier Campbell Robichaud. But I kept my thoughts to myself.

Despite his desire to see if he could sense any wonder-working buried deep inside Clarice, Campbell assured Aurelia he wouldn't be visiting any of the patients that night. He simply wanted to ascertain if someone else was nosing around where they shouldn't be. His eyes held a sad haunted look as he left the garden.

"I guess he isn't all bad, huh?" Specs handed me a canteen of water flavored with just a hint of citrus.

"He could be worse, I suppose." I grabbed the bucket in one hand and flung the other over Auri's shoulder.

"I hope you aren't referring to me." A clipped haughty voice came from the shadows ahead.

"You know, Little-bit, one of these nights, we're going to get to spend some quality time just you and me." I bit out the words as Holdan Listerman stepped onto the walkway as we rounded the corner toward the door.

"You're time is coming, I assure you. At any rate, I'd hate to be accepted by you now, Mr. Belstrohm. It would be quite the travesty of justice as I'm sure to be departing this lovely little hub soon."

"No worries then, Listerman. I still don't like you."

"Yes, well. . ." He held the door open for us as we entered the building.

"Hey, Holdan, Roe's coming over for my special nopales and walnut salad. Care to join us?"

Why, Auri? Why? I could have strangled her myself.

The grimace on his face was directed solely at me. "How could I refuse?"

We all gathered around the table in what I now thought of as Hale *and* Auri's apartment. She hadn't gone back to her own place except to grab her things since the night of the attack. I caught myself wondering if Medicus would spring for a larger apartment for them if they eventually got hitched. Asher and Gen had a relatively spacious abode. As far as I knew, all of the dwellings in our building were the same simple layout with an open kitchen and living quarters with an attached bedroom and lav. They ran up and down the central corridors in sets of mirrored pairs. I wondered how it would feel if they did move buildings? She was my best friend. I needed her close to me.

Chiding myself, I took a big bite of my salad. There was zero point in dwelling on things I couldn't change. We were never meant to live together forever. And if I had to choose someone for either of them, I could not have done better than my best friend with my brother.

The cactus and nut salad was actually pretty good. The beer was better. And Listerman? He was tolerable.

Auri ran the theory she and Campbell had concocted past him, and he took no time in replying. "It seems obvious now that you say it. I'm not sure how the two of us missed the possibility for so long. In theory, if the thaumaturgy can heal when directed, it might also heal when consumed."

"But this idea stems from the feelings I got when Nanette was throwing her magic about. You said she had no healing power despite her massive well of power. How could someone use the miracles to heal if they don't know how the healing works?" Auri was almost arguing against her own theory.

"Who says the people of the Avions don't know how to heal themselves? It could be purely instinctual. If they are able to draw the wonders to them, perhaps the mind and body do the rest without even knowing what they're doing? It is, of course, all hypothetical. I mentioned awhile back I was working on things outside the clinic. I've been trying to figure out how Nanette was able to do what she did. Hurt people the way she did."

Auri gasped audibly.

"Don't fret, Ms. Morris, I have no intention of becoming an even greater villain than I've already proved to be. However, it has got me thinking about the nature of the power."

The words were only just out of his mouth when the door banged open. How the hell had we forgotten to lock it again?

Jumping up, I stepped in front of Goldie-Locks.

It was Campbell, and he looked frantic.

"The clinic," he panted. He must have run all the way back here. "Aurelia, you need to come with me now."

Clarice needed a miracle. Judging from the slack jaw and the pallor of her face, if Goldie Girl's patient wasn't dead, she was certainly only a few heart beats away from it.

My brother stood at the head of the ashen teen, one hand on her carotid artery, eyes focusing on his watch. A bag and mask sat on the table edge. A look of helpless resignation was stamped on a face that few could say they ever associated with Hale Belstrohm.

An older man was on his knees on the other side of the table. Tears streamed down his worn cheeks. His large hands clasped one of the girl's limp ones.

Janet and Nora busied themselves with moving equipment and supplies off the table and from around the cramped space. Vials and tubing, packaging and syringes made a mess of the area. Any rush to continue lifesaving measures had been halted.

As we entered, Hale said by way of explanation, "I did everything I could." Whether he was talking to Clarice, her father, Auri as she rushed in, or himself, I couldn't say.

Auri slid to a stop at his side. She went briefly still as a look of utter shock was rapidly replaced by one of deep study and concentration. Behind the thick lenses of her glasses, her eyes flicked back and forth over the prone form of the girl. One hand rested at her clavicles, stroking the golden pendant, and the other pulled her hair back from her brow. I could practically hear the ticking and whirring of her mind as it shuffled from one thought, feeling, and plan to another.

211

"Can I borrow your stethoscope?" She held her hand out toward Hale but didn't take her eyes from the near lifeless teen.

Hale placed the bag over Clarice's nose and mouth and gave a gentle squeeze. The girl's chest rose and fell with the air artificially filling her lungs. "Sure," he said, "but I—"

"I'm sure you've listened, but I haven't," Auri snapped. In a measured tone, she continued, "Hale . . . just . . . please, can I borrow it?"

He slid the rubber and metal tool into her hand wordlessly.

She looked around, scanning the space as she placed the rubber nubs in her ears and the diaphragm on Clarice's chest. Auri's other hand rested on the forearm of her patient. It certainly wasn't necessary from a medical perspective, and I had a feeling Auri was trying to sense whether she could attempt to use her gift to save yet another life.

Giving Hale a significant look, I said, "Maybe we could give them a moment."

My brother either realized at the same time I did what Auri was on about, or he just read me the way he always did. His eyes shifted from fatigued to startled, but at least he didn't argue.

I knew he didn't want Specs to be in a position where she implicated herself and destroyed not only her career but possibly her life. He just wasn't fool enough to try to argue. He gave a brief nod and motioned to Janet and Nora. "Ladies. Your work here tonight has been exceptional. I think now we should just step out and allow Practitioner Morris to say goodbye." His eyes shifted to the broken man at the side of the bed.

I answered his unasked question with a shrug. I had no idea how to ask the man to leave his daughter's side.

Like the tiny goddess she was, Auri must have sensed our hesitation.

"I think Mr. Donahue should stay."

He never acknowledged her statement. I suppose in his mind, there was no question about him not being with his daughter for even a moment.

Aurelia's hand remained on the arm of her patient, but instead of the hard resolve and calm bedside manner I'd witnessed from her for the past several weeks, she was fidgety and agitated. Maybe she wasn't as blind to the threat of her actions as I'd assumed.

My attention focused on the scene by the bed, I'd almost forgotten both Campbell and Holdan had accompanied us to the clinic. Campbell had drifted off with the assistants, but Holdan stood a few feet away, looking as uncertain as I'd ever seen him. Auri noticed him lurking nearby, and I couldn't be certain, but I thought she mouthed the word "please" to him before Janet and Nora pulled the mobile privacy partitions in place. Unknowingly, the assistants had shut the two wonder-workers in with the dying girl and her grieving father.

Hale and I gently ushered the assistants away, and my brother—in an act of subtlety and skill I generally thought him incapable of—drew them to the desk with a rather inane discussion about paperwork and medical documentation of the events.

Knowing what Auri and Listerman were likely to attempt, I returned to the edge of the privacy screen ready to give some sort of warning should one be needed. Already I was concerned about what she hoped to accomplish with Mr. Donahue looking on.

Apparently my worry wasn't completely unfounded as in a hushed voice I heard her say, "Conrad. This is Mr. Listerman. He's going to assist me with something. What you may witness . . . well, Sandy told me some of your beliefs and I. . ." The

213

words were tumbling out in a fall of nervous energy. "What I mean is, I'd really appreciate it if you wouldn't say anything to anyone at the clinic?"

Her voice trailed off when he didn't respond. Despite his earlier anxiousness, Listerman seemed to have found his spine, and in a clear and confident, yet whispered voice said, "What Practitioner Morris is trying to so *eloquently* say is this—please keep what *I'm* about to do between us." Emphasis on the *I'm*. "Medicus does not appreciate my special set of gifts, and Practitioner Morris is simply attempting to protect me."

If I didn't know better, I'd say he was right back on those same dusty dead end streets where we'd first encountered him—pouring promises and potions from the back of the rickety wonder wagon.

I didn't have time to think on it further though. In the space of a heartbeat the quiet was broken by a sharp inhale and Auri's startled "Holdan."

Whatever was happening, it wasn't exactly what my petite friend had planned. I had to see. Peeking through the gap in the curtain, I almost didn't believe my eyes.

Listerman stood at the head of the bed, in nearly the same position Hale had been occupying only minutes before. He was bent forward at the waist as if to examine the still patient before him. With one hand, he clutched both of Aurelia's in a tight grasp, and with the other, he'd tilted Clarice's chin up in a position once again so similar to what Hale had done. This time however, Clarice's parted lips were not covered by the bag and mask used to assist her breathing. Now they opened just centimeters from Listerman's own.

Mr. Donahue sat motionless, eyes wide as Listerman seemed to exhale slowly into the girl's upturned face. The moment drug out for far too long. It seemed minutes, hours, days passed as the man who'd once held me captive attempted to breathe magic and wonder—attempted to breathe life itself—into the body of an all but dead girl. After an eternity, Listerman straightened and coughed delicately into his shoulder then drew a whooping breath. He swayed on his feet. Auri dropped his hands and grabbed him around the waist.

A muffled cry came from the side of the bed as Clarice began to choke and sputter. She, too, drew in a few ragged breaths, and her color moved from the pale slate hue it had been into a deeper warmer shade. She struggled to sit, her father crying in earnest now—this time with sobs of joy rather than sorrow.

I could have stood and watched all night, but the sound of raised voices near the entrance to the clinic had me spinning on my heel. Jassika Duncan and the ever-perky Cookie were bustling over.

In a voice which might have been a touch louder than was strictly necessary, I greeted them. "Practitioner Duncan. Isn't it your night off?"

"Cookie thought there was some sort of emergency that might need my attention." My eyes were drawn to the crown of Jassika's head. The hair there was sticking up in a silver and steel bird's nest. Maybe Jassika had been in one of the lounges all along. Otherwise, I couldn't fathom how the assistant had retrieved the older practitioner so quickly.

"Oh, well, Practitioner Morris is just finishing up with the patient she might be referring to."

Jassika's brow furrowed. "She says we lost the girl."

"Not at all. It may have been touch and go for a bit, but Hale was able to stabilize her. He may have overreacted, though. She's still here among the living."

I sent Hale an apologetic grimace. Anyone who knew him well would see the lie for what is was. He rarely, if ever, overreacted.

He shrugged in response.

"Excuse me. I was just leaving." Listerman was pushing out past the screen on shaking legs, doing his best to avoid eye contact with anyone in the area. The man looked awful. A sickly green tint hung about him, but I let him pass. We could help him out later. Jassika eyed him, and my gut sank.

Perhaps he thought no one would connect him to the miracle that had just been performed. Perhaps he thought it was time to step out from the shadow Nanette had cast over his life for the past seven years. Perhaps he'd known Auri would never convince Medicus she'd not used her special gifts to help save Clarice. Or perhaps he had seen a dying child and taken a leap of faith that this crazy act could save her life. Whatever the case might be, he had to know if he proclaimed he was performing a miracle and succeeded, no one would look too closely at Aurelia.

As he walked out past the shrewd eyes of Jassika Duncan into the hot desert night, I finally did what Auri and Geneva had been asking me to do for the past two months. I finally forgave Holdan Listerman for all the misery he'd caused us.

21

AURELIA

"There's no reason for me to stay." Clarice leveled her eyes at me and raised her delicately pointed chin. "I'm fine and you know it."

If she'd spoken those words to me a week ago, they would have been thrown out as a challenge. Instead, she was jubilant and impish. A healthy, smiling, carefree teen. I imagined this was the Clarice her father and Sandy had always known, and I understood why, when we'd first met, they'd been so sure she wasn't well.

Sighing, I took one last look at her chart and snapped the folder shut. "You're right. I see no reason to keep you in the clinic."

The girl popped up and danced around the front of her bed.

"But, Clarice, I need you to listen to me."

"I'm listening." She appeared to be doing anything but listening as she shook her hips and twisted her arms over her head.

I placed a hand on her wrist. "No, Clarice. Really listen."

The dancing stopped with a frown and a humph. She dropped onto the cot facing me. Pulling up a stool, I sat knee to knee with this beautiful girl who'd come so incredibly close to death under my care. I took both of her hands in mine and forced her to make eye contact with me.

"You almost died." Gone was the soothing voice and upbeat tone I used with my younger patients. This conversation was going to be serious and mature. "You. Almost. Died. You need to really think about that. Really and truly acknowledge it as a fact. Understand what could have happened if Practitioner Belstrohm hadn't found you when he did. What might have happened had Mr. Listerman not been here that night. Think about your father and what he would have gone through."

Chastised, she looked down at our clasped hands. "I do think about it."

"Do you?" My voice was laced with doubt. "Because if you do, you may want to consider how you came to be in that particular condition."

"He didn't mean it." Her voice was misery taken form.

"I'm sure he didn't." I don't often lie to my patients, but this was certainly at the very least, stretching the truth.

"All the times before, he stopped when I got weak. I think he just got carried away. And if I can help him, I want to."

"At what risk? Your life?"

She didn't answer.

"Look, Clarice. Wanting to help someone is noble. I can appreciate that. Really I can." I thought back to the evening in the desert when I'd wanted to help Geneva so badly, it had taken Hale tackling me to break the connection to her. "But he lost control once. Who's to say he won't lose control again?"

Silent tears streamed down her face. Minutes before she'd been up dancing and ecstatic to be going home. Now I'd leached the joy from her in a matter of minutes. It broke my heart a little, but these things needed to be said.

"I can't control what you do after you leave this building. But I am asking you—imploring you. Please think about what you're doing."

She wiped the salty streams from her cheeks and nodded. It was the best I could hope for. With any luck, Campbell and Asher were out there right now, tracking down the boy who'd done this. His actions might not have been malicious, but the reality was he was a danger to Clarice and possibly other young woman as well.

Despite the uncomfortable conversation, I wasn't in the mood to go home. When I was done with my other patients, I elected to spend the afternoon working in the pharmacology lab.

Hale had used up quite a few of our most important medicines in his nearly futile attempt to bring Clarice back from the brink. A few of the preparations had to be delivered from Medicus on one of the supply runs from Renfield. Several others though could be brewed and distilled right here in the clinic.

The space was nearly as big as the lab at our Medicus training facility, and while each of the practitioners had access, it was really run by a team of technicians whose sole purpose was in preparing the ointments, tablets, elixirs, and solutions we used daily.

Bottles and jars, tubes and flasks covered the wooden shelves. The tables for mixing and heating were constructed of marble slabs. Scales and pipettes littered several of the surfaces, and the whole room had an acrid chemical meets earthy fungal smell. It was more than a little off-putting unless you happened to be accustomed to it.

The door creaked open and shut softly. I didn't take my eyes from the pipette and flask in my hands.

"Practitioner Morris. Might I have a word?"

I finished measuring the faint amber liquid in my pipette and shot it into one of several tubes in a wooden rack, then turned to find Jassika Duncan standing just inside the door.

"Of course. I'm finishing up a few preparations. Two minutes." I measured out the rest of the solution and capped the tubes before washing my hands and sitting on one of the metal stools. Jassika pulled over another and groaned as she sat.

"The shifts don't get any shorter the older I get," she said. "Not sure how much longer my body will allow me to keep up with the pace of this place."

"You aren't thinking of retiring, are you?"

"The thought had crossed my mind, but I'm not quite ready to call it quits just yet. Maybe just an eventual relocation to a smaller settlement."

"Theo would never let you go." The two seemed attached to each other, and I couldn't imagine losing both seasoned veteran practitioners.

"You might be right." She nodded as she spoke. Then, shifting gears completely, she asked, "How is young Clarice Donahue doing?"

I smiled. "Quite well. I sent her home today as a matter of fact."

"And you never figured out the cause of her symptoms? Aren't you worried she'll just bounce back in again?" The question was innocent enough. We often had patients return quickly to the clinic if they weren't fully recovered or didn't follow the prescribed treatment when discharged. But something in her tone spoke of a deeper question. It was almost as if she knew all that had happened and was trying to get me to admit it.

"No." I drew the word out and held her gaze. I was a terrible liar, but I needed to sell the story as best I could.

"I see." She studied her nails. The movement caused the lamps to bounce sickly yellow light off her short ashen hair. The effect made her look younger but unwell.

"The young assistant, Cookie, thinks there may be more to the story than what Practitioner Belstrohm has documented."

"I can't speak for Cookie, but Hale is an exceptional practitioner and I trust him completely."

"I agree. He's always been quite proficient in his duties here. And the two of you?" She drug out the word and looked up from her hands, a single eyebrow raised in question.

"Are no one's business." The words came out more strongly than I'd intended. Softening my tone, I added, "However, if there is something between Hale and me, Medicus should be pleased. They match teams they hope will be long standing and cohesive. It's why Roe and I got matched together in the first place. And with Roe came Hale. It's no secret."

"Quite true," she agreed.

"And it's my understanding, the assistant you were referring to was working that night and neglecting her duties. But I'm sure you already know that. If you've reviewed the chart."

"I am aware, yes. It's how the topic was brought up, in fact. When we called her on it, she shifted the blame to Practitioner Belstrohm." She stood. "I'm only trying to do my job, Aurelia."

I softened a little and stood as well. "I can appreciate that. But really, Hale saved her. I have no idea what happened to get her into that state." The lie felt like ash on my tongue. "But his quick actions and expert training pulled her back to the land of the living. At least for now."

221

She started to speak but hesitated. She looked both tired and unsure. Not a combination the steel-spined Jassika Duncan typically wore. "Look. You seem determined to ignore my warnings, but I'll give you one more. Watch your actions—and those of your friends. I won't elaborate, but even I am electing to tread lightly around that woman."

"What woman? Cookie?"

She set her lips in a tight line and glanced over her shoulder.

"Why?" Of all the people to be leery of, Cookie certainly wasn't at the top of my list.

"Because of her father of course."

"Her father? I'm sorry, but I'm not following," I admitted.

"Yes. Her father. Cookie Welchel? Her father is Donald Welchel?"

She must have seen the confusion on my face. "Donald Welchel's been with Medicus for years. Longer even than me and Theo. He's stationed in Big Lake, but it's not a clinical position. He's on the board."

The Medicus Corpus Board made, if not all, then certainly most of the decisions in my life. They told me what I would learn, where I would practice, who I'd work with, and how I'd treat my patients. They *were* Medicus.

"I had no idea. I thought she was just a new hire. She never mentioned any other connection."

"I imagine she wouldn't. I don't believe she really wants to be an assistant. From what I gather, after a bit of family drama, she and her brother were banished from Big Lake and came here to gain some insight or maturity or something. He—the brother—works in the mail depot, I believe."

I couldn't suppress the groan that escaped me. Gary. Her brother was Gary, and he worked in the mail depot. All of those communications with Lita.

My parents. Holdan and his appeals to Medicus Corpus to be reinstated. Gary Welchel could easily have read any or all of it. My heart sank.

Mentally I flashed through each of the letters I'd written and received. I didn't think I'd put anything on paper that was overly incriminating, but I just couldn't be sure.

The site visit from Medicus couldn't be pure coincidence.

"I like you, Aurelia." She placed a hand on my shoulder and gave me a small smile. "You're hardworking, bright, and compassionate. All good traits for a practitioner. And you advocate for your patients. You might need to start advocating for yourself though.

"Medicus Corpus exists to correct some of the wrongs done in the world, but make no mistake, they will do everything in their power to make sure their practitioners stay out of the spotlight. Think what might happen if word spread someone here was able to cure the uncurable. History has taught us normal folk can become fanatical overnight.

"My understanding is the upper echelon of Medicus has decided to do a site visit to Devil's Meadows." Of course I knew this already thanks to Asher. "They plan to inspect the entire clinic sometime this winter. Please don't give them anything interesting to find."

Two days passed and things were beginning to feel almost as normal as they could in the bustling desert hub. With Desmond tucked up tight in his dark cell, the threat of other girls turning up dead had lessened. Despite this, a disquiet came with knowing he wasn't the man who'd nearly killed Clarice.

Campbell insisted he was still on the hunt, but it was abundantly clear to everyone—especially those within earshot of the howling screams coming from the detention cells—that the sooner he was on his way with his quarry the better. Only my friends and I were less than anxious to see him go.

Geneva would miss Asher terribly, and while she was more than capable of holding things in check here, we all knew the pair would be unhappy to be apart for so long. Roe too seemed on edge about the plans for the small group to head out. He'd played it off as worry for Asher, but a small part of me thought there might be a bit more to it. As rocky as the initial meeting between Campbell and my friend was, I couldn't help but hope they might end up close.

I was happy to see the valilier when he showed up with Roe for dinner. I expected to hear about the supplies and tram he was arranging so was a little taken aback when he mentioned his attempts to speak with Clarice earlier in the day.

Patient privacy was paramount, but as he pointed out, public safety was also important. Asher had smoothed the way at the clinic for Campbell to gain access to the contact information he'd needed. Conrad Donahue agreed to meet with him but had asked that Clarice not be involved unless absolutely necessary.

The story he got was more than a little disquieting. According to Conrad, Clarice began seeing a young man three or four weeks before she fell ill. In fact, she'd met him just a stone's throw from the bridge I'd waited on in an effort to trap Desmond.

Clarice and a group of her friends had gone to the old dilapidated area to run among the crumbling buildings. It had become somewhat of an event for the youth in the settlement. Despite the danger, the area had a certain mystique, not unlike the boneyard Roe loved so much. Brightly painted bits of wall, old statues, and even a rusting sky wheel gave the area a carnival-like feel. The teens loved it. Many of the spots were death traps, but that just added to the sense of adventure.

Between the relics and the main inhabited area of settlement were the work camps. They lay next to the tram stations where all of the loading and unloading of supply trams and passenger carts in and out of Devil's Meadows took place. The area was highly transient with people coming and going at all hours of the day and evening.

The young man was new to the settlement and had signed on at one of the camps. A day after his arrival, he was assigned to a scavenging crew. He was tasked with going through the old sections of ruined city, collecting any and all workable metal, wiring, or glass he found.

Likely because he was from somewhere other than the desert, Clarice quickly became enamored of him. The young man told her about lakes and green grass covered hills, rushing clear rivers, and snow in the winter. He'd told her he had to leave his home due to a family illness but would never elaborate despite the number of times she'd asked. He told her she was beautiful and how drawn to her she was. He didn't speak much of his past. Clarice was curious, but at the end of the day, she didn't really care about whatever secrets the boy had.

After a few weeks, he was around the small apartment Clarice shared with her father nearly all the time. That's when Conrad said Clarice began to get ill. He told his daughter she needed to focus on her health and demanded the two stop seeing each other. Initially she'd protested, but after a few days she acquiesced, and he thought that was the end of it.

Then Conrad saw the boy leaving the clinic the night his daughter had nearly died.

I could have kicked myself for not having gotten any of this history in my initial evaluations of Clarice. Not that I would have immediately jumped to the idea that her boyfriend could be contributing to her illness, but because now it was so obviously connected.

Campbell understood my frustration. "You think you feel bad. I missed the whole thing, and it was right under my nose all along."

"But you'd never even met Clarice. You wouldn't have been able to sniff out any thaumaturgy in her or"—I waved my hand in the air—"whatever it is you do."

"I might not have met her, but I've certainly met her boyfriend."

Roe and I looked at him in surprise.

"His name's Wes. He's Desmond's kid brother."

"What's going on in there?" Hale asked as he lightly tapped on my temple.

"Just thinking about everything Campbell told us."

"Yeah it's all a little on the absurd side. I feel terrible for the guy."

"Me too."

We'd climbed the stairs to the rooftop to watch the sunset. When I'd first found the stairwell opening up there the first week after we'd arrived in Devil's Meadows, I was amazed no one had taken advantage of the space before. It wasn't hard to con Roe and Hale into dragging some cushions and a tarp up the steps, and now I had a great space to hide out when I needed a break.

Holdan and I had done some of our earliest practice sessions up there, but since he'd deemed it no longer needed, he hadn't returned.

Hale rested on the dusty cushions, arms stretched back to hold his weight. Sitting cross-legged beside him, I watched the sun sink behind the western mountains. Almost on cue, as the light dimmed, the cicadas began their evening buzz.

"Do you think he'll wait around long enough to catch Wes?" I asked.

"Not sure. I know both Asher and Gen seem to think it'd be better to get Desmond out of the settlement and worry about Wes if he starts causing problems."

"What do you think?"

"I think I almost watched a girl die because of that little shit," Hale ground out, "so I'm in favor of his not hanging around Devil's Meadows."

"Even if he couldn't help it?" I was worried about Clarice just as much as anyone, but a part of me felt for a young man who couldn't control his genetics.

He groaned. "I get it. It's an illness. Probably makes me sound like a stone cold asshole." He grinned at me. "But I'd be happier if I knew he wasn't around."

"What do you think they do with them? In the Avions?"

"I can't imagine. Roe says Campbell mentioned being responsible for executions. That's a pretty heavy load to carry."

I shivered. I could not imagine what that must be like for him. Nanette had died in the desert as a result of her own actions, but I'd had a hand in her end whether I'd intended it or not. Plenty of nights, I still woke thinking of her face as she strangled on an invisible noose. I'd grown to really like Campbell, and I couldn't wish that sort of life on him. Especially knowing how close he and Desmond had once been.

Getting up on my knees, I scooted behind Hale. I nudged him upright and wrapped my arms around his broad shoulders. He put his hands over mine and squeezed.

"Maybe we could try to focus on something a little less . . . unsettling," I suggested.

He chuckled but agreed. "All right. What should we focus on then?"

"The fact that it isn't a hundred and ten degrees out?"

He nodded. "That sounds good."

"Or the fact that I'm not actively running right now? You were so disgusted with me at the dry lake. I remember. Angry that I couldn't run fast enough."

"I was not!" His indignation was comical. "You thought I was disgusted with you? I was disgusted that Jude wouldn't let you ride in the tram."

"Huh. Really?"

"Really. Damn, Auri. I knew you didn't think much of me, but I never thought you had me pegged as that big of an ass."

"I didn't. I mean, I kind of did, but. . . Sorry. Okay happy thoughts again. How about we focus on the fact that it's a beautiful night and neither of us are stuck in the clinic?"

"Fair. That's a good thing to focus on." He was quiet for a minute. The smell of his hair near my face was soothing. The way he rubbed his thumbs over the backs of my hands even more so. "Hey. Did I tell you I delivered a baby a couple of weeks ago? It was pretty amazing."

"No. You didn't." I smiled into the back of his head, trying to envision those deft surgeon's hands handling a tiny, squirming newborn. They're a lot more slippery than people imagine.

"Or," he said, breaking the image in my mind. "We could focus on me kissing you."

A fluttering started somewhere between my heart and my stomach. An utterly splendid feeling.

"That would definitely be worth focusing on." My voice was breathless and wispy, and maybe just a tinge on the squeaky side.

Hale turned his head, trying to look at me over his shoulder. "It would, of course, require you to come around this way."

"Oh." The squeak again.

I dropped my arms and walked on my knees until I was next to him. I mirrored his position with my legs straight out in the opposite direction, our hips touching. He bent toward me, but it became abundantly clear, with the vast difference in our heights, the position would be ridiculously uncomfortable for both of us. So I threw caution to the dry desert winds and moved myself into his lap, straddling him on my knees.

He cupped my face and smiled. "I could focus on you all night."

Despite the fact we had essentially been living together for the past several days, we hadn't spent any measure of quality time with one another. Like the sun and stars, we'd pass each other for the briefest of moments and share a quick kiss or a comforting hug when we could. Or, even worse, we'd be together but at work or surrounded by people, and Hale was even more anti public affection than I was.

On the rooftop and away from prying eyes, I finally got what I'd been craving since the day at the dam settlement. Or rather since somewhere out in the desert when I'd come to not only respect Hale but to feel a connection with him I'd never expected.

The kiss was sweet and lingering. He smelled like the summer sun and the desert sand. But he felt like comfort and home and safety.

Pushing him back on the cushions, I deepened the kiss and ran my fingers through the short loose waves of his golden hair. My glasses slid

229

down, and when I moved to push them back up, he pulled them off and set them out of reach before running his hands down my sides.

We stayed that way, until he broke the kiss and in a hoarse throaty voice said, "We should probably stop."

Sitting back on my heels and looking down, I asked, "Should we?"

He studied me for a minute and laughed. "No." In one fluid motion, he pulled me back toward his chest, then rolled, trapping me beneath him. He rested his weight on his arms and placed his hands on either side of my face, using his thumbs to stroke my thick curls back from my eyes.

"Someone might come up," he offered.

"No one ever comes up here," I countered.

"I'm trying to be a gentleman."

"I don't need you to be a gentleman, Hale."

"Auri, have you ever even—"

"No. But I'm a grown woman."

"Yes, you definitely are." A twinkle in his eye.

I smiled. "I'm afraid to ask, and I assume I know the answer, but have you?"

He turned his head away, avoiding eye contact, but nodded. "Yeah. A few times. Never like this though. Never when I felt like it really meant something." He looked at me then. "Does that bother you?"

"No. Does it bother you that I haven't?"

"Absolutely not."

"All right then."

The starshine was bright, and the desert air a welcoming breath on my skin as I looked up into the green eyes of the man I'd been falling in love with for the past few months. That night was magical, and for the first time in my life, I experienced a new kind of wonder.

22

HALE

If I knew anything, it was that there was no justice in the world. For all the stars in all the heavens would attest, that if there was, I had done nothing to earn the look I saw on Aurelia's face that night.

Six months prior, it never would have occurred to me that I'd be falling for my kid brother's adorable little best friend. Now there I was sharing what was easily the best night of my life with her. In the hellhole that was Devil's Meadows, on a dusty rooftop, amid questionable cushions, she was making me the happiest I had been in . . . ever.

It was all a little surreal, but I wouldn't change it for all the miracles in the world. We stayed on that rooftop half the night—Auri dozing on and off in my arms—and only when the wind picked up in earnest did we slip back down the stairs.

Since Desmond had been caught, Aurelia could relocate back to her own space, but there wasn't an ice cube's chance in Devil's Meadows I'd be the one to bring up the subject. If she decided to broach the topic, I'd accept whatever she chose, but I'd be eight thousand kinds of fool to suggest it.

Besides, Desmond might be snugged up tight in that cell, but the kid who'd done so much damage to Clarice was still roaming the streets. Best not to chance anything too soon.

I'd been thinking about the night of the code quite a bit. Mostly because I still felt so awful—such a complete failure—for not being able to save the girl on my own. It rang the same bells as my near failure with Geneva. But also because of what Jassika Duncan had told Auri about the reports she'd received regarding the night in question. The awkward encounter with the assistant left me feeling off kilter. Part of me just wanted to forget the entire thing, but I'd be lying if I didn't say I felt I should report it to someone. Given the fact she'd apparently tried to sell me out in what was likely an odd attempt to deflect from her own actions, I didn't want to come off as being retaliatory.

As was typical for me, I was brooding on it as Roe and I headed to work.

"What is *wrong* with you?" Roe asked when I didn't laugh at whatever joke he was telling me.

"Who says anything is wrong?"

"Oh please. The patented Hale Belstrohm grouse face has returned after a weeks-long absence and you think I'm not going to notice?"

We were walking past a series of small shop stalls set along the busy thoroughfare. We passed a vendor selling agave juice and lemonade, two with various bits of horse tack and wagon parts, and one very interesting stall piled high with cracked rubber gas masks, metal canteens and a collection of padlocks in various shapes and sizes.

"Just thinking about the other night." Dodging a pile of horse manure, I proceeded to fill him in on the encounter with the assistant.

"Was it Cookie?"

"Umm, yes. I think that's her name?"

"Shit, Hale. For being so smart, you can be a real dumbass sometimes."

232

I looked at him blankly.

"She's been drooling all over you for weeks!" he nearly shouted. "To be fair, at first she was drooling all over me, but then it shifted to you, thank the stars in heaven."

"I hadn't noticed."

"Obviously. You barely know the woman's name. Plus, you've been so focused on Shrimpboat, you wouldn't notice if half the assistants were walking around in just their stethoscopes."

He was right. I'd definitely been focused on Auri. The thought made me grin.

He looked at me and shook his head. "Anyway. Yes, you should address it, but by telling her you aren't interested. I'd leave it at that. No need to report it and kick a scorpion's nest."

We were approaching the clinic. Palm trees cast spiked shadows in the morning light, intermingling with the staff and snake logo to form a black-winged dragon climbing the exterior wall. The stucco on the building was dried and cracked, the paint long since faded. The windows too could do with a good washing.

Roe continued, "Besides, it isn't Cookie you should be worried about. So her dad's a Medicus big man. We can deal with that when the time comes. What about the kid? What he did? Sucking the life out of that girl like juice from an orange. Gives me the creeps almost as much as watching Listerman work his mojo." He gave a theatrical shiver.

As if summoned by my brother's voice, the kid—Wes—came into view at the clinic's entrance. Hands shoved in his pockets, he appeared all nerves and darting eyes.

"You." I pointed at him, and he took an involuntary step back. I swear his eyes were taking up half of his acne-dotted face.

I had at least six inches and probably fifty pounds on the guy, but I didn't let it stop me. I grabbed the front of his shirt and twisted, lifting the young scumbag off his feet.

"Wait. . ." he choked out. "Please."

Time and again I've told myself I'm meant to be a professional. Each time I vow that I'll change. That I won't let the sins of my father continue to dictate the kind of man I'm going to be. That I can be better than a scared little kid defending the defenseless. I tell myself I can be the calm composed *professional* practitioner. Then I see someone who's caused misery and pain to another living being. Someone who's come close to killing an innocent teen, or beaten their partner, or brutalized a child, and I simply cannot do it. The professional Practitioner Belstrohm slips through my fingers like sand through the cracks in my windows.

My brother thankfully is able to listen to his inner voice. He can become my conscious when I need it most.

"Hale." Roe was there pulling on my arms. "Not like this."

I twisted the shirt one more time and heard a seam pop in protest. Then I released my hand and watched as Wes dropped and scrambled back.

"I'm sorry," he blurted again.

I'd heard the word sorry too many times for it to truly hold any meaning. Sorry would not have brought Clarice back. Words of any kind wouldn't have saved her. I hadn't saved her. It had been Listerman of all the damned people to show up and save the night.

"Sorry isn't good enough," I ground out.

Roe, every bit the professional I wasn't, stepped between the boy and me.

"I know. I know. I can't tell you how much. . . I just. . . it was horrible and I don't deserve, I mean I

234

don't. . ." He took a shaky breath and looked up at me, water shining in his red-rimmed eyes. "I wanted to say thank you for saving her, and I . . . I want you to tell Campbell I'd like to go home."

23

ROE

The packed tram brought back a torrent of memories. Mostly good. Others, distinctly bad.

This tram, although smaller, was similar to the lumbering fiberglass carriages that had transported us across the vast desert and from one life to a wholly other one. It had the same scooped hull and large rubber tires. The same coachman's seat above the horse tack and harnesses. The same metal steps to the cargo bay. And although there were only two horses instead of four, they were both marvelous strapping beasts.

Really the trams had only two stark differences between them. The first was in the size of the thing. It was perhaps half as long as the trams we'd occupied earlier in the summer. The load was considerably lighter without all of the medical supplies and equipment we'd drug from Renfield to Devil's Meadows. But still it was laden with enough food and water to sustain the travelers for at least the three weeks it would take to traverse the eastern expanse of desert and begin the climb into the distant mountains. Once there, the availability of clean drinking water and fresh food would be more than adequate along the way.

The second major difference was the dividing wall a third of the way back from the driver's bench. The reinforced divider created a cubicle large enough to accommodate the sleeping bench running along the forward wall. A thick metal door fit with a small solitary barred window provided the only access and the only light to the cramped space. Desmond would spend his days on the road there, bouncing along, confined between the horses and the supplies.

Aurelia hadn't arrived at the depot yet. In her absence, Hale and I studied the transport. I had odd mixed feelings about the morning. While I was certainly glad I wasn't packing my own things to join the group, and happy both Desmond and Wes would be leaving our part of the world behind, part of me was sad to see the small band go. They would need to travel relatively quickly as autumn was around the corner to avoid the mountains in winter, and it would be a strenuous journey. I was worried about Asher and—despite myself—Campbell.

Geneva had assisted the two men in making the arrangements even though I was sure she was even less pleased with Asher's commitment to the journey than I was. Hale too seemed concerned; although with my brother, it was often hard to tell what was worry and what was just his cranky brooding mood.

"Ha, look at that!" I elbowed him as I saw Luc climb atop the driver's box and check the reins. "Wonder how they talked him into this trip." The last I'd known, all three of our previous tram masters were returning to Renfield after making the final leg of the journey to Jave with the second half of our group. Apparently at least one of them—Luc—had not.

"Asher must have pulled a few strings to get him to stay on in DM for a while."

"Not me," Asher commented as he approached us. "Decided on his own."

I nodded. "Where's your bag?"

"As it happens, looks like I'm sitting this one out." He placed his thumbs in the band of his cargos and rocked back on his heels.

I looked to his wife who was grinning from ear to ear.

"You're leaving Campbell to shoulder this on his own?" My voice held a hint of accusation.

Hale frowned. "I believe what my charming brother is trying to say is, aren't you the least bit worried about Wes trying something and Desmond getting loose?"

"Maybe you docs should worry about your jobs and let me worry about mine." His voice carried the same salty no nonsense timber I'd come to expect. His eyes flicked from me to Hale and back again, then he sighed as if we would be his demise. "Yes. Of course we have taken that into consideration."

"So you think what? Luc is going to jump in and kick some ass when needed?" I prodded.

"If you'd let me finish, I'd tell you." The sound of wagon wheels distracted us all. Asher looked over his shoulder, and we looked with him.

A small wagon laden with trunks and assorted household goods was pulling into the depot. An overstuffed armchair, upholstered in fading pale pink fabric, sat perched among pots and pans, a fringed lamp, and a heap of something covered in a thick canvas tarp.

"Ah, here they are now. Or at least some of them." Asher looked at us and raised his eyebrows. If he expected me to understand everything based on the new arrivals, he was sorely mistaken.

Sitting on the driving board of the sturdy little wagon, I was surprised to find Conrad and Clarice Donahue. Sandy was walking alongside the spotted grey horse, pulling it along. Her eyes were red and her nose was running. She clutched a handkerchief in one hand and a basket of what appeared to be wrapped sandwiches in the other.

"I don't get it." I looked to Asher then Gen.

"What's not to get? The Donahues have elected to make the journey as well."

My lips turned down. "But you can't expect them to take your place. Conrad's fit enough, but he certainly couldn't subdue Desmond."

"No, I don't expect he could."

"Plus there's the whole 'Wes is willing to kill his girlfriend and she's willing to let him' bit."

Asher raised his hand. "I'm going to let the valilier tackle that particular subject. I still can't entirely wrap my brain around how the whole thing works."

How what works? I wasn't aware of anything working recently.

"And," Gen spoke up, a small furrow between her eyes, lips in a tight straight line. "They aren't the only recent additions to the travel roster."

"All right." I drew the words out, looking around the depot. Horses and wagons, trams and people littered the open lot. Campbell—having gone to retrieve his prisoner—was nowhere in sight. "But someone is going to need to explain soon, or I just might die of curiosity."

Gen sucked in her lips and twisted them to the side. Despite the fact Asher wouldn't be traveling out of the hub that day, whatever the new arrangements were, she wasn't overjoyed with them. "Holdan," she finally said. Hale and I looked at each other, his surprise mirroring my own. "Holdan's also going along."

My lovely brother, never the most eloquent, raised his brows. "No shit, huh?"

"No shit," Gen responded.

239

"But why?" I blurted. He'd been right. Just when I found the man tolerable, he was leaving. It would be no huge loss to the hub, but I thought both Geneva and Specs might actually miss having him around.

"Medicus sent word. It's a full denial of privileges," Asher answered. "I suppose he's decided he might be able to use his other gifts in a more meaningful way. Especially if he's out of Medicus's line of sight."

After witnessing his treatment of Clarice, I certainly couldn't argue the point. What would I do if I could no longer practice medicine? Hiding out in tunnels and treating people in secret didn't seem like a fabulous alternative.

"And Valilier Robichaud tends to agree. You know," Gen lowered her voice—not that anyone was around to hear. "He told me he can't sense any sort of wonder-working in Holdan. Not like he can with Aurelia. Isn't that odd?"

"What about with Clarice?" Hale asked.

"Nothing with her either."

"Yeah, but that doesn't necessarily mean anything. He was never around her before Wes did whatever Wes did to her," I said.

Geneva agreed.

Asher crossed his arms over his chest. "At any rate, he thinks they'll both be safe with his people. Even Wes, who apparently claims he's been cured. Of what I have no idea. This is why I wanted Campbell to explain the whole thing himself. I just wish the guy would show. Daylight is wasting."

Hale stayed tight lipped as Asher and Gen wandered over to talk with Luc, then he too left me by the tram as he went to speak with Clarice. He shook hands with Conrad and spoke with Sandy briefly. Under the din of the depot, it was impossible to tell what they discussed, but knowing my brother, he was giving them tips on how to defend themselves should something go awry on the road.

The horses were set and the bulk of the cargo loaded. Only the personal belongings of the absent travelers, and the most important bit of cargo—Desmond—were missing. I was beginning to think I'd better head off to check on Auri when she arrived with Listerman. They strolled in side by side, her carrying a small medical bag and him with a large duffle over one shoulder. Neither seemed overjoyed to be there.

Without a word, he walked to the back of the tram and hefted his personal effects into the hold, then turned and accepted the bag from Aurelia. A glossy shine rose in her hazel eyes as she handed it over. Despite everything we'd been through, his absence was going to affect her.

"Listerman," I said, extending my hand to him.

I expected some sort of condescending remark, but he surprised me yet again. Shaking my hand firmly, he dipped his chin a fraction. "Mr. Belstrohm. I'm sure I owe you some sort of apology, but I can't think of what to say. Instead, I'll leave you with this: it's a strange world we live in, and one day, I hope to see you along its roads again."

Hale had meandered back to us and stood with his arms crossed over his chest. Listerman turned in his direction and nodded. Hale frowned, and I could see the struggle in his eyes. After all, this was the man who'd kidnapped his brother and had been willing to trade his now-girlfriend to a sadistic woman in exchange for his own freedom. It couldn't have been easy for Hale, but despite it all, he stepped forward and extended his hand. It was brief, but a handshake nonetheless.

No handshakes or brief nods for Specs. Her face was grim, but in one swift motion, she stepped forward and wrapped her arms around Listerman's waist. The embrace was typical for the tiny badass she was. Listerman looked uncertain for a moment, arms akimbo, a frown on his face. Then, as this simple act of magic hit him, he relaxed and hugged her back. I wasn't sure, but some liquid might have been leaking from his eyes as he turned away to fuss with his boots.

She grabbed at his elbow to keep him from getting too far, then rose onto her tiptoes. Holdan leaned sideways to allow her to speak against his ear. He looked momentarily confused. Without speaking, he studied her and nodded.

After he walked away I asked Specs what she'd told him.

"I told him not to come back this way. To find a happy life in the Avions and to forget about Medicus." She looked utterly wretched as she said it.

I wrapped my arm around her shoulder and planted a kiss to the top of her head. "Ah, Shrimpboat, don't be so glum. Listerman's like herpes. You might think he's gone, but he'll pop back up when you least expect it."

"Nice." Hale's voice was dryer than the dirt at our feet.

Auri didn't even bother to respond.

Through the din of the depot, a loud hoarse string of obscenities could be heard drawing nearer.

"Sounds like the guest of honor's finally arrived." It took me a moment to understand Hale's comment. Then looking over Auri's head, I saw the horse and rider walking between the gates.

Campbell sat astride a handsome dun horse with a mane and tail that matched the rider's dark locks. Marching beside him, Wes carried a backpack and decent-sized canteen. It wasn't the rider or the kid walking next to him that caught everyone's attention however. It was the third member of the group—head back, mouth open, vulgar words slewing out—that had members of the team and casual bystanders gawking. Desmond's hands were tied in front of him and tethered to Campbell's saddle by a moderate length of rope. He shuffled along without a fight despite the torrent of filth coming from his mouth.

At some point during his incarceration, someone—my money was on Campbell—had seen fit to have him bathed, shaved, and decently cared for. Even his hair had been cut into a short clean fade. It was much easier to see the resemblance to his younger brother once the matted hair and beard were gone. In fact, now that he was shampooed, it was easier to see his hair was actually the same golden brown as Wes's.

Campbell handed the rope to Wes, then dismounted the mare and tied her to one of several posts in the yard.

"Come on, old friend," he said as he took the length back from the teen and guided Desmond toward the waiting tram. "You'll be quite comfy here, I believe."

The valilier was gentle but firm in his direction to Desmond. Again, Desmond didn't fight but climbed the steps into the holding block of the tram and allowed Campbell to fasten the locking bolts on the door. He saved all his vigor for the hateful things that issued forth from his mouth—all of which could still be heard through the small barred window in the door. If he kept that up for any length of time, it was going to be an incredibly long journey for the entire group.

Wes took his own pack to the small wagon being driven by Conrad and stowed it in the back.

Campbell, having secured his cargo, approached us and thanked us for our help in apprehending his former partner. "I know I owe you all an apology for this." He glanced at me. "Some more than others." Seemingly of its own volition, my hand rose and rubbed at the side of my face where I'd taken his punch weeks ago.

"Apology accepted," Auri said. "I do hope you know what you're doing though." She glanced at the wagon Conrad and Clarice were occupying—Wes standing to the side looking extremely ill at ease.

"Wes has always been a good kid but more than a little impetuous. It's a shame he didn't stick around and let one of us help him. I'd always assumed Desmond took off to go after Wes. It never occurred to me to think it might be the other way around." He explained how Wes had known Desmond was getting worse and had kept it to himself. After his older brother disappeared, Wes had been consumed by guilt, and rather than asking for help, he'd taken it upon himself to track him down. Unfortunately, Wes had remained a step behind the entire way, and only caught up to Desmond when he'd stayed in Devil's Meadows.

"But . . . Clarice. . ." She didn't need to voice it any further. We all knew and shared her concern.

Campbell grimaced but nodded. "Like I said—impetuous. We've talked. He really does have some strong feelings for her. And that combined with a total lack of self-control. . . Well it led to what you all witnessed."

"So she'll still be at risk?" I asked.

"I wish I could say for certain she won't, but I feel like the risk has passed."

"What the hell does that mean?" Hale growled.

"He says he doesn't feel a draw to her like he did before."

"And you believe him?" Auri asked.

"I do. I know I'm not supposed to say this"—he smirked at Specs—"but I can still feel the pull toward you."

Hale drew in a deep breath through his nose but didn't say anything.

"That pull you have, Aurelia? Wes says he felt that same pull from Clarice and it isn't there anymore. I checked her out myself." He shook his head. "That came out wrong. What I mean to say is, I don't pick up on anything from her, like I do from you, so I believe if she had a touch of wonder in her veins, it's gone now."

"So like he drank it all up when he almost killed her, and now it's just not there?" It sounded crazy to me.

Campbell shrugged and twisted his lips to the side. "Maybe. I don't know. I've never seen anything like this before. It may just need to recharge. But it does seem that Wes has benefited from this also."

Auri looked skeptical. "What about Holdan? Can't you sense it in him?"

"Fortunately, no. But that could be for a number of reasons. Maybe they both need to recharge after what he did for her, but I don't think so. My speculation is it's more to do with his ability to control his miracles. Keep them guarded and possibly undetected. My understanding is he was in a difficult position until recently?"

"Yeah, you could say that." I didn't intend to sound so sarcastic. If you could call being prisoner and slave to a woman who enjoyed teaching lessons through magical lashings difficult, then, yes. He'd been in a difficult position.

"I know Conrad will keep an eye on Clarice, but promise me, if you see any signs of Wes treating her badly, you'll intervene." Aurelia was asking for a lot, and she knew it.

"I have every intention of doing just that, Aurelia." He stepped forward and took both of her hands in his. "I have hopes that between your friend Mr. Listerman and the effects his work have had on

245

both Clarice and Wes, there may be hope for others in my community. If that proves false, I will assist Clarice and her father in any way I can."

Auri nodded. "In that case, Valilier Campbell Robichaud, I wish you safe travels." She glanced at me, a sly smile spread on her face. "And I really do hope to see you again one day."

24

HALE

It was just before noon when the small train left the depot. The tram driven by Luc and carrying a sick man toward his home in the east was joined by two riders on horseback and a small wagon. The riders both looked comfortable atop their mounts, and the occupants of the wagon—a father looking for a new start and a daughter aglow with budding young love—both looked hopeful.

It was more than I could say about the two people I was walking with. My brother looked just shy of miserable, and Aurelia looked thoughtful and anxious.

The sun was high. The heat was merely uncomfortable rather than unbearable. We passed several crumbling facades along our route back to our housing complex. Auri sighed for perhaps the fourth time in just under two minutes.

"Do you want to talk about it?" I asked her.

She pushed her glasses up on her nose. "Talk about what?"

"About whatever it is you aren't telling us."

"What makes you think there's something I'm not telling you?"

I tilted my chin down and raised my brow.

"He's learned all your tells already, Specs. It took me years, and he's got you figured out in a matter of months. Impressive." Roe punched me lightly on the shoulder.

She sighed and fished something out of her pocket. It was a rumpled sheet of thin paper, torn at one corner.

"The envelope it came in had been torn and resealed when I got it," she said as she handed me the letter.

Unfolding it, a sudden fear ran through me. I didn't want to read what was written there.

I looked at her, a question in my eyes.

"It's not as bad as it could be, but it's still not good. Just read it, Hale."

Only my training kept my hands from shaking as I read the words in a vaguely familiar script.

Aurelia,

Thank you again for all of you support. Jonaten is not doing well. He has grown weaker as each day passes. I've taken your advice and found a train heading south. We leave in three days. With any luck, the post will travel faster than we do, and you'll receive this in advance of our arrival. With even more luck my sweet boy will survive the journey. Your hope of a cure has sparked an even greater hope in my heart, and I look forward to seeing you soon.

-Lita

"I got it yesterday. She should be here by the end of the week."

And the envelope had been opened. That bastard Gary had probably already reported to his father what he'd read. And the site visit was approaching.

"Asher was pretty clear. No miracles. No wonder-working. Auri, you can't do this."

"I know, Hale. I know I can't. But I'm going to anyway."

FROM THE AUTHOR

It's hard for me to believe I've finished my third book. It has been such an honor to know there are people who enjoy reading these little stories of mine. For those of you who've made it this far, I am humbled and honored by you.

Aurelia, Hale, and Roe have been such fun to imagine up and put down on paper. More of their story is out there, floating in the synapses of my brain, and I am looking forward to seeing where their journey goes next.

As always, there are a few people I need to acknowledge. Karen Robinson, my line and copy editor, is amazing. Thank you for keeping my errors in check. Lily Larsen, my brilliant daughter, provides valuable developmental insight and keeps the story on track. Thanks for sharing your wisdom with me. Addie Fern, thanks for sharing your energy on the days I need it most. To Brian, my biggest supporter in life as well as all things computer related, you know I could never dream of any of this without you. Thanks also to the rest of my family—Mom, Jen, and Ralph—for always cheering me on.

I'd like to end by thanking my real life Nora, Janet, and Sandy. While the namesake characters in this book are fictional variations of the women I work with, the hard work and dedication is spot on. As any physician, advanced practitioner, or other medical professional can attest to, the support we receive from nurses, medical assistants, respiratory therapist, and other office and hospital support staff is the foundation on which we practice. I for one, could never do what I do without you.

Also by Kami King Larsen

A Simple Tale of Water and Weeping

Blood and Wonder
A Medicus Corpus Novel

Let's Connect!

Visit me at kamikinglarsenbooks.com and join my mailing list for updates, early reader opportunities, and other goodies

Find me on Instagram
For all things bookish @klarsenmd_booksandbits
For author updates @authorkamikinglarsen

On Amazon: amazon.com/author/kami_books

And on Facebook @KamiKingLarsenBooks

ABOUT THE AUTHOR

Kami King Larsen is a native of the desert southwest and studied biology before attending medical school. Although she is a practicing pediatrician by training, she is a bibliophile and lover of great stories and all things whimsical by birth. Kami lives in Nevada with her husband, two daughters, and two dogs.

www.ingramcontent.com/pod-product-compliance
Lightning Source LLC
Chambersburg PA
CBHW020317200626
46814CB00006BA/2286